Lyric

Also by
Molly McAdams

A Rebel Novel

Lyric

Molly McAdams

Molly McAdams
www.mollysmcadams.com
Cover Design by *RBA Designs*
Photo by ©*Regina Wamba*
Editing by *Making Manuscripts* & Shannon
Interior Design & Formatting by Christine Borgford, *Type A Formatting*
Custom Illustrations by DeepFriedFreckles

The characters and events in this book are fictitious. Names, characters, places, and plots are a product of the author's imagination. Any similarity to real persons, living or dead, is coincidental and not intended by the author.

Print ISBN: 9780998420073
eBook ISBN: 9780998420066

Disclaimer: A very small portion of this book was originally titled "Rebel" in the *Once Upon A Rock Star* anthology. If you supported the anthology and read my short story in there, I encourage you to still read that portion as alterations have been made that are key to the rest of the story.

George and Donna, Johnny and Marjory . . .

Your extraordinary lives and enchanting stories fueled a passion that became a dream.

This is for you.

Prologue

Libby

I WASN'T SEEING ANYTHING IN that room.

I was reliving last night over and over like a never-ending nightmare.

I ran to my room, intent on looking for something I prayed wasn't there, and rushed for my bathroom at the last second. I only made it to the sink by the time my stomach lurched, ridding my body of bile.

A sob wrenched from my chest. I stumbled back to the wall and lowered myself to the floor.

Maxon settled next to me, his face a mask of worry and confusion. "Libby, what—what the hell's going on? Are you okay?"

I nodded weakly.

It was all I could do.

I was the furthest thing from okay, but I couldn't tell him the truth.

Deep down I think I'd known all along. But I'd wanted it to be anything else—anyone else.

Any real threat could be twisted into a prank when that's what you wish for it to be.

After so many years of denying myself—denying *us*—I would've dismissed any threat to our relationship.

Because that's what this was.

It wasn't a simple claiming. It was an open threat to the man I loved.

It was a dark blanket on the happiness I only found with him.

It was mocking the future I wanted.

I'd worried over what might happen to Maxon and me when he found out.

Now, I knew that ending was inevitable. The one I'd agonized over.

We'd dealt with enemies before—faced assassins silent as the night.

But this family wasn't silent. They were ghosts.

One

Maxon

RAN A HAND THROUGH my hair repeatedly while the phone rang in my ear.

"Pick up," I said through clenched teeth. "Pick up, pick up."

Libby's voice filtered through, happy and free . . . and recorded.

I fisted the phone in my hand, my arm shaking with the strength it took not to launch it across the room.

Six months of this bullshit. Six months of no response.

And I had no idea why.

The last day we talked was like any other. Better actually. The guys and I had just received our schedules for this tour. Tours meant seeing her.

Our conversation had been the same as always.

Teasing that made me ache for more. Left me counting down the hours until I could get home and call her.

ME: *Gonna be busy for a while. Tour starting soon. But I'm coming back for you, Rebel.*

I'd bit back a groan and shifted lower in the chair when she responded with a close-up picture of her biting on her bottom lip.

ME: *Those are mine.*

LIBBY: *It's cute how you think I'm waiting here for you or that you own any part of me.*

The corners of my mouth had twitched up in a smirk as I tapped out another message to her.

ME: *I do, and you are.*

LIBBY: *Is that so? Guess we'll see . . .*

But there was no answer when I called that night. There hadn't been one since.

Once the beep sounded on her voicemail, I growled, "Just played the last show. Closing out at The Jack in two nights. But I guess you know that." I laughed, the sound bitter and pleading at once. "But *I* don't know if you'll be there. *I* don't know if you'll be backstage before it begins. I don't even know why you've ignored every one of my fucking calls."

A strangled groan got caught in my throat when I dropped to the hotel bed, and I let my head hang between my shoulders.

My eyes slipped shut when a memory crept into my mind, taunting and torturing me.

She lifted the shirt teasingly, revealing her bare ass. Glancing over her shoulder, she twisted her full lips into a smirk. "Catch me, and you can have me."

"Just . . . just be there, Rebel."

I fell back on the bed and calculated the hours until I got to The Jack. I'd been counting down to this night since the last day I talked to Libby.

Our manager, Nate, had just dropped the tour schedule in our laps. The other members of my band were going over it while he looked on silently. I tuned them out.

Because I didn't care that he'd gotten us bigger venues.

Or that he wanted us to play more shows in the same amount of time.

And I sure as hell didn't give a fuck about how fast he'd scheduled us to move from city to city.

All that mattered was the tiny bar in an even tinier town at the bottom of the list, closing out the tour.

Every tour closed out in that bar.

The Jack.

The place where we'd first started out—sometimes playing for drinks or barely enough cash to keep our shitty apartment—and where Nate found us. Shortly after, he'd signed on as our manager and introduced us to a life we'd only ever dreamed about. He also became the only father figure any of us had ever had.

With our only family being each other, we'd left that town with no ties.

Except one. *Mine.*

A girl who was as wild as they come.

There wasn't a man alive who could lay claim to her heart. Not like that stopped me from telling her for most our lives that one day I would—from planning a future with her again and again.

And then we left.

Whenever I made it back to our hometown, I tortured myself by claiming her body for a night or two, knowing that was all we could offer each other then. Knowing no one else would ever compare.

Every time, I told her that one day I would come back for her and not leave without her.

And every time, she smiled that damn smile like she was enjoying the game we always played—that wild, free spirit shining bright and reminding me exactly what girl I was trying to hold on to.

For the first time, I was terrified she'd slipped from my grasp.

Two

Him

A CRUEL GRIN CROSSED MY face as I watched the man sluggishly come to.

"Wha—" He tried to move, his face morphing into panic when he realized he was chained to the chair. "What the—what's—who're you?"

I didn't respond. I stayed a few feet from him, arms folded over my chest, coaxing his panic to increase.

I wanted his fear.

I wanted his adrenaline to negate the effect of the drugs in his system.

I wanted him to know exactly what was about to happen.

Because I'd been waiting for this night for a very long time.

"Where the hell am I?" he demanded on a roar, his voice now clear.

"Thought that was obvious," I finally responded after watching him struggle with the chains for another minute.

"I asked where the fuck am I?"

I let my eyes touch on the exposed metal beams and metal siding. "Looks like a warehouse."

"What do you want, you sick fuck?"

My only response was the slight widening of my grin.

I knew to wait.

I knew exactly what would come next. It always came.

These men were all the same.

So I stood there, watching in amusement while he thrashed and tried to escape.

And then it happened.

A strangled sob burst from the man a few minutes later and his body sagged. The adrenaline fading from him just as quickly as it had come.

Before he had a chance to look at me again, my cousin slipped up beside him and yanked his head up by his hair.

"This girl," I demanded, my tone filled with rage and possession as I held a picture in front of him.

"W-w-what the—what about her?"

"Tell me about her."

"I don't know her, man," he cried out.

My grin turned into a sneer. "You sure about that?"

"I mean, I-I-I hooked up with her. Like once—"

"Twice."

"Fuck, man, I don't remember. It was a long time ago." Tears rolled down his face. "I don't even remember her name."

I nodded at my cousin to release him and slowly backed away. "Doubt she remembers yours either."

His face fell, leaving only terror and confusion warring in his eyes. "What?"

"Her name's Elizabeth Borello," I said as my cousin took aim. Before the gunshot rang out in the warehouse, I dropped my voice to a snarl. "And she's mine."

Three

Libby

PICTURES FLASHED BEHIND MY EYELIDS like unwelcome reminders of my grief. Little snippets of everything I lost.

I flinched and automatically tried to push them from my mind but stopped and clung to them instead. Used them to fuel my anger.

Anger was good. It was better than what I'd been drowning in. It was necessary to get through the coming days.

Get through the next forty-eight hours.

Feel nothing.

Get through—

I blinked quickly and looked at the table to see what had hit my face.

A sugar packet. Assholes.

My gaze drifted up and around. Everyone in our group was staring at me from where they were all piled into one of the booths at Brooks Street Café.

I didn't react to their expectant looks. I couldn't.

I was treading a fine line between anger and agony and blissful nothingness.

My heart raced and it felt difficult to breathe.

Shit. I don't have time to panic.

Feel noth—

"Libby," my brother pressed, as though he'd been saying my name for a while.

"I'm not hungry," I responded automatically.

"Yeah. No. We got that when you didn't order."

I glanced at the table again—to the empty plates there—and wondered when everyone had ordered and eaten.

How long have we been here?

"Libby."

"What?" I snapped, and immediately regretted it when Dare's face fell into a look of understanding.

"Have you heard anything we've said?"

"Yeah, that's not likely," my best friend, Einstein, murmured from beside me.

When I didn't respond, Dare said, "I asked if you're working the Henley show."

My chest hitched and throat tightened.

Einstein gave me a knowing look before turning back to her conversation with the twins.

Feel nothing. Feel nothing. Feel nothing.

"No," I wheezed. "No, I'm not."

Dare's stare shifted to his wife before settling on me again. "Are you *going?*"

Everyone except Einstein went still.

She already knew the answer.

It felt like a bubble was suddenly surrounding our booth, encasing us in deafening silence while they waited for my answer.

And I couldn't breathe.

He pressed his body close to mine and framed my face with his hands.

"This," he said softly. The word was almost lost in the roar of scream-ing fans waiting for Henley to take the stage of The Jack. "This is what's missing from every day and night. From every show. You here with me."

Funny. All that was missing from my life was him *here with* me.

I smiled coyly and let my eyes drift to the door of the room. "Your fans are waiting for you. Go play so I can have you to myself for the night."

"For always." He kissed me soundly, dragging my bottom lip through his teeth when he pulled away. "It's gonna be you and me forever, Libby."

My chest ached so badly it felt like my heart was literally breaking.

I struggled to find the anger I'd been grasping like a lifeline, but that brief memory had ripped open my wounds, making them feel so fresh and so raw. My pain was consuming and blinding, and it was impossible to feel anything else in that moment.

"No," I said on a shallow breath.

The twins shifted uncomfortably while Dare and his wife, Lily, shared another quick look.

"Do you . . ." Lily cleared her throat. "Do you want to talk about it?"

No. Because then it would be real.

I tried to stand even though I was farthest in the booth, then hurried to press against Einstein in a silent and frantic plea for her to move.

She settled in deeper to her seat.

She'd bribed me with caffeine from our favorite coffee shop to get me in the car after literally dragging me out of bed this morn-ing . . . and brought me here instead. Considering we all ate together a few times a week, and my family owned this café, I hadn't known why she'd lied about the coffee.

I got it now.

I should've known an ambush was waiting for me since Henley's show was tonight at the bar where I worked.

"Libby," Dare said gently. "He'll be back tonight."

"I know," I said through clenched teeth.

Feel nothing.

Get through the next forty-eight hours.

Dare gripped my wrist to stop me from leaving. As if he knew I was about to crawl over everyone to get out of the booth.

He was younger by a few years, but he'd always seen me as his responsibility. At a young age, he'd been forced into a role no one outside our life would ever understand.

He'd taken care of an entire family. Become a father figure and boss to many and kept us together no matter the threat we faced. He'd kept me with the family no matter how many times I'd tried to rebel and run.

"I know you're hurting, Libby," he said. "Jesus Christ, I know. We've given you time, but it's gone on long enough. This isn't you."

"What does it matter? They'll be headed back to LA in a couple days anyway, and I'll be fine."

"It matters because *this* won't change when they leave." Dare gestured to me with his free hand, his eyes a wild mixture of worry and anger. "You're a goddamn zombie. You barely talk. We hardly see you. When we do, you pick up Beckham and walk into another room to hold him and cry."

I glanced at the wriggling baby in his wife's lap, then looked away.

"We just want you back," Lily said. "We're worried about you."

"You're faking every smile and word to get through work," Dare continued. "You're forcing movements to get through days. But life is going on around you, and you aren't seeing any of it. And now you want to hide because fucking Ma—"

"Don't," I pleaded. "Don't . . . just don't."

Don't say his name.

He nodded for a few seconds. When he spoke again, his tone was gentle. "You've been through shit most the world will never have to experience. Nothing broke you. But you're letting this."

His hand tightened on me. "Talk to us. Let us be there for you."

I ground my jaw to keep it from shaking and prayed for the tears pricking the backs of my eyes to dry.

What did they want me to say? They wouldn't understand.

Einstein was there when I found out. I knew she was waiting for me to pull myself together. I knew she didn't agree with the way I'd reacted.

But I hadn't just been devastated. I'd been wrecked.

It was one thing to be consumed by overwhelming heartache. To live life on autopilot. It was another to admit to my friends—my family—that a man had the power to ruin me so completely by doing nothing.

Absolutely *nothing*.

Because in hindsight, I should've expected this. I'd been unwillingly pushing him toward it all these years.

That doesn't make it hurt any less.

"I always love seeing these tables filled with my favorite kids."

I bristled at the voice behind the sentiment and focused my stare on the table when everyone else looked at her and exchanged greetings.

She sighed gently, the sound like nails on a chalkboard, and murmured, "Seeing all of you together like this gives me hope that one day soon, you'll stop pretending to be something you aren't."

"Mom," Dare groaned when a soft laugh escaped Lily.

"Who's pretending?" Einstein asked with a huff. "I'm still doing me, thank you very much."

"You sure about that?" Maverick, one of the twins, mumbled under his breath before shoving out of the booth.

I looked their way in time to see Einstein's wounded expression before she could cover it.

"For a good reason," Dare cut in, his voice now stern. "Not for the old ones."

"Whatever you say, Boss," Einstein said wryly.

The look Dare gave her in return promised so many horrible things. "Call me that again. I dare you."

"Rain check?" she asked as she slid from the booth and followed Maverick out the front door.

"You should've never asked them to stop calling you that," Mom said.

I rolled my eyes.

And here we go. Just another meal with our family.

"You don't understand the repercussions of what you've done. Of what you're *attempting* to do. You're all naïve if you think you can escape that life. It can be days, months, or years . . . but eventually, that life will find you and bring you back."

"Enough," Dare said gruffly.

"Your father wouldn't have been careless enough to try. Or turn his back on his promises."

I faced her for the first time since she walked up, and she was staring right at me.

"I said *enough*."

She didn't flinch at Dare's harsh tone.

She held my gaze unwaveringly, making sure I knew her last words were meant for me.

As if I had any doubt.

If there was anything I was sure of in my life, it was my mother's disappointment in my decisions.

To be friends with Ma—with *him*. To love him. Choose him.

To turn my back on my dad's choices for me. To rebel against my family's lifestyle, and to support Dare when he disbanded it.

It was his plan and decision to disband the family, yet somehow, I was the one Mom blamed.

I could take the blame. I had most of my life. Like I said, I'd always rebelled against the lifestyle. Dare had kept it together—kept all of us together—for over fifteen years after our dad was murdered.

To our mom, he was the one who could bring it all back.

After all . . . mob families need bosses.

And Dare was ours.

I cleared my throat and broke away from the staredown. "Well, this has been fun," I mumbled dryly. "I think I'd rather go back to sleep though."

Dare caught my wrist again when I began sliding out of the booth. "We still need to talk."

Everything in me seized.

For a few precious moments, I'd been able to forget what was coming. What was happening.

I guess I could thank Mom for that. For once.

"No," I whispered. "We don't."

"Say the word, and I'll talk to him," Dare said in a low tone that assured me there would be more fighting than talking. "Say the word, and none of us will go."

My shoulders sagged and a lump formed in my throat. "I want you to go. I just—" My gaze drifted to where Mom was listening to our conversation with rapt attention. "Can we not do this? Please."

Dare's hand tightened when I moved. "Libby."

"Nothing," I said urgently as tears filled my eyes and raced down my cheeks. "He *literally* did nothing."

"Let her go, Dare," Lily said softly when I tried to pull my hand free again.

I could tell from the look in Dare's eyes that he didn't want to, but the instant he released my wrist, I slid from the booth and didn't spare another glance at them.

I didn't make it halfway to the door when the gentle, sweet, awful voice of my mother sounded next to me. "I may not know what the two of you were talking about, but I've seen the papers and the flyers. I know that boy is coming back to town."

I ground my jaw and stood there, stiff as a board, trying my hardest to stop the tears.

"If you know what is good for you, you will not see him. You will go nowhere near him. Do you hear me?" There were a few seconds before she hissed, "Libby, you are playing a dangerous game with him, and one day it will be your ruining if it doesn't come for him first. Tell me you hear me for once in your life."

I shot her a sidelong look. "I've *always* heard you. That didn't mean I was okay with what you expected from me. That didn't mean I could've stayed away from him. But it looks like you finally got your wish. He made it loud and clear that we are done."

She didn't even have the decency to look sad for me. "Maybe now you'll fulfill your duty to this family. It should've been done long ago."

I laughed in disbelief. "I'd rather die."

"Don't be dramatic."

"Oh, but I learned from the best," I drawled, giving her a meaningful look. I took a couple steps toward the door before turning back to her. "My heart has been torn from my chest. I have been in *agony* the last six months. And you can't show even the slightest hint of sadness for your only daughter when she's in the worst kind of pain. What the hell is wrong with you?"

She swallowed thickly, her head bobbing slowly.

I hated that she looked so sweet and caring, and yet she couldn't spare those emotions for me.

"I *am* sorry you're hurting. But I tried to keep you from this, Libby. If you had listened to your father and me, your heart would've never been put in this position with the James boy in the first place. And I'm more concerned about what's coming for you."

"It was dealt with ten years ago. It's over, Mom. *Nothing* is coming. If they do? I'd rather die," I repeated the words slowly, then turned and walked outside.

There was that anger. And I was going to hold on to it like my life depended on it.

Four

Libby

"WHAT ARE YOU DOING?"

"There you go, Gabe." I set the Moscow Mules on the wooden bar top in front of one of my regulars and then flashed him a sly grin when he left a hefty tip in their place—as he always did. I made a show of slipping the note he'd hidden under the bill into my pocket and then stuffed the cash into one of the nearly overflowing tip jars.

"I repeat. What are you doing?"

"See you around, Libby," Gabe said and turned to go.

Finally letting my eyes shift to where my best friend had situated herself on a barstool, I gave her a dry look. "What does it look like?"

"It looks like you're failing at avoiding someone." Her eyes glinted with a tease. "Not that I'm disappointed."

"Can't avoid you when we live together, Einstein."

She snatched a cherry from my garnish tray before twirling it between her fingers. "Was I talking about me? I don't think I was.

Then again, I think you already knew that because you aren't an idiot." She placed the cherry between her teeth, smiling knowingly at me as she tore the stem out. "So . . . whatcha doing here?"

Instead of responding, I began making drinks for the people I knew wouldn't be far behind her. Our friends—our family.

Einstein and I were too similar. If we wanted to know something, we didn't stop until we had our answers. The only difference was Einstein was a genius—hence the nickname—and she usually already had all the answers to her questions. She just wanted the person to confirm them.

"Last I heard, you were taking tonight off and staying as far from The Jack and downtown as you could get. And by *last I heard*, I mean *just this afternoon.*"

I slanted a glare at her but didn't comment.

This morning my pain was too overwhelming.

This afternoon my anger was too unpredictable.

I had had every intention of hiding in my apartment until Henley left town.

But I knew how to work the bar on pure adrenaline and heartbreak until the doors closed. I'd been doing it for months. I was determined to do it tonight.

So I spent an extra hour getting ready—not that I'd admit to that—and my fixed smile was as wide and as fake as they came.

"Yet, here you are," Einstein continued. "In the same lovely establishment a certain band is playing at tonight. A band a certain Max—"

"Someone needs to take home all the tips we're gonna make tonight." I sent her a smirk. "Might as well be me."

Lie.

I had no doubt tonight's tips would be better than I'd ever seen them. The Jack was overflowing with fans who were eagerly waiting to see Henley perform in the bar they'd started out in. But I wasn't here for the tips.

The truth was, I'd been to every one of Henley's shows in this bar . . . and part of me couldn't imagine being absent for this one.

Another part swore I was standing tall because The Jack was my home, and I refused to let any man run me out of it.

And yet, the biggest part was aching to know I hadn't made it up. Begging to know it had been real.

"When are you gonna let me give you my last name, Rebel?"

I raised my arms out wide, letting the breeze play through my fingers. "Told you I'm never letting a man tie me down." A laugh ripped from my throat when Maxon grabbed my waist and pulled me to the ground with him.

He rolled on top of me and nipped my neck teasingly, his fingers racing up the inside of my thigh. It didn't matter that we'd just finished not long before or that we were outside. We were somewhere no one would ever find us . . . and this was Maxon and me. We'd never been able to stay away from each other, and we only had days before he left again.

"I remember a few times you begged me to tie you down," he murmured, his voice dripping with seduction.

My eyelids fluttered shut, and my legs opened for him. "You know that isn't what I meant," I said breathlessly when he pressed a finger inside me. "I don't want to be owned. And you've never owned any part of me."

From the laugh that shook his body before he kissed me, I knew he could hear the lie in my voice.

Because he had *owned me for as long as I could remember.*

Heart. Body. Soul.

"And the show?" Einstein leaned forward and snagged another cherry.

I lifted a shoulder and set the drinks on the bar. "There's live music nearly every night. Tonight isn't any different."

The tick of Einstein's brow let me know she wasn't buying it.

Because it *was* different. It was so different.

Maverick slipped up behind Einstein and snatched a drink off the bar. "Are these for us?"

His identical twin squeezed into a space near Einstein and offered me a grin as he grabbed the wrong drink. "It's like you knew we were coming."

I pointed at Einstein. "I did. Clearly. And that isn't yours." After taking the drink from his hand, I set it onto the bar and slid him his whiskey. "Where's—" I looked up, a ghost of a smile crossing my face when I saw Dare leading Lily toward the bar.

"This is insane," she yelled to me once he had her pressed against the bar and was blocking anyone from getting too close to her.

"It usually is when they come back to town," Dare responded, concern for me shadowing his eyes. "I'm not surprised you showed."

"Get me if you need anything else," I called out, but as soon as I turned to help more customers, Dare snatched my wrist and forced me to look at him.

His gaze darted over my face, studying me.

I knew he was worried. Knew they all were.

There wasn't a need to be. I'd be fine the morning Henley were on the road to California.

At least, that was what I kept telling myself.

"How long has it been since you've seen him?" Dare demanded, his tone low and barely reaching me over the roar of the crowd.

Eight months and twenty-seven days.

I wasn't counting.

I forced myself to stand naturally, to stare at him as if I had no idea who he could be asking me about. This was just another night. Just another band.

There was nothing special about any of it.

"Seen who?"

Dare's eyes locked on mine, and his lips pressed together in a weak attempt to hide his grimace. And I knew in that short answer I'd already given myself away.

I turned when he released me but didn't make it a step before he said, "Maxon."

His hand twisted in my hair and pulled until all I could do was stare above me.

My knees shook and belly swirled with white-hot heat.

"Rebel," he whispered in my ear, a plea and a question.

A ragged breath tore from my chest, mixing with my whimper. "More . . . Oh God, more."

I glanced over my shoulder and shrugged. "Why would I care?"

From where she stood in Dare's arms, Lily gave me a soft, understanding look. He must have told her the entire story, and I hated him for it.

It wasn't his story to tell.

I stilled when screams and yells started pouring through The Jack, crying out for Henley and its members.

Each time I heard his name called louder than the rest, it was like a shock to my system and a knife to my heart. Pride surged through me just as heavily as my bitterness, leaving electricity dancing along my skin and a sick feeling racing through my veins.

Don't look. Don't look, Libby.

And then he began, the bass leading them off, sending a rush to my core. Each deep note worked through me the way his fingers had so many times before.

I reached out to steady myself on the back bar and hesitantly turned my head, keeping my eyes downcast until I could no longer stand it.

And there he was. Maxon James. Eyes locked on me. Fury and possession streaked across his devastatingly handsome face, making my knees weak.

The rock star who frequented my dreams and haunted my sheets.

The boy who vowed to be my forever.

The man who shattered my world.

I hated him.

I gritted my teeth against the emotions threatening to overwhelm me and lifted my hand in the air, flipping him off. Not waiting to see if he reacted, I turned and threw myself into making drinks for the next hour.

Refusing to look at the stage.

"Libby, I love you."

Acting like I couldn't hear his voice mixing with the others.

"Your heartbeat will always be my favorite song."

Pretending not to know every aching word by heart.

"Every lyric I write, I write for you."

Accepting goodbye was already here.

"It's gonna be you and me forever."

Five

Maxon

WHEN WE FINISHED OUR ENCORE, I lingered a few seconds after the guys leaped off the stage into the waiting, screaming crowd of The Jack. I silently begged her to turn from where she stood like my own personal siren. My jaw clenched tight and my blood buzzed.

When there was nothing, I unhooked and dropped my bass to the stage, ignoring the shocked gasps as I stormed off stage to the back rooms.

After most shows, the four of us exited the stage to celebrate with each other for a few moments. Reveling in the sounds of our fans screaming in the crowd as we took a shot and wondered *still* how this had become our lives before we ventured into the chaos of paparazzi and eager women and parties.

Not at The Jack.

We played. We jumped off stage so the guys could drink with the fans. And I slipped away with Libby to whatever secluded place awaited us.

It's how it had always been.

Then again, we'd never played a show here when she wasn't waiting for me in the back before we went on. Even before the fame and money. Even before Nate.

Until tonight.

And she'd flipped me off and fucking turned from me.

I stalked across the back room, my long legs eating up the distance too quickly no matter how often I turned. Until soon, the room felt too small and I felt caged.

It'd been nine years since we'd left Wake Forest and Henley had blown up bigger than we'd ever imagined. And in those nine years, Libby had always been right here. Teasing me with kisses and touches and telling me she wouldn't be waiting the next time. And I was fucking terrified *next time* had actually come.

A weight settled low in my gut, and it felt impossible to breathe.

I let out an animalistic roar, shoving my foot into a metal folding chair and sending it flying across the room.

I turned at the soft gasp that came from behind me. My body tensed when I saw the girl standing just inside the room, the door shut behind her. She was wearing shorts so damn short the pockets were sticking out. And I was pretty fucking sure the only piece of material under the leather jacket she was unzipping was a bra.

"So . . ." she began just as the zipper passed her waist. "You looked a little angry out there. I thought you might need someone to cheer you up."

The guys wouldn't think. They'd finish tearing off the jacket for her and take her against the wall.

But I wasn't them. And Libby was out there with my goddamn heart.

"You thought wrong," I responded, my tone practically a snarl.

She tilted her head as she shrugged the jacket off one shoulder . . . and then the other. Her lips twisted into a sensual pout.

"Are you sure about that?"

I jerked my head toward the door behind her. "You can leave, or I can make you."

Her pout turned into a hungry grin as she moved deeper into the room. "I won't say anything to the press."

My teeth gnashed so hard it made my jaw ache. I closed the distance between us, ignoring the hopeful look that lit her eyes just before I snatched her arm and dragged her back the way she'd come.

Yanking open the door, I forced her out of the room. "You aren't gonna say anything because there's nothing to talk—" I sucked in a sharp breath when I saw the group of people lining the hall just outside the door. Oxygen filled my lungs for what felt like the first time since we'd begun our set . . . only for the air to rush out just as quickly. "Where is she?"

The girl I'd just shoved out of the room looked from the group to me, her face set in frustration and embarrassment as she pulled her jacket over her shoulders and stomped down the hall.

I looked back at the group of people. Some I'd grown up with, others had come to town a handful of years before I moved away. There was a girl I'd never seen tucked close to Libby's brother, Dare. At the moment, I didn't care to meet her. She wasn't the girl I wanted to see.

"Where is she?" I demanded again when no one said anything.

Dare exhaled slowly and scowled at me. Tipping his head to gesture down the hall, he said, "Well, it looks like you're doing just fine."

I laughed in frustration. "Nothing happened. But I need to know what *is* happening with Libby. She's been ghosting me since I told her about this tour. And then . . ." I flung my hand out like Libby was standing there. "Shit, I don't know."

Libby's best friend snorted but didn't look up from where she was tapping on her phone. "I was hoping you'd realize by now how badly you fucked up, but apparently you're too stupid. Bummer.

I've rooted for you from the beginning."

"How did I fuck up?" I asked incredulously. "I just got here."

Einstein glanced at me before looking back at her phone and pushing from the wall she'd been leaning against. "Exactly."

My hands curled into fists when she and two of the guys walked away, leaving me alone with Dare and his girl.

"I'm Dare's wife, Lily," she said after an uncomfortable silence.

I blew out a pent-up breath and raked my hands through my hair. "That's nice."

"Watch it," Dare growled at me.

"I've heard a lot about you," she continued as if we hadn't said anything.

I sent a glare in her direction to find her staring at me like she was trying to figure me out. She wasn't looking at me like she wanted to unzip my pants and suck my dick like so many women did—even with their guys clinging to them. She simply looked at me curiously as she burrowed deeper into Dare's side.

It was a welcome change.

I cleared my throat and said, "The media lies."

She pointed to Dare and clarified, "I've heard a lot about you from this one and the others. But none of them said you were such an asshole." The words were said so smoothly they caught me off guard.

I don't think I'd ever been called an asshole in my life.

A breath of a laugh rasped from my throat. "Yeah, well, you caught me on a bad night. A long time ago I ripped out my heart and left it with a girl. And now she's refusing to talk to me."

"For all your talk about what my sister means to you, you're all over the news for your relationships with other women," Dare taunted.

"The media lies," I repeated. "Not that I claim to be a saint when I'm gone . . . but do you think your sister is either?"

"Not something I want to think about."

"I've begged her to come to California with me from the be-ginning, and she's refused. And every time I'm here, she makes it clear she won't be leaving with me or be waiting for me the next time I come back." I leaned against the doorjamb and crossed my arms over my chest. "She always was until tonight."

Dare was shaking his head slowly, almost like he didn't realize he was doing it. "You really don't get it, do you? You fucking ru-ined her."

I already had an idea how mad she was. But hearing that sent a punch to my gut—and I still didn't have a clue what I'd done.

He pushed away from the wall, taking Lily with him. "For the record, I've never rooted for the two of you."

One of my eyebrows ticked up. "Not a secret."

"I like you, Maxon. Always have. I just don't like you for my sister," he said unapologetically.

It was how he'd talked since we were kids.

Straight and to the point.

No bullshit.

No shame.

"I didn't know Henley would turn into what it has, and I'm happy for you. But I knew even if you guys never hit it big, you'd try to go somewhere . . . and that still would've led you down a road surrounded by drugs and other shit I didn't want her around."

I let out a heavy breath when he turned to leave. "You should've known I'd never let her near that." When he looked back at me, I explained, "The guys go to parties and clubs constantly, and maybe drag me to a bar a couple times a month. Most of my time is spent at the house when we're not busy. Ask your sister. She gets off work around the time our shows end or we finish practicing. Half my nights were spent talking to her before this tour."

Dare huffed. "Not what I meant. You think you could've kept *Libby* from that life?"

Libby was impulsive and wild and free in everything. The way she thought. The way she lived. The way she loved.

If you told her not to do something, she'd do it just to show you that you couldn't stop her.

She was my rebel.

But she craved the way my calm clashed with her wild, and she came to me to escape the world.

Libby ran to me when she needed space from her family. I was the one she ran to when she needed peace injected in her life . . . like she knew I had the ability to keep her tied to earth.

"I would've never let her near that shit," I repeated slowly, coldly.

With a slight nod, they left, and I stood there wondering what the hell I was going to do.

When the show ended, I'd wanted to stalk over to the bar and pull Libby away from it and out of The Jack until we were far from people and she had to talk to me.

Now that I'd had a chance to calm down somewhat, I knew what was needed.

Patience.

And, Jesus . . . if anyone could be patient, it was me.

I'd waited most of my life to make her mine.

Six

Libby

MY HEART STUTTERED AND MY feet faltered when I turned and found Maxon sitting on the stool in front of me. Light brown eyes locked with mine, jaw clenched tight, hands fisted on top of the bar. The look in his eyes was so primal I thought he'd pull me onto the bar and have his way with me.

My belly swirled with heat and my heart twisted and splintered a little more.

I wanted to ask one of the other bartenders to take this customer, but they were slammed. And even though I didn't want to see Maxon, I wasn't that sort of girl.

I didn't hide from men. Not even Maxon James. I just . . . maybe didn't have to speak to him.

I poured him two fingers of whiskey and slammed the tumbler onto the bar top with more force than necessary before moving on to the guys in the far corner.

And for the next two hours, it continued like that.

Maxon never moved or took his eyes from me. Even when people came up to him and asked for his autograph or a picture, those eyes the same color as his whiskey stayed hooked on me.

And I failed at ignoring him.

His presence was overwhelming despite the crowded bar.

He made it hard to breathe. He made it hard to concentrate. He made it hard to remember why I hated him, when all I wanted was to fall into his arms and tell him how much I'd missed him.

But then my eyes would burn with tears when another girl wearing next-to-nothing would try to climb into his lap. Even if he ignored them or pushed them away, it was those moments I remembered exactly why I hated him.

Fuck you, Maxon.

But even when the other members of Henley left for parties and The Jack thinned to its normal numbers, he never moved from his seat. And that overwhelming presence became suffocating.

"Head out, Libby."

I froze, my horrified gaze sliding to Zeke, the owner of the bar. "I'm fine," I said, silently begging him to take back those words.

He nodded to where Maxon sat behind me. "I know you've got somewhere to be. Now get out of here."

"I'm really fine."

He gave me a look like he was doing me a favor when it was the furthest from it. "I'm not asking. We can handle closing tonight. Go . . . hit the town. Or whatever you kids do."

"Stop talking like you're ancient," I said as I ducked under the bar to grab my things from the cabinet.

Zeke was forty, not seventy. On more than one occasion over the years, I'd tried to pass the time in his bed.

But not only did he have a huge problem with casual hookups in the workplace, he was also not into *casual*. If he had a woman in his bed, she belonged to him. So, in Zeke's mind, I belonged to Maxon James. Hard to argue that when he'd been there for every messy part of our twisted affair.

It was better this way. I typically only slept with men I would never see again.

I couldn't exactly avoid my boss.

Once I had my bag in hand, I stood and stormed out from around the bar, never looking in Maxon's direction as I stepped out of The Jack and headed to the side parking lot.

"What now?"

I stumbled to a halt and sucked in a sharp breath, a shiver rolling down my spine at the sound of his voice so close to my ear.

Unable to stop myself, I looked up and found him standing right beside me. Eyes furious and face unbelievably handsome.

Before I could take another step, he grabbed my arm and hauled me back so I was pressed up against the building and he was caging me against it. "We're talking."

I licked my lips, my heart racing having *this* body so close to mine. "Who said I wanted to?"

"*I* want to. What the fuck is going on, Libby?"

"What's going on is you're stopping me from going home."

He pressed closer and dropped his forehead to mine, his words all growl and carnal sin. "You know that's not what I'm talking about. You're ghosting me, and I need to know why."

I pressed my hand to his stomach to push him away . . . but my body betrayed me. My fingers slowly fisted in his shirt, blasting me with memory after memory of skating my fingertips along the defined muscles of his abdomen.

"Libby . . ."

My knees shook at the plea in his voice.

"I told you," I began, my voice nothing more than a whisper. "I told you that you would come back and I wouldn't be waiting for you."

"You've said that for nine years."

"And I've meant it," I said through clenched teeth.

He huffed, the sound between a laugh and a sneer. "Could've fooled me." He pushed away from the wall and took a few steps away before quickly eating up the distance between us again. "Every time I've come back we've picked up where we left off. *Every* time."

"So, in your head that means I've been here, doing what . . . ? Pining after you like some naïve girl? Dreaming we would be together in the end?" I asked, trying to hide the waver in my voice as I confessed realities and fantasies I wished weren't true. I sidestepped him when he reached for me and held up a hand to stop him from trying again. "No. You've had your disgusting groupies—"

"Groupies?" he asked in a lethal tone.

"—and I've had men keeping my bed warm."

He grabbed my outstretched hand and pulled me to him, his head dipping so we were eye level. "You and I both know I would never go near a *groupie* just like we both know nothing can change the fact that you're mine."

I stared into his fierce, pleading eyes for a few moments, a sad smile pulling at my lips. "Now who's naïve?" When his hand tightened around mine, I said, "You think I'm yours, but you're never here. You've always expected me to leave with you, but this is where I want to be."

"Where you want to be?" he asked with a disbelieving laugh. "You've always told me that you wanted to get away from your family . . . and then when I gave you chance after chance, you told me you couldn't leave them."

"Just because I didn't want any part of them doesn't mean I can leave them or want to."

He dropped my hand to rake his through his hair. "Do you hear yourself, Libby?"

"You didn't have a family. You don't understand." As soon as the words left my lips, I wished I could take them back.

Maxon stood there, fingers locked at the back of his neck, staring at me with an unreadable, shattering expression.

"I have a family," he finally said. "I have the guys. And I always had you . . . until now."

Maxon and Lincoln, the lead guitarist of Henley, were in the same foster home from a young age. One that, around the time they aged out, was investigated for parental physical and drug abuse.

They spent most of their lives away from that house, both forming the band with the other two members . . . and Maxon with me.

He'd been there through everything. My dad being murdered. Trying to resist what my family was . . . even if Maxon wasn't allowed to know the extent of it or our dynamic. But he'd been there.

My silent support.

First crush. Kiss. Love. Everything.

He was supposed to be the last.

And then he left.

"Maxon, I'm sorry," I whispered when he started walking away. "I didn't mean it."

"Why are you here, Libby?" he asked suddenly, then turned to face me. Gesturing at the building behind me, he laughed sadly. "You said you always meant it. So, if you weren't waiting for me, why'd you start working at The Jack when I left? Why are you still here?"

I bit back my automatic response and shook my head.

As far as everyone knew, it was another way to rebel against my family—against what we were. But Maxon would see right through that.

"You hated the bar scene," he continued. "But you were there for every show. I left, and two weeks later, you were working here. So, what was it? Did you want to find another bassist who played here? Maybe a frontman?"

"Oh, fuck you."

He flung his arms out to his sides. "Give me something, Libby. I've been going out of my fucking mind the last six months. I've been on edge and picking fights with anyone and everyone. And now it feels like I can't breathe because you're taking my goddamn heart and slowly crushing it."

"I'm crushing *your* heart?" I asked, the words sounding strangled. I nodded quickly. "Right . . . right. Okay, you wanna know
why I'm here? I'm here because I gave some asshole my virginity
on the stage of that bar after a show. I'm here because *my* heart was
brutally torn from my chest in the back room when that same jerk
told me he was leaving when he was *still inside me*. And I wanted to
be surrounded by those memories so I'd never forget you. I wanted
every high and every low. And then you fucking destroyed me."

Maxon looked lost. His arms hung limply. "Destroyed you . . ."

"But I'm done," I said through the tightening of my throat. "The
Jack has become my home away from home. And those highs and
lows are now just memories that will haunt me in my home. For
so long, I told myself I wouldn't wait for you. But now I really am
done. I can't do this anymore, Maxon. Not when it feels like this.
I won't keep waiting for you to come back and stay here when I
know you never will. I want someone who wants to *stay* with me.
Who wants to settle down and start a family *with* me."

"Settle—fam—Libby. You *never* wanted to settle down," he
stammered, his face ashen. "You never wanted a family. You refused
to be tied down."

"Things change," I cried out. "I'm thirty-one, Maxon . . . I'm
allowed to want something more than this."

"Then you should've told me," he yelled, hitting his chest. "I've
wanted to give you that for as long as I can remember. I've *told* you
I'd give you that one day."

"You *wanted* to give me that," I whispered. "You wanted to give
me that before you became the biggest secret the world wanted
to reveal."

"Nothing has changed," he said earnestly, even though everything had.

He wasn't my Maxon anymore. He wasn't the boy who wrote
songs about me while I lay with my head in his lap, and then sang

them in my ear while slowly undressing me.

He was *Maxon James: America's mysterious rock star*. He had people crawling over each other for a chance to unravel a piece of the silent, solemn Henley in the group of wild bad boys.

I thought they'd never be able to. I was wrong.

"I promised myself that I would stop waiting for you when I turned thirty," I said, my voice trembling. "Thirty came and went, and yet I *still* waited for the nights when you'd call. And then—" A sob wrenched from my chest. "How can you tell me you're coming back for me? How can you stand here demanding to know what happened like you didn't wreck me?"

"Because I don't know what happened," he yelled, exasperation leaking through every word.

"I was here, Maxon. I was here just like I've *been* here . . . and you were in California getting some groupie pregnant."

He went still, his face falling into a hardened mask. When he spoke, his tone was low and grave. "This better be a fucking joke."

"Funny. That's what I said."

He ran his tattooed hands over his face, his light eyes burning when he looked at me. "From the beginning of all this, what's the one thing I've told you?" When I didn't respond, he yelled, "What's the one fucking thing, Libby?"

The media lies.

I didn't respond. I kept my head high and held his furious stare.

Because he *had* told me that. He'd told me that repeatedly over the last nine years.

It'd been easy to believe him in the beginning. Even easier because the news had been flooded with reports of the Henley boys, each more outrageous than the last. Because Maxon had spent so many nights talking to me until I'd fallen asleep in the early hours of the morning, I knew each new story was just that. A *story*.

But as the years passed, more of the reports went from outrageous to factual.

Like when the guys had spiraled into a life of destruction a few years after they hit big. The drummer, Ledger, smashed his car into a concrete divider . . . and he really *had* been three times over the legal alcohol limit with drugs in both his pockets and his car.

Or when Maxon and Lincoln were arrested for a bar fight . . . and he refused to tell me why, only saying, "Don't listen to anything. The media lies."

With each news article that held more fact than fiction, it became harder to ignore the media. Easier to believe that Maxon simply liked knowing I would always be there.

I hated thinking I was *that* girl. The girl waiting for the rock star.

I'd refused from the beginning to be her. It's why I'd always told him I wouldn't be waiting when he came back. It's why I found guys to occupy my time when Maxon was gone.

But it didn't change what we had.

It didn't change the swarm of butterflies in my stomach on the nights my phone lit up with his name. Or the rush of emotion when I finally saw him after months. The way my body responded to his touch or the way my soul cried out when we separated.

Then everything came crashing down around me six months ago.

Not twelve hours after he'd told me about the tour—told me he was coming back for me—it was everywhere:

"Maxon James Has Been Rocking More Than Just The Stage. Henley's Mysterious Bad Boy To Be a Dad!"

"Women Everywhere Are Crying. Maxon James Officially Off The Market."

"Henley's Mystery Boy a Mystery No More! Maxon James Revealed."

"See The Glowing Parents-To-Be! First Photo of The Lady Who Snagged Maxon James."

That's when I *knew* I'd become that girl. It didn't matter what I'd always claimed . . . I was that naïve girl waiting for the rock star to come home and spend forever with her.

The butterflies and the rush and the connection—everything that got me through to the next phone call or visit—they were nothing more than a fantasy I'd desperately clung to.

Because like the article said . . . women everywhere were crying.

I was simply one of many.

Maxon held up a finger, indicating one. "I've never touched a groupie. You know that."

Before he could lift a second finger, a bitter laugh touched my lips. "I don't know you at all anymore. You're just the guy I gave my virginity to a long time ago and made even more mistakes with after."

The hurt and shock that tore across his face echoed in the recesses of my chest, but I refused to back down.

When he stood like a statue of heartache, I folded my arms around my stomach, as if that might hold me together, and spoke through the knot in my throat as I took a step away. "Goodbye, Maxon."

"Rebel."

I faltered, my legs unsteady when I prided myself on standing strong.

I always had until he'd broken me.

"You don't get to call me that anymore," I whispered through my pain.

"And you don't get to call us a mistake because of something you clearly don't understand. I've called and texted you every fucking day, and I never heard a word from you."

"Why would I want to talk to you?" I asked with a disbelieving laugh.

"Libby . . ."

I jerked away from him when he tried to grab my hand. "No, let me go, Maxon," I nearly shouted. "Don't you get it? It's over. We're done. Let me walk away and let me move on from you."

"We're never gonna be done. You're mine."

Always. I'll always be yours.

"I've never been yours." The lie was thick on my tongue, tears filled my eyes. When he started talking over me, I cried out, "I'm getting married."

The words hung in the air like the tiniest devastation.

Maxon stared at me, unseeing, his face void of any emotion as seconds dragged with a slowness I knew well.

His chest heaved, and he swayed slightly before steadying himself. His stare drifted to where my left hand was hidden from his sight. Denial filled his eyes and was quickly replaced with rage.

Because this was never part of our agreement.

Sleep with other people? Fine.

Date them? No. Never.

Marry them? Hell no.

Pregnancies? Fuck no.

It was always supposed to be Maxon and me in the end.

"Does it feel like the ground was just ripped out from beneath you? Does it feel like you're hollow?" I asked through my tears. "Imagine being me and seeing it everywhere. Seeing pictures of you with *her*."

"Who is he?" he asked, his words gruff.

"I couldn't escape it," I continued. "I couldn't tell myself they were all lies when the headlines and words and pictures were shouting so loudly." My hands moved sluggishly toward my head as a cry sounded from deep in my soul. "It got in my head and twisted my gut. Laid brick after brick in the empty space where my heart used to be."

"You don't know what you're talking about."

"Because the media lies?" I mocked with a huff. "Yeah, well . . . not all photos do. Some of those pictures are hard to dispute."

Maxon didn't stop me when I turned and walked to my car. And I didn't bother asking for my heart back.

He could keep it.

No one else would ever come close to deserving it.

Seven

Maxon

WALKED THROUGH DOWNTOWN WAKE Forest without paying attention to where I was headed or how long I'd been walking. I was stopped a few times for pictures and autographs, but for the most part, I was able to blend into the people still lingering on the streets and spilling out of restaurants.

Blending in was something I'd always been good at. It's why paparazzi rarely got pictures of me unless I was out with the guys. Because the guys . . . they were another story. It was as if constant spotlights followed them around, begging for people to see them.

I didn't like that part of this life—being seen. Being noticed. Being followed and picked apart until there was nothing left. Until the entire world felt like they knew you.

There was only one girl who had known me. Only one girl I'd ever let really *see* me. And she was fucking engaged.

The feeling of loss and emptiness crawled through me, slow and agonizing and consuming.

I groaned and raked my hands over my face. I wanted to go back in time and try to prevent her from meeting whoever this guy was. To go back when her wants for the future shifted and be here to remind her that I had always wanted to be her forever.

"Hey, rock star."

My steps slowed, and I glanced over the tips of my fingers to find the owner of that voice.

I dropped my hands, my arms falling heavily to my sides when I saw Libby's brother and friends sitting at a table outside a coffee shop.

"Glad I got to see this look," Einstein continued. "Told you I rooted for you from the beginning."

"What look?" I asked, exhaustion weighing down my words.

"The *I-fucked-up-so-hard* look."

I lifted my hands, only to let them fall again. A breath of a laugh escaped me, but there was no humor behind it. "I've told her forever that I wanted to marry her. I've told her that I was *going* to. She told me she didn't want that. How the hell is any of this my fault?"

"Never mind. He still doesn't get it," she muttered and quickly drummed her fingers on the table. Each drum bringing her hand closer to the pile of cell phones in the middle.

"Apparently not," I mumbled.

"Leave it," Dare barked at her, then looked to me. "You talked to her?"

I looked at him, letting my expression answer for me.

"You fucked up the minute you got someone pregnant."

"Jesus," I said on a groan.

Einstein laughed, then looked at Dare with surprise. "Wait . . . you're serious? You're all mad because you think he got someone pregnant?" When no one responded, she said, "Sometimes I hate being the only smart one."

"Again . . . the media lies."

"That's not Maxon's baby. It was never a question of if it was his baby." Einstein's revelation was said with a hint of annoyance as she kicked a chair out in my direction. She waited until I dropped into it before grumbling, "It really didn't take being a genius to figure that out."

Everyone except Einstein was staring at me, their expressions ranging from shame to confusion.

I ran my hands through my hair. "Libby knows that. I called her and left messages explaining what was happening—*who* that girl is."

Dare's head snapped to Einstein. "Why the hell have you been mad? Why did you think we were?"

"Because Libby shut Maxon out *and he let her*. And like I've been saying, *I* rooted for him." She glanced at me with a careful expression. "And I doubt Libby knows. She ignored every call and deleted every message without reading or listening to them. She hasn't let anyone talk about you—including me. I was sure you'd show up, but you never did. Six months?" She scoffed. "Figured you were too stupid to realize you'd lost her or you didn't care."

What the hell?

She doesn't know? She really thinks . . . fuck, Libby.

Those months of silence had been torture. Impossible to get through.

It had been hard to breathe earlier when Libby wasn't there before the show and then flipped me off. Turned from me.

But nothing compared to the excruciating pain I felt now.

Nothing compared to the weight on my chest, making every breath a struggle, knowing I might've been able to prevent this.

And now she's engaged.

"I thought she knew . . . she *should* have known." I shook my head and rubbed at my empty, aching chest. "But Libby and I went days without talking—sometimes even a week. And we'd been so slammed prepping for the tour that I hadn't realized she was ghosting me until the tour started. I couldn't just leave. But I called and texted her every fucking day we were on the road. Kept telling myself I'd see her at the end and . . ." I swallowed thickly and choked out a laugh. "Doesn't matter anymore."

"Idiot," Einstein mumbled.

"She's engaged, so how the hell do I compete with that?"

From the utter silence and stunned looks from every person at that table with me, it was clear I was missing something.

"The fuck did you just say?" Dare asked, his tone low and threatening.

"She's engaged . . ."

Once again, Dare's head whipped in Einstein's direction, but she just burst out laughing and dug through her bag before tossing a set of keys at me. "I can tell you with one hundred percent certainty that Libby hasn't so much as looked at another man that way since your supposed daddy status made headlines, and she sure as shit isn't engaged. I'm also positive she won't let you in the door, but I'm still rooting for you, so"—cupping a hand around her mouth, she mock-whispered—"my car's the red one behind you."

My hand fisted around the keys and my chest rose and fell with uneven breaths. "She's not engaged?" I asked slowly.

"She better not be," Dare bit out.

Einstein rolled her eyes and ignored him. "You tell us. In all the years I've known her, she's only ever mentioned marrying one guy . . . and he's sitting at this table instead of fixing things with her."

"She better not be," Dare repeated through clenched teeth, earning a smack on his arm from his wife.

I was going to shake that damn girl.

I was going to shake her and yell at her. Then I'd kiss her and spend the next few days buried inside her. And yeah, I was going to fucking marry her.

I looked at Dare, my head shaking subtly. "You know me. You've known me forever. No one can or will take better care of her than me." I stood from the chair and took a few steps back. "She might not be engaged now, but one day she will be. And it'll be to me."

Eight

Libby

LISTENED FOR THE SOUNDS of Einstein's talking when our apartment door opened and shut. She had a habit of walking in, already mumbling about things she needed me to know.

Or just mumbling to herself.

But it was silent.

I twisted on my bed and placed my feet on the floor, my movements halting and stomach dropping when the voice that sounded in the hall wasn't Einstein's.

"Why'd you say it?"

I sat there, frozen, watching in horror as Maxon rounded the corner to my doorway.

His whiskey eyes locked on mine, his expression a mixture of frustration and need. "Why, Rebel?"

Air rushed from my lungs like I'd been punched. "How are you here?" I asked, the words barely more than a wheeze.

He held up Einstein's keys only to drop them on my dresser as he moved deeper into my room. "I heard you didn't read or listen to any of my messages, so you're going to listen to me now."

My head was already shaking, my eyes filling with tears.

I didn't want to do this with Maxon. Not now, not six months ago, not ever.

"That's not my baby," he said slowly, like he wanted to make sure I heard and understood every word. "That girl? Jesus Christ, Libby, did you ever look at her face?"

I jerked at the frustration in his tone but didn't respond. I couldn't. My throat was so tight I could barely breathe.

I'd seen pictures of them. They'd been everywhere.

Pictures of them walking with Maxon's arm hooked around her neck. Pictures of them hugging. Another of him kissing her cheek. In every one, she had a very clear baby bump and a diamond on her ring finger.

But I couldn't recall her face.

Maxon dropped to a crouch before me so his face was directly in front of mine. When he spoke again, his tone was soft. "The media lies, Libby," he whispered, echoing words I'd heard thousands of times from him. "That was *Ava*."

"What?" I choked out, my head shaking and mind racing.

I knew Ava. Knew who she was to Maxon. She was in the foster home with him and Lincoln.

"She lives just outside LA now with her husband . . . remember? Lincoln and I see her sometimes."

I already knew that . . .

My stomach ached and twisted with guilt.

I tried again to remember the girl in the pictures with Maxon, but there was nothing.

I never looked at her face. I couldn't bear the thought of seeing the woman he'd chosen over me. Just as I couldn't stand to hear his words.

There'd been too many photos over too many years, and I hadn't been able to go through it again.

I felt like the worst kind of idiot.

"Those pictures were taken when we met up to have lunch with them. Her husband and Lincoln were right next to us, but just out of the shot, in *every* picture. Her husband called me laughing when he saw them, and . . . God, I was *positive* you would've recognized her and done the same. I had no clue you actually thought the girl and the baby were mine. None, Libby."

I blinked quickly in a vain attempt to stop the tears that were steadily slipping down my cheeks, then dropped my head into my hands when a sob broke free. "Oh God."

I'd been sure he'd thrown our life away without a single thought. It had slayed me. Wrecked me. Because nothing in my life had ever felt as right, as perfect, as Maxon.

To know I was the one who ruined us . . .

He grabbed my hands and pulled them down so he could look into my eyes. "Why'd you tell me you were engaged?"

"I wanted you to know what I'd been going through. To feel what I'd felt." I laughed weakly. "It's the same reason I always left before you woke up. I wanted you to have a taste of what it felt like when you left me."

"Fuck, Libby." He curled his hands around my neck and pressed his mouth to mine in a slow, passionate, claim.

And it was just like it always had been between us . . .

Right.

Perfect.

My body buzzed beneath his touch and my soul sang. I was finally whole. It was a feeling I didn't think I'd ever get enough of.

"What about the rest?" he whispered before raking his teeth across my bottom lip. "Was everything else you said a lie?"

I pressed my forehead against his and released a stuttered breath. "I said a lot to you tonight that I didn't mean." When he only looked at me, prompting me to go on, I said, "That we were a mistake.

That I wasn't yours."

"Settling down . . . the family?" he asked as he slowly pushed me back on the bed.

My face pinched with grief.

Because I wanted that, but I knew I would never find someone I wanted to give my life to. Not like the man currently kneeling above me, reaching for the band of my sleep shorts.

"I do want that," I admitted. "But that doesn't change the reality of our situation. That doesn't change that you're on the other side of the United States or that I want a family here."

He stilled, his eyes searching mine. "You really want to be here?" When I dipped my head, he blew out a stuttered breath and nodded resolutely. "We'll figure it out. Whatever you want. Ask me to leave Henley, and I'll do it."

"I don't want that," I said quickly and struggled to sit up on the bed. "I've never wanted that. Those guys are your family. You said it earlier."

"They'll be my family if we aren't a band, but they know what you mean to me. They know what it's been like for me since we left here and how much the last few months have nearly destroyed me."

I lifted a hand to his face, pressing the tips of my fingers to his lips. "I'm sorry."

He grabbed my wrist to put more pressure to his lips, then pulled my hand away. "They know my life doesn't make sense without you."

"I would never ask you to stop playing, and I don't want you to."

"But you've been waiting for me to come back and stay," he said, recalling my earlier words.

I smiled sadly. "I never claimed to be easy to handle."

The corner of his mouth curled into a smirk that made my stomach swirl with need. "I think I handle you just fine," he murmured. "I also think Henley needs some time off . . . after that I can figure out the fucking long commute to LA from here."

I barely had time to register his words before his mouth was on mine again.

"Are you serious?" I asked against the kiss, my tone a mixture of disbelief and pure joy.

"Rebel," he said with a soft laugh. After brushing another kiss across my lips, he laid me back on the bed, his mouth moving across my jaw and down my throat. "I've always known I wanted forever with you. Just been waiting for you to get there with me."

Our next kiss was a slow claiming. Our touches nothing more than faint, teasing brushes as we unhurriedly removed clothes. When Maxon spread my thighs at an achingly slow pace, those faint brushes became hard and demanding, our kiss rough and pleading.

I clung to his muscled forearms as he shifted his body to kneel between my legs, and tried to follow him when he pulled away from the kiss.

"From now on, you don't leave before I wake," he said in a low, serious tone.

My head dropped back, and my mouth opened with a whimper when he pressed his thumb to my aching clit.

"If you see something that bothers you, you ask me about it. Don't fucking ghost me."

I started to nod but cried out when he pushed two fingers inside me, pumping me roughly, thoroughly, exactly the way he knew I liked it. "Oh God, Maxon . . . yes."

"The next time you tell someone you're engaged, you're gonna have my ring on your finger."

My lips twitched into a smile, excitement swirling in my chest just as his mouth covered me, sucking and licking and teasing me while his fingers fucked me. I secured my fingers in his hair, pressing him closer and shuddering when he groaned against me. The heat in my belly suddenly intensified when he raked his teeth over my clit, my back arching away from the bed as my orgasm tore through me.

My mouth opened with a silent moan as wave after wave of pleasure rolled through me until I was nothing more than a trembling mess weakly attempting to cling to what I'd almost lost.

A shiver ran down my spine when he swiped his tongue against me one last time and then pushed himself up to press his mouth to my stomach.

"If they want to print about me being a dad, it'll be because *this* belly is round with *my* child."

I pulled him close and whispered, "Yes. Yes, to everything."

"About damn time."

A laugh rolled up my throat and turned into a whimper when his thick length pressed against my entrance. "Please," I whispered, my fingers tightening in his hair and legs wrapping around his hips. "Maxon, please."

My head fell back when he slowly pushed into me. His mouth and teeth trailed up my neck at the same torturous pace until he was fully seated inside me, bare for the first time.

This was how it was always meant to be. Us. Together. Completing each other in a way only we could.

How I ever thought I could live without this—without *him* . . .

And then he moved.

Each roll of his hips was powerful and demanding. Each thrust pushed me to a high I was sure I would never come down from.

I moaned when he pressed his mouth to mine—devouring me—begging me for everything I was. Making me crave more of the intoxicating mixture on his lips and tongue of whiskey and me. A silent proclamation. A heady claim.

This man was mine.

I whimpered in protest when he moved back to sit on his knees and pulled most of the way out. He gripped my hips and lifted me so only my upper back and head were touching the bed, a wicked grin playing on his lips when I tried to move against him and wasn't able to. A frustrated cry fell from my lips and ended with a sharp whimper when he roughly forced me onto his cock, sending me spiraling into a bliss that pulsed from deep in my core.

"Fuck, Libby," he growled as I trembled around him. Each shudder had him tightening his possessive grip on me. Each ripple of pleasure through my body silently urged him faster and harder until he found his release inside me.

His body tensed, his muscles straining as he slowly pumped inside me once . . . twice . . . and then shakily set me on the bed and lowered his body to mine.

I laced my fingers through his hair, pulling him closer and pressing his forehead to mine as our chests moved with our ragged breaths. "I love you."

A brilliant smile pulled at his mouth before he was brushing it across mine. "When are you gonna let me give you my last name, Rebel?"

The high I'd been on immediately dipped.

Maxon's smile faded when he saw my expression. "Libby . . ." he began warily. "What—I thought—"

"No, no. It's not that. It's not what you think," I hurried to say when he moved to sit in the middle of the bed. I pulled the sheet over my chest and licked my lips as my mind raced. "If you ask me to, I will leave with you in the morning and take your last name."

His face fell into an unreadable mask. "I've been waiting to hear that since we were eighteen . . . but I know there's a *but* coming."

"You started calling me Rebel so long ago. That name fits me better than you realize." I hesitated for a second, my tongue darting out to wet my lips. "I never wanted to leave my family, Maxon. I was just *rebelling* from what they were—what *I* was. But I couldn't tell you."

"You mean the mafia?"

I stilled, my breath catching in my throat when Maxon said the title so casually. "How . . ."

Maxon laughed softly, his face cracking with relief. "Jesus, Libby.

I've been in love with you for as long as I can remember. You think I wouldn't catch on that something was going on with your family?" When I stared at him in shock, he asked, "Is that what you were worried about me finding out? Is that the *but?*"

"Well, yeah . . ."

A fuller laugh left him as he placed me on his lap. His eyes searched my face, amusement dancing in them. "This?" he murmured, passing his fingers across the tattoo on the back of my neck. "You told me about it when we were in second grade. You drew it and said, 'This is me. I'm a rebel.'" Maxon's smile stretched wider. "You rebel against everything, Libby, but I call you Rebel because of that day."

I automatically reached back to touch where his fingers had just been.

Four horizontal lines, each shorter than the one above it, with a vertical line slashing through, longer than the others. All centered in an outline of a circle.

It was our family's symbol. We adopted it when they rebelled from a different mafia family long before I was born. Now every Borello member had it tattooed or branded on them to show their allegiance with pride.

I'd never been proud of what we were, but the blood pounding through my veins had marked me a rebel from birth.

I just couldn't believe I'd told Maxon.

"But I didn't really know what you were until your dad was murdered," he continued, his tone solemn. "No one in town seemed to know or talk about it. Your brother immediately dropped out of school, and you acted like it wasn't a big deal. And whenever I saw him over the next few years, he had adults straight out of a mafia movie hanging on his every word. But I'm pretty fucking positive I wasn't supposed to see any of that since I was usually sneaking in or out of your window."

A breath of a laugh escaped my lips, and my head shook in

disbelief. "I just—I can't believe you knew all this time."

"Would it have changed our relationship before?" When I only offered him a pained smile and shook my head, he shrugged. "Then what does it matter?"

"Doesn't it matter to you?"

He placed a teasing kiss on my lips. "Is Dare gonna have me killed if I marry you?"

I tilted my head to the side and pretended to think about it before leaning in for another kiss. "No. He'd just do it himself." My chest shook with a laugh at Maxon's stunned expression. "He wouldn't. Dare dissolved the gang over a year ago. He doesn't want anything to do with that life anymore."

"Really?" he asked, surprise coating the word. "Why?"

"That's another story, and it's not mine to tell," I whispered against his lips. "Knowing all you know, you still want to marry me?"

He nipped my bottom lip then pressed his mouth to mine, kissing me tenderly. "Always, Rebel. I'll always want to marry you."

Sorrow and grief still pulsed through me from how much the probability of losing him had affected me. My heart still felt bruised from the months of believing there was no hope.

But it made my love for him undeniable. It left me assured our lives were irrevocably intertwined.

And I felt whole for the first time in so long.

He twisted me around so I straddled his lap, his eyes burning with need when he gripped my hips to position me over his hardening length.

My head dropped back, a low moan building in my chest when I sank down onto him. I rocked against him slowly, letting my head roll forward to hold his heated stare. "So, Maxon James, about my last name . . ."

Nine

Libby

STRETCHED LAZILY, RELISHING IN the aches that accompanied two blissful nights in bed with Maxon, my movements halting when the person behind me burrowed closer.

Someone too small to be Maxon. Someone smaller than me.

Someone with ice-cold feet pressed to my ankles.

My eyes flew open, a demand for my best friend to get out of the bed on the tip of my tongue, until my brain suddenly caught up with the situation.

If Einstein was in bed with me . . . that meant Maxon was gone.

And Henley was scheduled to return to LA today.

I was out of bed and storming out of the room before my chest had a chance to start aching.

My gaze touched everything as I moved . . .

The leather cuff I gave him when he first left Wake Forest wasn't on my nightstand.

The clothes I'd ripped off his body last night weren't scattered on my floor.

The acoustic guitar Lincoln brought over yesterday was no longer propped against the couch.

There wasn't a trace of him anywhere.

He wouldn't.

He wouldn't, he wouldn't, he wouldn't.

Cruel, unwanted thoughts reared in my head, saying *he would.*

Saying Maxon did this—did everything—to get back at me for all the times I told him I wouldn't be waiting for him. For all the times I left before he woke. For the last six months.

But every promise and plea, every touch and kiss, were quick to push those thoughts away, making his disappearance that much more incomprehensible. That much more painful.

I didn't realize I was gripping at my chest and my hair until I heard a loud, obnoxious yawn from behind me.

I turned, my breaths coming out rough and ragged when I saw Einstein watching me with a look of annoyance.

"Kinda hard to cuddle when you jump out of bed like it's on fire."

"He's gone," I said, the words nothing more than a breath.

"Well, who would stay when that's how you sleep? Jesus."

"He's gone."

"Calm down," she mumbled as she passed me, wrapping my comforter around her tiny frame before plopping on the couch. "He'll be back when he's done."

A wounded laugh punched from my chest. "He was supposed to be done, Einstein. He wasn't going to go back—not for a while. We were going to—" I bit at my lip, unable to say the words as pain seared my chest.

Einstein stared at me like I'd grown another head. "Have you always been needy and whiny and insecure? Because I feel like we wouldn't have been friends if I'd realized this before now."

I straightened, my expression falling into something I was sure would've made others cower.

Not Einstein.

"I thought I lost him to someone else," I said through gritted teeth. "Now after having him back for a couple nights, he's gone. And you're calling me—"

"Yeah, and like I said, he'll be back. Do you want him to talk to Dare or not?"

My head jerked back. For a few seconds, I stood there watching Einstein. "Wait, what?"

"You honestly think the two of you can be together without Dare's approval? Dare hates him."

"He's . . . he's talking to Dare?"

"Yeah." She waved a comforter-covered hand toward the hall-way. "If you wouldn't have jumped out of bed and ran, I would've told you that."

"I didn't—" I laughed faintly and ran my hands through my hair. "Considering I didn't fall asleep next to you, I wasn't expecting to wake up with you there."

"Well, don't sound so butt-hurt about it. I'm an awesome cuddler."

"You only cuddle because you're cold."

"Doesn't change the fact that I'm awesome at it," she shot back. "Anyway, I was about to make coffee when he left. I figured cuddling was better than coffee."

My mouth twitched into a smirk. "Cuddling in the bed I'd had sex in all weekend? On and under that comforter?"

Einstein's face went void of any emotion. After a few seconds, she pushed the comforter away from her body and stood from the couch. "If you need me, I'll be in the shower. Scrubbing my skin with steel wool."

I laughed when she passed me, light and free.

Now that I knew where Maxon was and knew he was coming back, it felt like a weight had lifted off my chest. It felt like how it always should've been.

Maxon and me.

Together in Wake Forest.

The dream I'd always had but could never touch, wasn't only in reach now, I was living it.

Over the next two hours, I moved around the apartment on a cloud.

I washed the bedding and took a shower. I dressed in something other than clean pajamas since Maxon would be back soon. Made coffee and breakfast for a still-scowling Einstein and myself.

And when Maxon knocked on the door as he opened it, I ran for him and jumped into his arms.

But the way he gripped me, arms like steel bands around my body, like he was afraid of what would happen when he let go, had me leaning away.

I gripped at his hair and pulled his head away from my chest, searching his whiskey eyes, my heart sinking as he slowly lowered me to my feet.

"Maxon . . ." My unspoken question lingered in the air between us.

"Holy shit," Einstein said from somewhere beside us, drawing out the words.

But Maxon didn't respond or look at her. He stared at me with eyes like fire as the muscles in his jaw worked.

When I started to look toward Einstein, she asked, "He said no, didn't he?"

"What?" I searched Maxon's expression for any indication that what she assumed was wrong. My stomach dropped moments later. "No. No, tell me this is a joke."

The corners of his mouth twitched into a weak smile. "It'll be okay."

"You have to be fucking kidding me," I said through gritted teeth, trying to shove from Maxon's arms so I could get to the door and to my brother.

But his arms only tightened, and then his mouth was on mine.

When my body relaxed, he moved his lips to my forehead and placed a gentle kiss there. "It'll be okay," he repeated. "You're mine, and I'm not going anywhere. He'll change his mind eventually."

I nodded against his lips, but I didn't plan on waiting for *eventually* to come around.

Dare couldn't give me my freedom only to control my life.

He couldn't stop me from being with Maxon after waiting nine years for him to come home to *stay*.

Dare would change his mind sooner rather than later, or he wasn't going to have a say at all.

Ten

Maxon

TWIRLED A FRY BETWEEN my fingers then dropped it in the basket. "I just can't believe you're actually serious."

"Dude. If you're all in, *we're* all in. And if we're doing this, then we're fucking doing this right."

"Don't say *we* like we all agreed to this," Jared said.

"You didn't disagree," Ledger said matter-of-factly.

"I said it was dumb to make that kind of split-second decision when there's no motivation for us like Maxon."

I held a hand out toward Jared, as if to show one of them had sense.

"You were heard. And you were outvoted," Ledger continued. "This is our hometown, that's all the motivation we need." A smirk slowly pulled at his mouth. "What better way to say 'welcome home'?"

Something that resembled a laugh left me as I ran my hands through my hair, leaving my head hanging when I mumbled, "Jesus."

I should've known.

I should've fucking known.

I'd had no doubts the guys would support my decision in wanting a break to spend time with Libby. To slow down for the first time in too long.

But I hadn't expected *this*.

"We're family," Lincoln said with a shrug when they dragged me out there, like that explained their need to be over the top and impulsive with everything in their lives.

I'd turned and walked away, unable to respond to what I was seeing. What I was hearing.

What they were planning would make my life a hell of a lot easier on so many levels.

With work.

With having them around.

But, fuck, if Dare didn't want me with Libby before . . .

I knew it was pointless to have another conversation with him. He'd made his opinion clear and wasn't changing it anytime soon.

So in the few days since he'd crushed my dreams of marrying the girl I'd waited a lifetime for, I'd tried to silently prove I wasn't going anywhere.

That I wasn't simply good enough for her . . . but that I was good *for* her.

And then my bandmates—my brothers—dropped a bomb on me.

A gift and a goddamn death sentence.

"I need to talk to you."

I looked up when Libby's voice suddenly came from beside the table, my blood heating and body responding just having my girl so close.

Her dark eyes were full of fire and fixed on me.

She looked like a lethal combination of sex and wrath.

Fuck me if I didn't get hard.

"You hear the news?" Ledger asked, his earlier smirk now stretched wide.

"Yeah. Maxon. Now." Every word was said through clenched teeth, her gaze never leaving me.

Einstein walked up behind her, for once not on a phone or tablet, her expression grim as she mouthed, "You're so fucked."

"Shit," I mumbled and slid out of the booth.

Libby was stalking away before I straightened, and by the time I caught up with her near the other side of Brooks Street Café, she whirled on me, already yelling at me below her breath.

"Have you lost your fucking mind, Maxon James? You really think you can do *this* and Dare will be okay with us being together?"

Not what I expected.

I stilled, wondering what news she'd heard and why she was so damn mad.

"You're pissed about what I'm doing?" When she lifted an eyebrow in confirmation, I nodded, an edgy laugh scraping up my throat. "Right. Right, because first you were pissed that I wasn't staying here with you. And now you're pissed that I *am*?"

"I'm pissed that you think you can come in here and try to ruin us with a decision that could've been avoided if you would've just talked to me."

Funny. She nearly ruined us by not talking to me.

I glanced over my shoulder to make sure no one was looking our way as her accusations got louder and louder.

Locking my gaze with hers, I stepped into her space, leading her backward until she was pressed to the wall without ever touching her.

"I get that for the last decade we've been apart, and for the last five days, it's been you and me in each other's faces. That takes time to get used to. I know. Now, if you need to bitch and scream, I'm here to calm you. But if you're gonna come at me because you feel a little trapped after being free for so long, don't expect me to lie down and take it."

"Wouldn't dream of it."

"You said you wanted to settle down and have a family, and, Rebel, that's what I'm trying to give you," I murmured, my voice dropping low as I ran my hand over her flat stomach. The corner of my mouth twitched up when she trembled beneath my touch. "I've been waiting most of my life to spend the rest of it with you. You can't expect me to let your brother stop me."

"You're an idiot if you think he *can't* stop you. If you think he *won't* stop us. And he *will* if you plan on buying that godforsaken prison and trying to make me live there."

My brows pinched, and I wondered how Libby knew that I'd been looking at houses at all. "Prison," I stated dully.

"The Holloway Estate," she said with a sneer. "That place is a prison."

I stared at her for so long, her anger started to fade. "The Holloway Estate . . . that's what this is about?" Before she could answer, I gave a light laugh. "I don't know, Libby, that place is perfect. It has a guest house away from the main house . . ."

Her jaw clenched.

"There's a huge row of rooms that can be turned into a recording studio on the other side of the property."

That fire in her eyes was back, burning brighter than before.

"And the house—it's massive and extravagant."

"It should be leveled to the ground," she seethed.

I cocked my head and finally allowed my growing confusion to saturate my tone. "And it's everything *I* hate and everything the *guys* are drawn to."

She jerked against the wall and blinked quickly. Her anger fading just as fast as it appeared.

"The guys are buying it, Libby. I'm not." I studied her stunned face for a second before asking, "Considering I found out an hour ago . . . how do you already know? And what the hell do I need to know about that mansion before they buy it?"

"You're not buying it?" she asked softly.

"No. Why the hell would I want a place like that?"

A faint smile played on her lips before disappearing, and her body sagged against the wall. "Einstein has that place covered. Completely. Anyone sets foot on it, she knows. Not that anyone has, but if they would've shown interest during the last year, she would've known. She knew the real estate agent got a call, but she didn't think it would be for Holloway, so she hadn't looked into it yet. And then there was a cash offer not long before the four of you set foot on the grounds this afternoon." She gave me an accusing stare.

"The guys decided if I was going to stay here, they wanted to be around too." Leaning into her, I softly demanded, "Tell me why you're mad at the thought of me buying a house."

"It's *that* house."

Relief filled my veins, but I didn't let it betray my expression, I only pressed closer to her. "Why that house?"

Her dark eyes searched mine. "That place? It was Holloway owned."

"Something about the name clued me in." Despite the amusement coating my words, Libby's face stayed carefully composed.

"They killed my dad," she finally admitted on a breath, almost too low for me to hear. "They killed Dare's fiancée, Gia. They killed dozens of Borellos." Before I could react, her stare dropped to the floor. "And we killed even more of them."

I stood there, pressing her against the wall, as the weight of her life and her family crashed around me.

When I didn't speak, she risked a glance at me. "Irish," she explained. "They were our greatest enemies. Lily, Dare's wife, was one of them. They kept her hidden there. That's why I called it a prison. That's why Dare would lose his mind if *you* bought it. That's why I would've refused to live there."

I pushed away from her and scrubbed my hands over my face.

"Jesus Christ."

"There's so much blood on that property—blood that can never be washed away."

"And there's not blood on your house?" I asked darkly.

The same pain and shame I'd seen throughout our lives filled her eyes. And I hated it.

She'd always despised what her family was. The weight of what they did shouldn't rest on her shoulders.

"They're gone now?" I asked. "These Holloways?"

"Sort of." She lifted a shoulder in a shrug. "Some of them rebelled from within and took out the leader. They disbanded not long after we did. Most of them scattered. A couple of the good ones are still here, like Lily's ex. Einstein works with them."

I stared at the girl I'd loved since I was a kid . . .

And suddenly wondered if I knew her at all.

I'd known about her.

Known what her family was.

But knowing was different than hearing. It was different than listening to her talk about it like it was everyday life.

To her, I guess it was.

But now, all I could see was the shame dripping from her expression as she'd said, *"They killed dozens of Borellos. And we killed even more of them."* Had she ever been behind any of the deaths?

My wild girl begging to be free.

My Rebel.

Fuck.

"Libby . . ."

She opened her mouth, hesitation and resilience warring on her beautiful face, as though she already knew what I was too worried to ask.

"Maxon."

I blinked, pulled out of the bubble Libby had put us in that felt too insane to be real, and turned to see our manager, Nate, standing halfway between us and the rest of the guys.

With a jerk of his head, he turned and headed toward a booth away from everyone else. A silent offer and demand.

I slowly looked to Libby, her expression now full of worry.

"I never claimed to be easy to handle," she whispered.

The air fled from my chest. "Fuck if that isn't the truth." I closed the distance between us and grabbed her chin between my fingers, tilted her head back, and pressed my mouth to hers for a quick, hard kiss. "We'll finish talking about this," I assured her as I stepped away.

She nodded but didn't look any less relieved.

I turned to leave, then looked at her. "Two stories. Four bedrooms. Three baths."

Her brow furrowed. "What?"

"Big trees and backyard. Wraparound porch. Shutters on the windows."

Her eyes widened in question and excitement.

A corner of my mouth lifted. "And you thought I would buy a mansion. I know you, Rebel." With a wink, I headed to where Nate sat, impatiently drumming the tips of his fingers together, and slid into the booth opposite him. "Surprised to see you in North Carolina."

His fingers stilled and his gaze locked on mine. When he spoke, his voice was calm and soft . . . and spoke volumes of his frustration. "I was told via text that my boys weren't returning home as scheduled. I found out from the *others* that you wanted to take time off and planned to settle here. About an hour later, Ledger hung up after shouting that they were buying property here too. And you thought I wouldn't show?"

My stare dropped as shame unfurled in my gut.

Nate was more than our manager. We didn't really know much about his past, but just as he'd been a father figure to us, he saw us as his own sons.

"I should've called," I admitted. My stare dragged to the booth that held the guys, Libby, and Einstein. "I've been busy."

"I heard." He dropped his hands to the table and shifted closer when I looked to him again. "I'm happy for you, Max, I am. You've been my easy kid from day one, and I know it's because of her. I know the husband and dad thing is what you've always wanted, and you've never made it a secret that you wanted it with her. But—"

"Don't '*but*' me." I let out a frustrated laugh. "Jesus, Nate, whatever you were about to say, don't."

"Maxon—"

"Don't." I sank roughly against the padded booth and looked around the café, my jaw aching from the pressure I was putting on it.

I knew the tone he'd suddenly taken on.

I knew that expression.

The one where he was about to deliver shit news and was trying to soften the blow.

I already had Dare trying to stop me from being with Libby . . . I didn't need Nate on his side.

"It would be one thing if you wanted that life in California while maintaining your image," Nate continued. "Or, hell, anywhere. But you don't just want that life, Max. You want to put Henley on hold for it. And that life you're wanting? It's not for a month or two . . . it's forever. You don't have the luxury of making those decisions."

I shot him a glare as I prepared to tell him exactly what I thought of his *luxuries*.

"You boys have appearances on news stations and late-night talk shows. You have shoots for covers. You have a new album to continue promoting. There are benefits and awards shows. You can't just *take a break* and move back to your hometown to hide and play lovebird."

Wanna bet?

The words reverberated in my mind, lashing and begging to be said.

Begging to voice their defiance. Begging to show their weight.

Because Nate and I both knew I could walk away without looking back, and he'd have nothing. Our original contract with him stated five years before any of us could walk at any moment—everything after was to be dealt with, and decided upon, as it came up.

We'd given almost double that.

But I couldn't do that. *Wouldn't.*

Not to Nate. Not to the guys. Not to our fans.

All reason had fled my mind the moment I'd finally gotten a taste of what I'd been waiting for my entire life.

Because a future with Libby was all I wanted, but I had a life I couldn't abandon either.

"I've waited for her forever," I said, the words rasping up my throat.

Nate dipped his head in acknowledgement.

"I'll do anything to keep her now that she's mine."

His hands lifted off the table in a placating gesture. "Bring her with you. She can come to anything. Be at everything. I'll make it happen."

My head was shaking before he finished. "She can't."

He watched me, mouth slightly open in a look of confusion and defeat.

"The reason she never came back with me before? It's because she wanted to be here—wanted to settle down and have a family here," I explained, then leaned forward to drop my elbows on the table and my head in my hands. "Her brother won't *let* us be together because of my profession and the life that follows it. If I want any chance of being with her, she *can't* come with me."

Nate was silent for so long I finally looked up at him. "Her brother," he stated dully. When I nodded, he rubbed a hand over his face, muffling his strained laugh. "Am I missing something, Max? She's your age. Her brother shouldn't have a say."

I breathed a laugh. "Yeah . . . it's complicated."

He eyed me warily. "Are they close? You know . . . *too* close?"

I swallowed the bile that immediately rose at the thought. "Fuck. No, Nate. Jesus. Their dad died when they were younger. He's protective."

"That's a little too protective."

"Tell me about it." Not that it would change anything. I didn't feel like being on an ex-mafia boss's shit list. "But I want to be where she is—and she's gonna be here."

"Max . . ."

"You said I could have that life anywhere if I maintained my image. I will. I'll go where you need me to for whatever is scheduled. Shows. Shoots. Ceremonies. But I'll be coming back here, and I want things to slow down so I can make up for the time I missed with Libby."

Nate was silent again for a while. "If anyone deserves the whole love and marriage thing, it's you. But if it's making you say *slow down* today . . . will it have you saying *stop* tomorrow?"

I knew what he wasn't asking . . . what he was wondering. Was Libby the one pushing me to take a break?

But she'd already made it clear she didn't want me to leave Henley, just as she'd made it clear what she *did* want for her life.

And I couldn't fault her for that.

"*Stop* will come eventually. It has to for everyone in this industry. Right now, all I want is time. Time she never asked me for. But time we need."

He leaned back in the booth. "I can respect that." After another moment, he said, "I'll have to look into studios around here for you boys."

"The place the guys are buying has a great building on the property that can be transformed into a space for both practicing and recording."

Nate nodded, an exaggerated sigh leaving his lips. "Of course it does. Loud and overstated, as usual?" When I only rolled my eyes, he asked, "And what did you find?"

"Something perfect for us. Exactly what she's always wanted. Under the radar."

A look of approval crossed his face. "Of course it is." He drummed his hands on the table. "Well, I guess I'll need to take a look at these properties and say hello to this girl of yours. I hate saying I didn't give her a second glance when we first met, since I didn't expect much of the two of you."

A smile quickly covered my face. "I could've told you how it would've played out between us. She's my wild one. I knew it'd take a while to catch her, just didn't know how long."

When I stood from the booth, Nate stopped me. "I *am* happy for you, Maxon," he said again. "I want the best for you, but it's my job to look at the bigger picture. I have to think about what's best for each of you individually, as well as the band. At the moment, that's continuing. And when it comes time to slowing down or ending, it's doing it the right way."

"I know." Like I was drawn, I looked toward Libby when her laugh rang through the café. My mouth twitched into a smile at the sound and the sight of her head dropped back as she laughed freely. "All I want is time," I whispered, my gaze never leaving my rebel.

"We'll figure out a way for you to have it—for you to do your jobs quickly and get back to her," Nate assured me. "We'll keep your move to Wake Forest quiet as long as we can to give you as much time as possible without people trying to pry into your lives here."

My smile fell.

I was used to prying eyes.

I was used to hiding from the world in plain sight in cities like Los Angeles.

Trying to hide in a town the size of Wake Forest—especially with the guys drawing attention? Or when the world caught wind of my relationship with Libby? It would be impossible.

If I hadn't considered it . . . I doubted Libby had.

If I wasn't prepared for it . . . I knew there was no way in hell she ever would be.

Eleven

Libby

INSTEIN'S FIST MET MY SIDE so suddenly and unexpectedly that my laughter ended on a wheeze.

My eyes cut in her direction to see what her problem was but didn't make it to her. Because there, just inside the front door, was my mother—stare wide with horror and rage as she took in the boys we were with.

"Shit," I choked out as I scrambled from the booth.

I didn't look back at Einstein or the guys—or to where Maxon was in one of the other booths. I wouldn't give her the satisfaction of knowing how worried I was that she might say something to one of them.

"What are they doing here?" she demanded when I walked past her, but I continued until I was outside. Her voice reached me before she caught up to me in the parking lot. "Answer me, Libby."

"They're eating. You know, I think you gave up the right to ask that when Lily started managing the place for you."

"This is still my restaurant," she said softly, her eyes glowering in a way she reserved for me alone.

"Technically, it's Dare's."

"Damn it, Elizabeth, don't push me. I want to know what they're still doing here. You said it was over between the two of you."

My head listed to the side. "Oh, you don't like when someone pushes you? Funny. Neither do I." I took a step closer to her and lowered my voice. "Especially if the person doing the pushing is supposed to love you unconditionally. Is supposed to protect you. But instead, is the one blindfolding you, binding your wrists, and shoving you into enemy hands."

"I *was* protecting you. I am *still* trying to protect you," she yelled. She cleared her throat, her gaze darting around as she lowered her voice. "You are putting yourself in danger. You are putting him in danger. You're putting us all in danger. You and you alone."

"Now who's being dramatic, Mom?"

"I sacrificed my life for this family, and I would do it again," she seethed. "The men have their roles and we have ours. It is our duty to do what needs to be done for the greater good, to keep the peace. And your actions incite *wars*. Your decisions destroy alliances."

Same argument. Different day.

I wondered if a day would come when we stopped having it.

I just prayed if the day came, it wouldn't be because her fears had turned to reality.

"Your precious Dare took care of it. I destroyed nothing." I stretched my arms out wide and looked around. "Would you look at that . . . no war."

"You are so naïve."

"I'm not the one who let an unfounded fear dictate her life for *ten years*." I rolled my eyes and looked away so she couldn't see the lie in my eyes.

Because I had.

I *had* let my mother's fears bleed into my own and rule my life for so long. Denying Maxon was proof of that.

I stiffened when I caught sight of Maxon starting toward us. Before he could make it to the door, he looked over his shoulder to where Einstein and the guys were.

"He needs to leave," she said gently. "They all do."

"That's not happening."

When I turned, Mom was shaking her head in disappointment.

"They're moving back here," I whispered, as if I was afraid of her reaction.

Not that I didn't know what it would be.

But I didn't want her to taint my excitement over Maxon coming home.

"Oh, Libby." Her eyes slowly shut and one of her hands covered her mouth. "What have you done?"

I looked in Maxon's direction again, to where he was now facing away from us. "I stopped worrying about the fallout. I let myself love him on the outside the way I've always loved him on the inside."

"You've always been defiant and headstrong. I didn't realize you were stupid too."

I looked at her as shock and hurt pulsed through me.

"The greatest hunter is silent, invisible, and attacks when you least expect it. I'll pray for the rest of my life that my fears won't become a reality. But I'm not the fool that blindly *hopes* that they won't. For you to laugh in their face . . ." Her head shook quickly before a quiet sob hitched in her throat. "I buried your father. Don't make me bury you."

She walked into the café without another word, and a few seconds later, Maxon touched my shoulder.

I cleared my throat and angled my head toward him, but kept my stare on the ground so he wouldn't see the conflict in my eyes.

"Wasn't that your mom?"

"Uh-huh."

Confusion coated his words when he said, "She didn't respond to me or look at me."

You should consider yourself lucky. I offered him a brief smile. "Sorry."

His eyes caught and searched mine. "What's wrong?"

"Nothing," I tried to assure him.

He studied me for a few seconds before hesitantly nodding. "Uh . . . Nate wants to meet you. But we can do it another day."

"No, today's . . . today's great."

Nothing like being reminded of every fear you overcame to make you want to live each day as if it's your last.

Twelve

Libby

WHEN I GOT HOME FROM work that Friday, the Henley boys and Einstein were spread out around the living room. The TV was on and the volume was up loud, but no one was paying attention to it.

Maxon was in the far corner with a pad of paper and his guitar.

Jared was on the couch on his phone.

Ledger was sprawled out on the couch opposite him, beer in hand and neck twisted to be involved in the conversation happening on the floor . . .

Between Lincoln and Einstein.

A very cozy-looking Lincoln and Einstein.

"You've got to be kidding me," I said under my breath.

Ledger caught sight of me when I stepped closer to the couches, a smile lighting up his face. "Hey, look who decided to grace us with her presence."

I watched Einstein's every move, noting the way she stiffened and refused to look at me.

I forced a smile. "Shouldn't you be at work, Einstein? Could've sworn you said there was a case being closed out tonight."

She shrugged and leaned in to whisper in Lincoln's ear.

Shrugged.

Einstein didn't know how to stop working. She'd also never bail on closing out a case.

That was where most of her genius was needed.

Her work helped people. Saved them.

My eyes fluttered shut when a strong arm curled around my waist and familiar lips pressed to my neck.

"Bedroom."

My mouth twitched into a smile. "Caveman."

"Something like that."

I twisted in his arms to kiss him slowly, letting my lips linger against his when I said, "Three minutes."

His heated stare raked over me when he released me and stepped away, his voice all gravel when he said, "Hurry."

I turned for the hall leading to my room, snapping at Einstein as I went.

I didn't have to look behind me to make sure she followed.

I could feel her guilt and pain.

"What the hell, Einstein?" I hissed as soon as I set foot in my room and whirled around in time to see her shut the door. I lifted my arms out to my sides. "I'm going to skip past the work thing and go straight to you practically sitting in Lincoln's lap and *whispering in his ear.*"

She just stood there, staring at me without giving anything away.

I huffed and pressed my fingers to my forehead. "I've never seen you whisper in someone's ear for the sake of flirting. God, I don't think I've ever seen you *flirt.* What are you doing? What about Maverick?"

Pain and panic flashed through her eyes and her body bowed slightly.

She recovered by leaning against the door.

"What about him?"

My shoulders slumped at the careless words following her obvious pain.

My heart twisted and ached for Maverick. For Einstein.

"Einstein—"

"Am I a horrible person for not missing him?"

I was so caught off guard by her question considering she'd seen Maverick recently that I stared at her for a few seconds. "Johnny?"

She jerked her head in a sharp nod.

How was I supposed to answer that?

Johnny had been family—Borello by oath. And Einstein's boyfriend for . . . God, forever.

But Johnny had also possessed the darkest, cruelest soul I'd ever encountered.

I missed the Johnny who had been there for nearly every day of my life. I *didn't* miss his sadistic mind.

But I hadn't loved him the way Einstein had.

Though I'd often thought if Johnny hadn't been so volatile, Einstein might not have stayed with him until the end. Then again, she was always surprising me. Tonight was testimony to that.

"I don't think so," I whispered. "I didn't know that you *didn't* miss him."

She looked at the floor. "There are days I do."

I nodded but didn't respond.

Einstein had slipped into my bed random mornings for as long as I could remember.

She was always cold and liked to cuddle to warm up.

Ever since Johnny's death a year and a half ago, I woke up to her ice-cold toes pressed to me more often than not.

I'd been sure it was from grief.

Now I wondered if I'd been wrong.

If it was a combination of emotions Einstein wasn't used to dealing with . . . and Maverick was at the head . . .

"I know letting yourself love Maverick doesn't make you a horrible person."

Her eyes flashed to mine and hardened. She grabbed the doorknob and jerked the door open. "He's better off without me."

"I—Jesus." I let my head fall when she stormed out.

I glanced up when the door clicked shut a few moments later and offered Maxon a brief smile.

"She looked happy," he mumbled sarcastically and pulled me into his arms.

"Yeah, I bet."

He searched my face, his tone hesitant. "Wanna talk about it?"

"I'd rather forget," I whispered and leaned close to kiss him slowly. "Think you can help with that?"

A laugh climbed up my throat when he grabbed my thighs and lifted me so I could wrap my legs around his waist.

Maxon's lips twitched into a carnal smirk then slanted over mine as he walked us into the bathroom. Pushing me against the wall and deepening the kiss when he leaned into the shower to turn the water on. Setting me carefully on the edge of the counter while he waited for the room to steam up.

His mouth never left mine.

The kiss turned frenzied.

Hands searched and breaths grew ragged.

By the time he pulled me into the shower, we were still half-dressed and frantically tearing at each other's soaked clothes.

His mouth and hands were everywhere.

Burning and branding me. Teasing and torturing me.

Until soon, I was trembling and pressing against him, silently begging for what he was keeping from me.

When he finally pushed into me, I shattered. I arched against the water-slick wall, my mouth falling open on a silent moan as my orgasm rolled through me. His thrusts took me higher and higher, demanding more of me until I fell apart again.

I dug my nails into his shoulders, trying desperately to hold on as he moved. Each roll of his hips was rough and relentless until he found his release inside me.

Tremors rolled through my body and passed to his as he carefully set my feet on the floor and pressed me harder to the wall.

His lips ghosted down the side of my neck to my collarbone.

Each rough breath brought my skin in contact with his lips.

Each kiss left chills in its wake, reminding me we had a lifetime of this to look forward to.

Thirteen

Libby

MY EYES FLASHED OPEN, MY body already hyperaware of everything that was wrong with the situation before I woke.

"Seriously?" I bit out, but she didn't wake from where she lay in front of me.

Ice-cold toes wedged between my legs. Hand wrapped in mine. Head taking up most of my pillow.

And Maxon was nowhere to be found.

I let out a sigh and carefully maneuvered out of my bed, wondering why I had taken so much care not to wake Einstein once I was standing. With a glare over my shoulder, I kicked my mattress before storming out of my room, forgetting I was in nothing but Maxon's shirt until I stumbled into the living room filled with sleeping Henley boys.

I tiptoed through the room to keep from waking them and made my way to where Maxon stood shirtless in the kitchen, watching me with that possessive and predatory stare of his that always made my knees weak. I pulled my bottom lip between my teeth as I closed the distance between us, my stomach warming with need and desire and the memory of what he'd done to me last night.

By the time I made it to him, I was trembling.

He pulled me into his arms and kissed me slowly, sensually. "I want to see you walk out in my shirt every morning for the rest of my life."

"Caveman."

He laughed low and gravelly and pressed his large hand against the small of my back, bringing me closer so I could feel his hard length against my belly. His lips brushed against mine when he said, "Something like that."

A tremor moved through me, and his mouth stretched into a smile in response. Then I was suddenly moving backward until I was against the counter and arching back—his hands searching and pulling and claiming . . .

A shuddering breath tumbled from my lips when his mouth moved down my neck and chest, my hands flying to grip his hair when he slowly dropped to his knees in front of me.

"Maxon," I hissed and tried to pull him up. "Everyone is asleep behind me."

His hands ran up my bare thighs as he prodded my legs apart, his tongue and teeth soon following the path. "Then don't make a sound."

My mouth opened on a silent moan when he teased where I was bared to him, only to do it again and again.

Each time bringing him closer to where I was aching.

Each time bringing me closer to begging him to put me out of my misery.

Then he was there—his tongue swiping against me before he was pulling my clit into his mouth and pressing two fingers inside me.

I released his hair and grabbed the counter when my knees buckled, a strangled whimper catching in my throat when he gently rolled my clit between his teeth.

"Oh God."

I felt the loss of him immediately.

But not a second later, he delivered a swift bite on the inside of my thigh before quietly hushing me.

And then he was spreading me to him. Devouring me and fucking me with his tongue in a way that had my eyes rolling back and my grip on the counter loosening as I tried to hold on to reality.

My core tightened.

My breaths turned ragged.

My limbs trembled.

My body yearned for the release that was so, so close.

And Maxon was suddenly standing and righting my shirt—his eyes full of panic and carnal need and fury—before heading to the sink, cupping water in his hands and running them over his face . . .

Are you fu—

My front door was unlocking and opening.

Shit, shit, shit.

I looked at Maxon in time for him to give me another heated and frustrated look over his shoulder before turning toward the door, my eyes already narrowed as it opened to reveal my brother and the twins.

Maverick stormed in, his stare searching the apartment and immediately falling to where the Henley boys were sleeping on the floor and couches of the living room. Pain and anger flared in his eyes, his hands curling into fists as Diggs barreled past him.

"Oh, *oh,*" he called out, headed straight for the kitchen.

"Can't you afford hotel rooms?" Dare asked, not bothering to be quiet either, his eyes locked on where Maxon now stood behind me.

An irritated laugh sounded in my ear, but Maxon didn't respond otherwise.

"We were hanging out. It got late. They crashed here," I explained, then smacked my hand on the counter to get Diggs's attention, causing the sleeping men to stir. "We already don't have any food because of you, so stay out of the pantry."

He shot me a pout from over his shoulder but didn't stop looking for food to steal.

"Yeah, I'm sure the rock stars don't have much experience with trying to find their way home after late nights," Dare said with a taunting smirk. He suddenly stiffened, his gaze darting over my body before flashing to Maxon's. With a quick, assessing look at my face, anger filled his eyes and his jaw clenched, the muscles straining. "Go put some fucking clothes on, Libby."

"I'm fine," I said through gritted teeth, mirroring his tone. "You can't come in here, uninvited and unannounced, and then tell me how I should be dressed. Actually, you know what? You can leave."

One of Dare's eyebrows lifted in surprise and challenge.

Maxon's fingers drifted over my waist. "Rebel," he murmured in warning.

"You've been hiding out ever since you told Maxon you didn't want us together. And the first time you show your face, you come in here with the twins as backup and immediately tell me what to do in *my* place?"

Maxon's fingers tightened.

Dare let out a sharp, dull laugh. "Backup? Yeah. Yeah, all right. Let's go with that."

"Oh my God," Einstein mumbled from the hall, her groggy voice stopping me from lashing out at Dare again. "Can you be any . . . louder . . ."

I looked toward her, noting the panic in her eyes as she stared at Maverick.

His frustration and pain filled the apartment and made me forget about my own anger for a moment.

After a few seconds, she locked her jaw and forced a look of indifference that faltered when he left the apartment.

The tension pressed down around us for long seconds until

Einstein took a few steps toward the front door, but Dare held a hand up to stop her.

"I didn't—"

"You didn't show up to work this morning. No one could get in touch with you," Dare said softly, darkly. "And then, of all fucking people, Kieran Hayes called *me* to see if I knew where you were, because you didn't show to close out a case last night. Maverick lost it after that." His gaze swept to me. "But the twins are *my* backup . . . yeah?"

Diggs snorted around a mouthful of pretzels. "Speak for yourself. I'm here for the food."

Dare gave him a look, and Diggs immediately headed out the door—pretzel bag still in hand.

With a sharp look at Einstein, Dare continued, "If you want to abandon your responsibilities and escape life, then find new jobs. If you want to continue pretending the rest of the world isn't there, then let Maverick know so he doesn't keep waiting for a girl who loses her goddamn mind when a few rock stars come back to town." He gestured toward her, his face twisted in disappointment. "I knew *you*. I trusted *you*. But this person you're turning into since Johnny died? Fuck, Einstein, I'm thinking even *you* wouldn't trust the stranger you've become."

"*Dare.*"

Einstein flinched at my harsh tone, but Dare simply eyed the guys now sitting up, staring at him in stunned confusion, before setting his glare on Maxon. "You haven't been here a week, and my family's already falling apart. And you wonder why I don't want you with my sister."

"Falling apart?" I asked, frustration coating my words. "Is that really how you see it?"

He looked at me for a moment before letting out a breath of a laugh and turning toward the door. "Funny that you can't."

I started toward him, coming to a stop at the entrance of the kitchen when Maxon's arm curled around me. "No," I bit out. "No, you don't get to do that. You don't get to make Einstein feel like shit. You don't get to come in here and say that stuff to Maxon and me and then leave."

Dare looked over his shoulder then abruptly turned, his eyes filled with rage. "I have a problem with guys keeping women where they don't want to be. Let her go."

"Jesus Christ," Maxon whispered. His hold loosened, but I grabbed his hand before his arm could fall away.

"Oh my God, do you hear yourself, Dare?" I asked incredulously. "I *want* to be with him. I *want* to be near him. Trying to stop me from going after you when you piss me off isn't keeping me where I don't want to be. Stop thinking every move and decision he makes is somehow a direct attack on you or our family, because that couldn't be further from the truth."

"Now that these guys are in town, Einstein isn't showing up for work and is ignoring all of us except you. That has two of the people I trust most in a silent war. It's causing chaos in our family and my business. And it has Kieran *fucking* Hayes calling me."

"Oh my God, Kieran Hayes," I said in mock horror. "Get over it. If she can work with him, you can handle a—" My shoulders sagged and some of the fight left me when I turned, only to find Einstein no longer there. "You need to apologize to her."

"She needs to wake up. She needs to know what she's doing."

"She *knows*," I said, seething. "She's trying to figure things out—she's *been* trying to. Einstein's hurting and scared and she doesn't know how to deal with having those emotions. She's going to fuck up now that she *is*. Give her a break and know that it has nothing to do with Henley being in town. But, speaking of, they aren't going anywhere. Maxon's not going anywhere. And that's something you need to accept."

"I have," he said simply, stunning me for a second. "Doesn't change my decision."

"Fuck your decision," I yelled.

"Libby," Maxon said gently.

I looked over my shoulder, my brows drawn tight, and lowered my voice to a whisper. "I won't let him do this. I won't let him dictate my life anymore when he gave up that right."

After a few seconds, Maxon nodded.

"No one tried to stop you and Lily," I said to Dare when I faced him again.

Amusement lit Dare's face. Like he'd been ready for this—waiting for it. "You sure about that?" Before I could respond, he said, "Johnny."

"That was different. He was crazy."

"Kieran."

"She was his girlfriend," I shouted. "Of course he tried to."

The guys in the living room all drew out hushed *Ohs*.

Maxon's grip on me tightened, and I knew he was putting together who Kieran was—what gang he'd been a part of—from what I'd told him the other day.

"Do you want me to go down the list?" Dare asked with a tick of his brow.

I knew he meant the list of Holloway members. "That's not what I meant, and you know it. Einstein and I, Maverick and Diggs . . . we didn't try to stop you." I didn't continue, but my unspoken words lingered between us like heavy weights.

Even when we found out she was the Holloway Princess.

Even when we found out she belonged to Kieran Hayes—the Holloway Assassin and Underboss.

When Dare spoke, his tone was reserved. "Everyone loved her. Everyone *fell* in love with her. No one knows Maxon that well."

"I do," I said, pressing my hand to my chest. "I know him, and that's all that should matter. Whether or not he was physically here, he has always been there for me. Through everything."

"He was your escape from your family. Why would I want him

around now?" His gaze flickered from Maxon to the other guys, then back to me. "We were Lily's escape. See the difference?"

"It's different now, you know that. You know what it was like back then. You *knew* I wanted to get away. Maxon's here because I want to stay. And you're still trying to prevent that."

"Trying?"

"Dare . . ." I pleaded with my eyes alone, but nothing in his expression changed.

"His life will only bring you harm, Libby," he said unapologetically. "Different kinds he can't understand. And he can't protect you."

"The fuck I can't," Maxon growled from behind me, his grip tightening.

"Trust me," he said on a grim laugh. With a nod, he stepped toward the door. "I already told you my decision. It doesn't matter what you do—how long you stay here or if you stay permanently. It won't change my mind."

"I don't care," I whispered when he opened the door.

He stilled, then slowly looked at me.

"Your reasons?" I laughed sadly. "They're not fair. Not to Maxon. Not to me. He's not a stranger I just met and am expecting you to be okay with. You've known him most your life. And the rest?" I shrugged. "It's not up to you to decide what I do with my life anymore, Dare."

"Libby—"

"The moment you stopped leading the family was the moment you gave up any right to tell me what I could and couldn't do," I said firmly. "I love you, and I've always respected you, and I know that's why Maxon went to you. But when you start pulling the shit you have the last few days, I stop caring about your approval. I stop worrying if you'll be angry. I stop caring at all."

Dare's face fell, and for a long time he stood there watching me with a look like he wanted to say a dozen things that couldn't be voiced in front of company that hadn't grown up in our life.

"Push me out of your life if you want. Stop caring, Libby. You've been my responsibility since I was thirteen. You all have. I don't know how to stop worrying about you. I don't know how to stop trying to protect you."

And then he was gone, his words lingering behind him.

Fourteen

Maxon

YOU COULD'VE HEARD A FEATHER fall in the seconds after Dare left the apartment.

No one moved.

No one spoke.

I wasn't sure any of us fucking breathed.

Libby's head dropped and angled to the side so she could look at me from over her shoulder, finally breaking the spell, her dark eyes a mixture of defiance and grief.

She swallowed, the movement slow and forced. "I think I, uh . . . I should check on Einstein."

"Are *you* okay?" I asked soft enough so my voice wouldn't carry to the living room.

Her gaze darted away and one of her shoulders lifted slightly. "He can't get away with saying shit like that." She glanced at the guys then whispered, "We'll talk later."

I lifted her hand to my lips when she began walking away, kissing the tips of her fingers and holding her stare before releasing her. As soon as she slipped down the hall toward Einstein's room, I hurried out the front door, ignoring the guys when they started talking and calling out for me.

I caught Dare just as he and one of the twins were sliding into a car.

The second he saw me, he climbed out and slammed the door behind him. The twins followed, naturally flanking him, as if they'd done it hundreds of times.

"Not backup, huh?"

Dare only cocked a brow.

I rubbed at my jaw, my frustration building. "Right. If that's how you want to do this. But we need to talk."

"We talked. If you weren't listening, my decision didn't change."

"Yeah, no, I got that. I didn't think it would anytime soon. Your sister knew that." I gestured to the building behind me. "But after the shit you pulled in there? You're *begging* her to go against you."

"And you're suddenly an expert on her?"

A stunned laugh left me. "I know her well enough. You can't tell Libby not to do something unless you want her to do the opposite. She allowed what you said before because she respects and loves you too much—but you just damaged that."

A cruel smile crossed his face. "I told you I didn't want you together. I told you your life would ruin her. Yet you somehow took that as an invitation to stay." He lifted his hand and pointed to the apartment. "And it doesn't take a fucking genius to know I walked in on something that shouldn't be happening."

"Jesus, give me a break," I said on a groan. "She's thirty-one years old, Dare. Are you gonna tell me you were a fucking saint until you married your wife?"

"You aren't good for her," he growled.

"Why?" The word was a taunt. I ran a hand over my jaw and stepped closer so my voice wouldn't carry. "Because I don't come from your world, *Boss?*"

The guys tensed, all eyes went wide before I was met with identical threatening expressions.

"Choose your next words carefully," Dare said in a dark tone.

My brows slowly lifted and my mouth twitched into a smirk. "You honestly think I could love your sister my entire life—be there for her through *everything*—and not figure out what your family was?" When a cold, detached look settled over his face, I said, "I've known since high school. I never told a soul because I don't care. I get that you think I can't keep her safe, and maybe in the way *you* keep people safe . . . I can't. Doesn't mean I can't protect her *my* way. Doesn't mean I can't love her. Provide for her. Doesn't mean we don't belong together."

Dare stared at me for a few seconds before rubbing a hand over his mouth, nodding as he did. "You're wrong."

"Jesus."

"It's not just the lifestyle. It's that you're in a spotlight Libby *can't* be in. She isn't just a Borello by oath, she's a Borello by blood. People know our family. Our name. I dissolved the gang, but enemies don't care. When you put her in the spotlight, you put a blinding target on her back."

My stomach churned and it felt like the ground was coming up to meet me.

I could wait out Dare. I could wait for Libby forever.

But this?

"You knew . . ." I shook my head slowly, then lifted my stare to meet his. "You knew we'd be together one day. You've never said anything until now. Why?"

"I knew you wanted to be with her. I knew how much you meant to her. But I was positive she wouldn't consider a relationship with you—let alone a future with you. Being with *anyone* isn't Libby's style." He huffed. "Then the last six months happened and I saw how ruined she was by you. I knew I'd had it all wrong."

I stood there, my mind racing, before I shrugged helplessly. "It was never a question of *if* we would be together. It was *when*. I've told her our entire lives it was going to be her and me forever, and it will. There's no ending us."

"I can't let you be together."

I nodded and turned, running my hands over my face and through my hair, gripping it as I paced away before turning around to face the guys. "There's no ending us."

For the first time since I'd asked if I could marry Libby, he didn't look angry. He looked like he felt sorry for me.

"She wants to settle down here with me. She wants a family. I plan on giving her those things, but I've been stalling because you aren't okay with the idea of us."

"How nice of you," he said with a curl of his lip.

"I said *stalling* . . . I didn't say I wasn't *preparing* for everything." I smirked when his hands fisted. "I could find ways to keep stalling and hope you'd come around, but even if you didn't, eventually I'd stop waiting. I asked you if I could marry Libby because you mean the world to her. I'm trying to respect you, but you can't control her life. She's not your daughter, she's your older sister."

"I'm aware."

"Then treat her like it. As much as you hate it, I *do* know her. She defies authority. She does what people tell her not to. After today, I know she's going to push for me to stop waiting for you to give me the green light. And she won't have to push hard."

Dare stared me down, his chest pitching with his rough breaths. After a few moments, his shoulders sagged. "I never wanted to lead. I never wanted to be in charge of the family. I was forced into it. But they all became my responsibility—*Libby* became my responsibility. All I ever wanted was to find a way to end it. Now that I have, I don't know how to stand back and watch my family make decisions I know will hurt them."

"I get it, man, I do. But you said it yourself . . . you thought I'd ruined your sister. That's what happens when we're not together. She'll hurt more if we're apart. Let Libby be mine. Let her become my responsibility. I'll take care of her."

"Didn't you hear a word I said?"

"I heard you." I shrugged. "Look, I won't lie to you. People will want to know about her in the beginning. They'll want to know who my girl is. But we have publicists for a reason. Everything can be monitored and pictures of her can be taken down if they need to."

"Hell of a lot of good that did you for the father-to-be pictures."

"There wasn't a reason to take them down considering it was *Ava* and we thought it was funny. Not to mention we made the decision to wait a day to give a statement. Libby's different. But she won't be caught with me until her last name's changed. No one needs to print the name *Borello*. No one needs to know who she really is."

He stared at me like I'd lost my goddamn mind. "That's it?"

"I love her. No one else can offer her better than that." He looked like he was about to disagree, so I hurried to ask, "What, would you be okay if I was someone *safe*? Some guy working in a cubicle who would piss himself if he ever found out about who you really are? Or would you rather me be from your life? Someone who could *keep her safe*? Someone who kept Libby pulled into that life after you spent so long finding a way to end it?"

Dare's jaw clenched, but he didn't respond.

"I'm her best friend. Her safe place. The guy she chose." I flung my hand out toward them. "I found out about all of you and didn't bat a fucking eye or run scared. I'm what's best for her. You can deal with the rest."

Dare nodded absentmindedly for a few seconds before heading for the car, the twins following without having ever uttered a word.

Once Dare was at the car with the door open, he looked at me and called out, "I don't ever want to walk in on something like I did today."

"Don't walk in without calling first," I shot back.

His laugh was loud and didn't hold a hint of his earlier anger. With a dip of his head, he slid into the car and turned it on.

I didn't wait to watch them leave. I walked into the apartment and found the guys standing in a tight circle, talking softly.

As soon as they saw me, Jared threw out his hands and mumbled, "The fuck, dude?"

"Yeah, what the hell did we wake up to?" Lincoln asked.

I blew out a harsh breath. "Honestly, I don't know half the shit they were fighting about."

"When did Dare become such an asshole?" Ledger asked, looking over my shoulder to see if the guy in question had followed me inside.

My mouth twitched into a grimace as I headed toward Einstein's room. "Right about the time I asked if I could marry his sister."

"Not like you haven't been fucking her for the last decade."

I paused and shot Ledger a warning glare, then looked to the other two. "Did the girls ever come back out?"

When they shook their heads, I continued toward the room, following Libby's and Einstein's voices.

With a knock on Einstein's door, I slowly cracked it open and waited to see if there would be demands to leave. When there was nothing, I stepped inside and looked between the girls.

"You both okay?"

"Who came in?" Libby asked instead.

I glanced behind me before realizing what she was asking. "I went to talk to Dare."

Her exhausted stare bounced over my expression. "Are they gone now?" When I nodded, she leaned forward to squeeze Einstein's hand, then stood from her bed and walked toward me. "My room," she whispered.

I let her lead me across the apartment, ignoring the questioning and confused looks of the guys as we passed them. I closed her door behind us, then leaned against it when she began pacing the length of her room.

"Dare's never been like this before," she said after nearly a minute. "Even when he was boss."

"I know."

"I think he's panicking because he doesn't have a say over anything now, and he doesn't know how to let us live our lives."

I watched her for a while, waiting to see if she would add to that. "He thinks you're going to get hurt, and he's trying to prevent it."

She stopped moving and turned to look at me. "It doesn't matter. He can't do what he's doing. He can't say the shit he said today. And Einstein—God, he doesn't even understand what's happening with her, and he's trying to place the blame somewhere else."

I knew better than to ask what *was* happening with Einstein.

I cleared my throat and shifted against the door. "I caught some of it," I mumbled, dropping my head against the door as I tried to remember Dare and Libby's fight.

"Kieran Hayes called because you didn't show to close out a case last night."

"Kieran—She was his girlfriend."

"But this person you're turning into since Johnny died?"

"I didn't know Johnny died," I whispered.

Can't say I'm sad about it.

He'd been Dare's best friend and Einstein's boyfriend. And like Libby said, he was crazy. Batshit fucking insane.

The kind of guy you knew would snap one day.

"Dare did it."

The fuck.

I don't remember moving.

But the next thing I knew I was away from the door and in front of Libby.

"Johnny had really lost it," she hurried to explain. "Worse than ever. Tried to kill Lily numerous times. One night it came down to Johnny or Lily, and . . . Dare had to make the decision."

"How the hell is this your life?" I whispered.

Her brows drew together and she seemed to fold in on herself. She looked terrified. Like she was afraid that anything that left her lips would be something that sent me in the opposite direction.

"We don't choose the families we're born into. This is never something I thought you would know." She held her hands out pleadingly when a sharp laugh left me. "Don't do that."

"Do what?"

"Look at me like you don't know me."

I closed the distance between us and pulled her into my arms. "I do know you. But you have to realize how crazy this sounds. I knew . . . but I never thought anything like this. I never thought there was another family living in the same damn town that was killing members of your family, and vice versa. And Kieran?" I asked, bringing up the guy Dare mentioned. "He's one of the Holloways, isn't he? You said Einstein worked with them."

"Yeah, he was the worst one." When I stiffened, she quickly added, "I mean, he's good. He's a good guy . . . but he was their assassin. And he's still absolutely terrifying to be in the same room with. I don't know how Einstein works with him."

I blinked slowly. "You're not joking, are you?"

Her head shook and mouth twisted in a sad smile. "You'll get used to the stories and old titles. It's just different from what you've ever known."

"That's an understatement, Rebel."

She relaxed deeper in my arms and whispered, "My world is born of shadows and kept hidden from view. Your world is in the spotlight and on display for everyone to see. To the average person, both seem unbelievable . . . doesn't mean they don't exist."

In the spotlight. For everyone to see.

"She's a Borello by blood . . . When you put her in the spotlight, you put a blinding target on her back."

Shit.

I trailed a finger down her jaw and back again. "I'll find a middle ground for us. I promise."

"You mean in between dealing with my brother?" she asked, defeat and frustration coating her words.

I started walking her toward the bed, my mouth curving up. "Already taken care of."

I pressed my lips to hers when her mouth popped open in surprise, teasing her tongue and swallowing her moan when I laid her on the bed.

She wove her fingers through my hair, gripping and tugging to break the kiss so she could look at me. Her breaths were rough and her dark eyes were full of excitement and need. "Maxon, are you serious?"

"When are you gonna let me give you my last name, Rebel?"

A soft laugh slid up her throat. "Now." She pressed her mouth to mine. "Now. Tomorrow. Whenever."

Fifteen

Maxon

"CAN YOU STOP?" JARED SAID with a frustrated huff. "Fucking hell, you're making me anxious, and I was chill as fuck five minutes ago."

I glared at him as I stopped drumming my fingers but didn't comment.

We'd been in New York for three days doing TV shows and appearances, and I couldn't get out of here until late tonight. The guys wanted me to stay for a last night of clubs and parties . . . I'd laughed.

I'd been counting down until I could get back to North Carolina and Libby since the minute I left.

One more photo shoot.

One more appearance.

And then I was on a plane.

I started drumming on my legs again.

"I'm starving," Ledger grumbled from where he was lying in

the back seat. "Can we stop for tacos?"

"You want to eat tacos before a shoot?" Lincoln asked him dully. "A shirtless shoot?"

"Fuck yes, I do. My stomach's eating itself."

"Jesus Christ, man." Jared hit my hands. "Stop. If you need to get laid that bad, we'll find you someone to bang."

"What the hell's your problem?"

"You've gone a year without her before. Try to go a few days without pissing me off."

"Fuck you," I snapped. "What's with you lately?"

"What's with me?" He bit out a sharp laugh. "I'm not the one changing our lives because of some pussy."

My fist connected with his face before I registered the movement.

After I got a second hit in, he grabbed the collar of my shirt and shoved me against the door.

"Fuck me. We need tacos before we kill each other," Ledger yelled. "Driver, *please*. Find us tacos."

"I don't care that she's there," Jared yelled, his face red from my fists and his rage. "I don't give a shit what she means to you. I left that town and I wanted to be done with it." He shoved me harder against the door before releasing me and moving across the seat to position himself against his own door. "That town is nothing but bad memories."

"It's bad memories for all of us," I bit out. "But Libby . . ."

"Man, *fuck Libby*."

I launched across the seat and was immediately shoved back when his foot connected with my stomach.

"Say that again," I said through clenched teeth. "I fucking dare you."

"She was supposed to come with us," he yelled. "We all thought when your bullshit deal ended, she was coming *with* us." He flung his hand toward the back of the car. "Not forcing us back to that damn town."

"No one's forcing you anywhere. The three of you can live anywhere. *You* can choose to live anywhere else." I leaned forward and lowered my voice. "I know your home life sucked. I know you wanted to get away. We all did. That's how we came together, Jared. Jesus."

"You're not the only one who had a shitty home life, man," Lincoln murmured calmly from where he sat in the front. "Maxon and I were beat and went without food half the time. Ledger had it worst of all. But we all got away from it, and those people are paying now."

"Tacos," Ledger whimpered.

"Shut up, Ledger," Jared yelled before turning on Lincoln and me again. "I have dealt with ending tours there. But I can't live in a place where every street is a nightmare. I can't act like I don't hate everyone in that town for pretending not to see what was happening to us."

"Sometimes you gotta face your demons to live your life," Lincoln said. "Can't let the past haunt you."

No one was closer to Libby than me . . . and I hadn't had a clue what was really happening to her family. In her world.

Right in front of me.

Right in front of all of us . . . in a town the size of freaking Wake Forest.

"You ever think maybe they really didn't know?" I asked.

"Uh, Max . . ."

"Shut up, Ledger," we all said.

"You need to check your phone," he said hurriedly. "Like, now. Driver, dude, we're definitely gonna need those tacos."

All three of us had our phones out, but I only had time to put in my code before it was ringing.

It was Nate.

"Yeah?"

"Have you seen it?"

The way he was talking instantly had my stomach clenching with unease.

"No, Ledger just—shit." My stomach dropped and heart painfully skipped a few beats when Jared shoved his phone in front of my face.

"Yeah," Nate said on a sigh. "I'm getting calls from the shows you boys just finished, wanting to know why they didn't have this scoop. I'm already getting requests . . ."

I didn't hear anything else he said.

I didn't hear what the guys were saying to each other or to me.

I could only focus on the pictures loaded onto the celebrity news site, with the headline: "Henley's Maxon James Heats Up The South."

The first picture was from last week in Brooks Street Café. I'd kissed her hard and fast . . . but she'd been pinned up against the wall.

The second was the night we left for New York. I'd gone into The Jack to say goodbye one more time. I was leaning over the bar, but the picture clearly captured exactly how long and slow that kiss had been.

"Shit," I said, cutting off whatever Nate had been saying.

We need to get these pulled.

I skimmed the article, and only breathed a little easier when I didn't see Libby's name anywhere on there.

He sighed, then assured me, "We're working on getting these pulled. But you had to know pictures were going to surface. Especially if you aren't worrying about public affection."

I ran my hand through my hair and groaned. "It's Wake Forest. *Public* isn't supposed to matter there, Nate. It's people we've known our entire lives. She knows that this kind of thing will happen, but I wanted to keep us just *us* for a little longer. That town should've been a safe space."

"I don't know what to tell you, Max. It comes with the . . ." He spoke away from the phone for a few seconds before uttering, "Uh,

I'm not sure what, uh . . ."

When I tried to scroll to the top of the page again, it stalled before disappearing completely, leaving the screen with a *page-not-found* error.

"Was that you?" I asked Nate.

I hit refresh, only to get the same error page.

"No. We're still trying to deal with legal."

My furrowed brow smoothed, and I laughed in wonder. "Einstein," I muttered, then handed Jared his phone.

And then it hit me that if Einstein got the page taken down, then Libby might already know, and I needed to call her. "I need to go, Nate."

"Uh . . . yeah," he whispered, still sounding confused by the disappearing page.

I glanced at Jared and shifted lower in the seat. "One more thing. Thought I should warn you before you saw proofs from the shoot. Jared's face hit my fist. Twice."

I hung up before Nate could respond just as Lincoln asked, "What happened to the page?"

"I think Einstein shut it down."

"Badass," Lincoln murmured.

Jared huffed a laugh. "She is kind of a badass."

"Dude, that little genius is the shit," Ledger agreed, then shouted, "*Tacos. Finally.*"

I rolled my eyes and called Libby, my heart pounding and fingers drumming on my leg.

Glancing at Jared, I said, "Sorry about your face."

He shrugged. "We're good. I'll pay you back later."

A weak laugh left me just as Libby's voice filled my ear. "You might want to avoid Dare for a few days. But hey, at least we look good kissing."

Sixteen

Him

GLANCED UP, ALREADY GLARING, when my assistant and cousin stormed into my office.

One dropped into a chair, dragging a hand through his hair, the other continued toward my desk.

"I'll have to call you back," I said quickly, and hung up without waiting for a response. "Please tell me there's a reason for—what the hell do you think you're doing?"

"I need—you have to—" My assistant held up a trembling hand from where he stood typing on my computer, then begged, "Trust me. This just went live on news sites."

As soon as a site was up on the screen, he shoved away from my desk and began pacing the length of my office.

I didn't have to ask what was wrong.

There, on my screen, were two pictures of Elizabeth kissing someone else.

Every dark need surged through me, making me want to lash

out at everything and everyone within sight.

She hadn't been with anyone in well over six months, and suddenly she was on a damn celebrity news site.

My body stilled and ice filled my veins.

"What the hell is this?" I asked on a breath.

"Sources tell us Maxon James has continued to frequent his hometown of Wake Forest, NC since the band first moved to California, all due to longtime love interest, pictured above."

"'If you've lived here for any amount of time, you know they've been together, for like, ever,' an anonymous source says."

I slowly looked from the screen to the men in my room.

My chest was roughly rising and falling with each exaggerated breath.

"How did this get past you?"

My assistant stopped pacing and cleared his throat. "We—"

"Christ," my cousin murmured from where he sat. "You have *us* watching every move she makes at work, and *my* assistant tracking any guy she fucks. We can't—"

I launched the computer across my office, the sound of it crashing against the window was overshadowed by my deafening demand. "How did this get past you? How did a *longtime love interest* get past you?"

"If he wasn't someone she picked up at The Jack, how the hell could we have known?"

"It shouldn't have gotten past us," my assistant said quickly.

"Every move." My teeth were clenched, the words sounded like a snarl. "Watch every move she makes from here on out. Not just at that goddamn bar."

My cousin barked out a laugh. "I have a job that doesn't involve following a girl."

"We have assistants for a reason. We have employees and money for a reason. Put them to use."

He sent me a seething look. "This is what happens when you

don't take care of your belongings. Other people pick them up to play with them."

I grabbed my keyboard and smashed it across the desk. "I want everything on that Maxon James," I said, my tone filled with rage. "*Everything*. And then I want to teach him no one touches what's mine and lives."

Seventeen

Libby

MY STEPS SLOWED AND BROW furrowed when I noticed the thick, plain, white envelope taped to my front door.

I stopped in front of it, then turned to see if anyone was watching me.

Everything was still and bordered on eerie in that way only the early hours of the morning could. It was my favorite time—when I got home from closing at The Jack—because there was *nothing*.

Just you and your thoughts, echoing back to you in the quiet of the night.

It reminded me of the calm Maxon exuded.

I ripped the card off the door and turned it over as I lifted my keys to unlock the door, but my movements turned sluggish and the quiet suddenly seemed too loud when I found my name printed on the bottom corner of the envelope.

My full name.

Elizabeth Borello.

I looked up and my gaze darted wildly around as I hurried to unlock the door. My heart pounded forcefully. It felt like any beat would be its last.

I rushed into my apartment and slumped against the door, my fingers on the deadbolt and head hanging low as shame twisted through me.

I'm Libby Borello, damn it. I don't back down from anything.

Men. Challenges. Hagglers. Threats. Death.

But two words on an envelope had fear spiking in my veins. Had me running.

I'd never been so ashamed of myself.

A weighted breath fled from me as I pushed from the door, but my steps halted when I looked up and found the Henley boys staring at me with looks of confusion.

Einstein looked horrified.

Maxon was halfway between the living room and me, his hands half-raised like he was approaching a trapped animal. "Are you okay?"

I let the envelope slip from my fingers into my purse. "Of course I am. There was a—" I cleared my throat and gestured to the door. "A, uh, spider. Huge one."

"Right." His brows pinched tight and voice lowered. "You look pissed . . . because of a spider."

"I'm not pissed." I was so pissed. "I guess I'm tired, or something."

He roughed his hand over his jaw and nodded. I knew he didn't believe me. "All right. Well, uh, do you want something to eat?"

I slipped past him and tried to ignore Einstein's assessing stare. "Yeah, sure. Just let me change first."

I knew I didn't convince anyone that I was fine. I didn't realize until I was almost to my room that I hadn't touched or even kissed Maxon. But I needed privacy to open the envelope before my earlier fear could return and consume me.

It could easily be nothing.

Could be my mom trying another way of talking to me.

But if it was from who I thought . . . then I couldn't let the others see it.

Maxon wouldn't understand. I didn't want him to have to *try* to understand. Einstein would involve Dare, and that would only start a war we'd been trying to prevent for so long.

I hurried into my room and snatched the envelope from my bag.

My hands shook and lungs screamed from the lack of oxygen as I stared at the offensive object.

I wanted to ignore it. I wanted to open it. I wanted to burn it. I wanted to laugh at my absurdity over a damn envelope.

Instead, I carefully pried open the lip. My trembling increased when I tried to look inside.

"You're such a wimp," I said as I loosed a shuddering breath.

With a frantic laugh, I stuck my hand in and pulled out a Polaroid picture.

"What the hell?"

The picture was of a note, with the words:

I have pictures too.

"Pictures of what?" I whispered, then looked into the envelope again . . . but it was empty.

I thought back to the pictures of Maxon and me that ended up online a couple days ago and wondered what else someone could've captured. Maxon and I had rarely been out in public together except for the two times that had already been sold to the celebrity news sites.

And who the hell in Wake Forest would do this?

I wanted to stare at the picture a little longer, try to decipher something from nothing. But I knew I couldn't have much time before someone came in here to see what was really wrong.

I shoved the Polaroid in the envelope and put it in one of my drawers under some clothes, then hurried to strip out of my work clothes.

My earlier shame didn't compare to now. I'd let some jealous punk scare me.

Me.

"Jesus, Libby."

I was shrugging into a large, comfortable shirt when Maxon stepped into the room with a knock on the door.

His face was impassive as he shut the door behind him and leaned against it. One of his eyebrows ticked up in bemused frustration when he slid his hands into his jeans pockets.

"So . . ."

I let a coy smile play on my lips and slanted my head. "So."

"Are you gonna tell me what's happening?"

I opened my mouth and suddenly found it impossible to speak. My stomach felt heavy as it churned with acid.

I cleared my throat and asked, "What do you mean?" I knew the feigned innocence in my question didn't fool him. It couldn't. He knew me too well.

An edgy laugh punched from his chest. "Let's start with you rushing into the apartment like you were being chased. Or the look on your face like you'd just seen a ghost. Or the way you wouldn't come near me, when the last two days, I don't think more than a few minutes passed before we started tearing at each other's clothes again and fucking on the closest surface."

I shrugged. "I missed you when you were gone."

"And now you're done missing me?" he asked wryly.

"I was trying to be respectful of your friends and Einstein."

Maxon looked like he didn't know if he should laugh or check to see if I was actually Libby. "You mean the friends you yelled at and wouldn't let in here. Today. Right after they got back to town."

"To be fair, they tried to break down my door at the worst time. It totally killed the mood."

Until Maxon joined me in the shower . . .

"And don't you guys sleep?" I asked, exasperated. "I mean, why were you even still up?"

"Wait—what? We're always awake when you get back. We were messing around with some new songs up until a few minutes ago." He ran his hands over his face and let out a soft groan. When he was looking at me again, he plead, "Libby, tell me what I'm missing."

I wanted to.

It would be so easy to.

This was *Maxon*. My safe place, my best friend, my everything.

It was just a picture from some asshole, letting me know that Einstein would probably have more work to do.

But something about my name printed on the envelope didn't sit right with me. It made me nauseous and left a knot in my throat whenever I even considered telling him the truth.

Because Elizabeth Borello was a dangerous name.

It was a name associated with blood and enemies.

I wanted nothing to do with it.

Anyone who grew up here—which was pretty much everyone— knew my full name. But to the town, I was just Libby.

And yet, *Elizabeth* was on that envelope.

Still, it could've been left by anyone.

Literally anyone.

I loosed a sigh and let my shoulders sag as I walked to where Maxon leaned against my door.

I pressed close and wrapped my arms around his waist. "Something scared me when I was walking to the door."

Maxon's brow furrowed and body went tight beneath me. "What?"

Instantly worried for me. Instantly transformed into my protector when I didn't need one.

"I don't know," I said honestly.

Because I didn't.

I didn't understand the meaning of the picture or who it was from.

"But that's why I was trying to get in here so fast. And I don't get scared."

"Libby, it's almost three in the morning. Anyone would be scared walking into the apartment alone. You could've called me and I would've met you outside. You *should've*."

"No, you don't understand. I *don't* get scared. It pissed me off that I let myself think someone was there. That I let anything scare me at all. And I just needed a second to cool down from that."

He watched me for a few seconds, then asked carefully, "Is this a mob thing?"

I gave him a deadpan look. "You should've seen how shocked Einstein was when I came in. I don't think she expected to see me like that as long as she lived."

He shifted me in his arms, pulling me deeper into his embrace. "You've never been scared . . . about anything? Thought you said that assassin guy scared you."

"He's terrifying to be near, but I'll still stand next to him without batting an eye. It's hard to explain unless you've seen him. He constantly has this look like he's thinking of all the ways he wants to kill you—and you know he could do it before you could take your next breath." I bit back a laugh when Maxon's eyes widened. "And he's the good guy."

"I'm confident enough in myself to say that I don't ever want to meet him. He would be the person I ran screaming from."

My next laugh was louder, richer—but ended abruptly.

The panic that had seized my heart from what seemed so long ago consumed me again. That grief swirled in my chest as if I was experiencing it for the first time.

I wondered if I would ever forget it . . . that pain from thinking I'd lost him forever.

Then thinking he'd left again.

I wondered if my heart would ever fully heal.

"I lied." I met Maxon's eyes before letting my stare fall to his chest. "I was scared the day you went to talk to Dare. You weren't there when I woke, and I thought you left . . . for California."

"Rebel . . ."

"Guess that's a different kind of fear," I whispered hesitantly.

He caught my chin between his fingers and forced me to look at him. "It's gonna be you and me forever. I'm not going anywhere."

Potential Polaroid Assholes

Literally anyone. Ugh.

Eighteen

Libby

"**G**ABE," I CALLED OUT, MY mouth stretching into a wide smile when I saw one of my regulars sliding onto a stool at The Jack. "It's been so long since I've seen you."

His signature crooked smirk turned amused, his head listing to complete the look. "Been a week, as always."

I faltered for a second, my smile freezing in place.

The online pictures and the Polaroid . . . all that had happened within a week?

I forced a laugh. "Longest week of my life." Drumming my hands on the bar, I asked, "What will it be tonight?"

"Haven't changed on you yet. Not starting now."

"You keep giving me free rein on drink choices, and one of these times I might just make you a girly cocktail with fruit and an umbrella."

"Whatever you're in the mood for, I want." His dark eyes burned as they searched my face, but just before I could look away from the piercing stare, he turned and glanced around the bar with a look of indifference.

I grabbed for the whiskey, since Maxon's return had the liquor on my mind constantly, and asked, "How many tonight?"

"Four of us." That stare returned to me. "How've you been?"

I shrugged, talking about work and not much else as I poured whiskey in four glasses. When I echoed his question, he kept his answer short, vague, and about work.

As always.

Gabe had been coming to The Jack every Friday night for about seven years now. From day one, he'd allowed me to make him whatever sounded good, never once asking for anything specific.

He was tall and built like a brickhouse. His face was permanently etched in a scowl, and I'd made it my mission for years to see that crooked smile cross his face—if even for a second.

Now he gave them to me freely.

But the man was something to look at, with or without the smile.

Dark, messy hair and penetrating stare. Full lips and a tall, hard body cloaked in his ever-present slacks, loosened tie, and button-down . . . forearms peeking out below his rolled-up sleeves.

I'd passed Maxon's absences with him a few times . . . a year.

But Gabe was just . . . *Gabe*.

He was attractive, and I could appreciate that, sure. But he had been nothing more than someone to pass a night with whenever I'd tried to pretend I was fine.

Fine that once again, Maxon had left me.

Fine that once again, I had been easy to leave.

We never got too personal with the details of our lives when we spoke. There was no emotional connection so our interactions didn't change after sleeping with each other.

I chose his drinks, and he alternated between staring at me like he wanted to devour me and looking around like he was both content and frustrated with the world. Business as usual.

But he always left a *very* generous tip, and underneath, a piece of paper with one, simple word on it.

Hi.

Sometimes it was on bar napkins or receipts . . . others it was on his business card or ripped pieces of paper. But it was underneath the tip every time.

Something about it made the solemn man with the presence of a warrior a little less threatening. A little more endearing. A little more human.

But now as I slid the tumblers toward him, I wondered about that note.

They had always seemed innocent—and were the motivation behind wanting to make him smile—but now I wasn't sure how I was supposed to accept them.

Hi had lost some of its innocence, because now . . . everything was different.

Maxon was back.

He was mine and I was his.

Most importantly, the deal between us had been destroyed. *My* deal, as Maxon reminded me over the years.

But I was the one who'd been left.

I was the one who had to choke down the knowledge that he was a famous rock star living across the country.

To expect or ask him to stay true to me for all those years when I couldn't give him what he wanted—a relationship. A life. A future—it would've been foolish. Naïve.

So, yeah, it was *my* deal. One that allowed needs to be taken care of. But it was the only way *I* knew how to protect my heart.

And we pretended it didn't wreck us to think of what the other might be doing.

Because Maxon wasn't just someone to satisfy physical needs when he was in town.

He was the other half of my soul. My heart.

Just as I was his.

"You okay?"

I blinked quickly and focused on Gabe for a second before realizing I'd stopped pushing the glasses toward him.

"Yeah," I said hesitantly. "Yeah, sorry."

Except I wasn't.

For the first time in years, I was acutely aware that one of my favorite regulars knew what I looked like naked.

The men I slept with were only in town for a night or two—usually coming in to The Jack for a show—because I knew I would likely never see them again. Gabe was the only exception. I'd justified it because he lived in the city.

I was now remembering why Raleigh men were too close for comfort. Why I'd had that rule.

It was also supposed to prevent the scene that was playing out in front of me . . .

Maxon walking toward me. Gabe staring at me like he wanted to devour me again.

Son of a bitch.

I should've known it would happen sooner or later. It was a miracle it hadn't happened before.

The few times Henley had played at the bar since Gabe started showing up, Gabe was always gone by the time the set finished.

Whenever Maxon came to town on his own, I spent those days holed up with him, away from the world.

Now they were side by side.

Maxon popped up on the bar, the muscles in his tattooed arms flexing as he leaned over to kiss me long and slow.

My unease at Maxon being near a man I'd slept with fled the moment his lips met mine, and I was smiling by the time he pulled away.

"Missed you."

"Always." He placed another quick kiss to my lips, then lowered himself to the floor. "We're headed to Raleigh to have dinner with Nate and some people he knows. Wanted you to know in case you beat me back to the apartment."

"And you had to come in here to tell me?" The tease in my tone offset the roll of my eyes.

"We had to pass by here on our way out and I wanted to taste you."

"Maxon," I hissed and grabbed a lemon wedge to throw at him.

"If you'd rather I didn't . . ." He shrugged slowly, his mouth twitching into a smirk. "I'll remember that when you get home."

My stomach turned into a flurry of butterfly wings the instant those last words slipped from his tongue.

Home. With Maxon.

Nothing had ever sounded so perfect.

"I'll change your mind when I do," I promised, my blood heating when he winked before turning away.

In a daze, I watched Maxon leave. My eyes slowly shifted to the side and my body jolted when I found Gabe's penetrating stare on me.

"Hi," I said awkwardly.

A ghost of a smirk flashed across his face. "Boyfriend?"

"That's my—he's . . ."

I'm going to marry him, but we're not engaged. "Boyfriend" doesn't begin to encompass what we are—what we've been through to make it to this point.

"He's my Maxon," I finally answered.

"He was here a couple weeks ago. He played," he said, his voice a low rumble. "And I think I've seen them play here a couple times before."

"Right. He's from here. Actually. They all are. Henley. They grew up . . . yeah. But he's back. Now. For good."

Awkward . . . it was all so awkward and I couldn't figure out how to form full sentences, because Gabe was still staring at me in that way he did, and we'd just talked about something other than work.

We'd gone into *personal* territory for the first time ever.

He nodded, just a slight dip of his head. "Understood." A breath of a laugh left him as he stood and reached into his pocket. "So I shouldn't give you these anymore?"

Relief pounded through my veins when he folded up a little scrap of paper, and I offered him a grateful smile.

"I've been with him my entire life," I explained when he placed the ball of paper on the bar.

Gabe's eyes flashed up to meet mine.

"When the band left for LA, Maxon and I were only *on* when he was home. It was . . . well, it's confusing and it's weird. It's just how we got through the time. We had a deal."

"Did you?" he asked, something like a challenge filling his tone.

"I'm sorry, this is weird. I'm shutting up." I waved off the awkward tension slowly creeping between us again. "We don't talk about our personal lives. I hope you and the guys enjoy your night. I'll see you later if you want another round—or next week."

Another dip of his head.

Another ghost of a smirk.

He placed a too-large tip on the bar top and palmed the four glasses in his large hands, his eyes locked on mine as he backed away. "See you around, Libby."

My breath caught, and I stood there watching him go, unable to move.

It was his voice—the deep tenor of his parting words.

They were the same words he said every time he turned away from the bar . . . but this time had been different.

They were no longer cloaked in seduction and mystery and intrigue.

This time those simple, innocent words had frozen fingers gripping my spine, and left me cold the rest of the night.

Because they sounded like a dark promise.

Nineteen

Maxon

JARED ROLLED HIS EYES AND tossed his pic down when Libby walked in from work that night. "Jesus, she's already back."

The hell?

Before I could say anything, Libby walked past the living room where we were all lounging, a forced smile on her face. "Looks like practice is going well."

"Are you fucking kidding me?" I kicked him when I stood and turned for the hall. Looking back over my shoulder, I called out, "You're welcome to find somewhere else to sleep in your favorite town."

When I reached Libby's room, I shut the door behind me and took my time drinking her in. "God, Rebel, look at you."

Short black shorts and a black lace, see-through top.

And I was frustratingly aware she went to work dressed like that.

"So, I guess Jared still blames me for moving here," she said offhandedly as she started pulling at her shorts.

"He'll get over it. He doesn't have a legitimate reason for blaming you." I walked closer when I realized how still she'd gotten.

"I know he doesn't. Doesn't make it any easier when he's been staying here—*in my apartment*—and his anger toward me is so thick and obvious I practically choke on it," she murmured.

"Again, not a legitimate reason for being mad. But I'll talk to him." I grabbed her arm and turned her to face me, my eyes raking over her. "Are you trying to drive me insane? Or just the guys that come into the bar?"

Her lips twisted mischievously. "What do you think?" She turned for her dresser and asked over her shoulder, "How was the meeting with Nate?"

Libby was standing in front of me in next to nothing . . . and she wanted to talk about the guys.

Right. Sure.

I roughed a hand through my hair and fought to gather my thoughts. "Good, I guess. Same as always. He wants to make sure you're not becoming too much of a distraction for me and that I'll keep doing what I'm supposed to."

She turned slowly, a sleep tank in her hands. "What do you mean?"

I let my hand fall to gesture to her. "My conversation with him that first day he came here. At Brooks Street."

She shook her head, her eyes shifted quickly as she tried to remember that day. "We talked about the Holloway house after you met with him. I met him, but we didn't really talk about your conversation."

"Shit, uh . . . it's not a big deal."

She laughed softly, hesitantly. "Your manager's worried I'm a distraction, and your bandmate glares at me. Right, not a big deal."

I closed the distance between us and pulled her close, letting her tank fall to the floor. "It's not. Really. It doesn't matter what they say. What matters is that you're home and wearing this." I ran the tips of my fingers down her chest and over her waist, gripping tight when I reached her hips. "And I need to spend some time taking it off you and tasting you."

Her face lightened and her laugh filled the room when I led her toward the bed. "Is that so?"

I answered her with a searing kiss.

Twenty

Libby

PRESSED A KISS TO Maxon's bare chest before quietly slipping out of my room and down the hall the next morning . . . and found the living room filled with sleeping Henley boys again.

"I'm ready for you to move to Holloway," I grumbled as I stepped over Lincoln's sleeping form on my way to Einstein's room.

I was used to living with a lot of people, thanks to Dare and mafia life. So I didn't mind having the boys in my space.

Just not every night, especially when I could practically feel Jared's resentment, even when he slept. One more snide comment, and I was sending him back to a hotel.

I came to a sudden halt when I opened Einstein's door. Her room was empty.

Again.

I wasn't sure where she spent her nights when she wasn't sleeping here, but for her sake, I hoped she knew what she was doing.

With a defeated sigh, I shut her door and headed to the kitchen.

Einstein wasn't like me—never had been.

She couldn't have meaningless sex. Not when her heart was already too invested in a man who was just as invested in her. But she had her mind set on destroying her heart in order to protect it.

Maverick was made for Einstein just as Maxon was made for me.

After Johnny's death, she'd briefly accepted Maverick's comfort before pushing him away.

I think she's afraid of what would happen to her heart if she let herself love someone again—only for them to be taken from her. She'd already lost too many people.

But I knew Einstein. I saw the pain she couldn't hide fast enough when she hurt Maverick.

Not that it would stop her from doing anything to make Maverick believe he meant nothing to her.

Maxon and I had been different.

Everything I had done was to keep him safe . . . alive.

I'd kept him at an arms-length and refused to let go. All while loving him as fiercely as possible every moment we stole away together.

I destroyed my heart to protect *us*.

I reached for the coffee maker and put a filter and grounds in the basket, then turned to fill up the pot with water.

My blood ran cold and my stomach dropped.

The apartment shifted and I struggled to stay upright.

There, propped against the faucet, was a thick, plain white envelope.

I stared at it for countless moments before my head whipped around, searching what parts of the apartment I could see from where I was standing.

But there was no one.

Just me.

The sleeping boys.

And the envelope.

I slowly stepped forward and set the coffee pot on the counter next to the sink, and shakily reached out to grab the envelope. Sucking in a deep breath, I flipped it over and tried to contain the full-body tremors that rolled through my body when I saw the printed name on the bottom right corner.

Elizabeth Borello.

I carefully worked the top open, my gaze darting up to make sure no one was waking or watching me, and tried to swallow past the sudden lump in my throat when I saw the top of a Polaroid picture peeking out.

But like before, I didn't understand what I was seeing.

Not at first anyway.

Then a cry left my lips that sounded like a siren in the weighted silence pressing down around me.

Because that was me in the picture.

Sleeping in my bed.

Maxon lay shirtless beside me, holding me close.

That shirt engulfing me? It was his. I'd pulled it off him last night . . .

And I was still wearing it.

On the bottom of the Polaroid, written in Sharpie, were two words.

You're mine.

I couldn't process what I was seeing or what it meant. That photo had been taken within the last five hours. Which meant . . . which meant the person leaving me the pictures could still be in the apartment.

Shit.

I shakily shoved the picture into the envelope, then grabbed a chef's knife from the butcher block. I checked the pantry and guest bathroom before hurrying to Einstein's room again and checking it.

When I passed through the living room on my way to my room, I glanced at the guys long enough to make sure they were all breathing, then paused.

I turned, suspicion building and spreading as I studied Jared's sleeping form.

"He'll get over it. He doesn't have a legitimate reason for blaming you."

The first picture arrived the day Henley came back from New York.

Any of them could be playing a joke. Hell, even Einstein could.

Lord knew she liked to cuddle and Maxon was in her spot. And she could've slipped into the apartment and left before I woke.

But there was something about these that felt personal now.

Something that didn't feel like a joke.

And I would know if Einstein had a Polaroid camera.

I quickly turned and rushed through the rest of the apartment, checking every place anyone could hide.

The dread in my stomach intensified no matter how many times I chanted it was one of my friends playing a prank.

Because this was clearly no longer just some jealous punk in Wake Forest.

You're mine.

You're mine.

You're mine.

I returned the knife in the block and started the coffee maker, watching Jared for long minutes before forcing myself to my room to get dressed and grab the first envelope.

Once I was ready, I sat next to Maxon and gently shook him. "Maxon. Maxon, wake up."

He rolled to his back and cracked his eyes, his hand moving to grab for me. "What time is it?"

"I'm not sure. Hey, I have a question." I kept my voice at a whisper, but my tone bright. "Do you have a Polaroid camera?"

His head jerked against the pillow and his already heavy-lidded eyes squinted a little more. "What? They still make those?"

"Yes. So, I'm guessing you don't?"

"No, I don't even own a camera." He rubbed a hand over his face then propped up on his elbows. "Do you want one?"

"No," I said a little too quickly. I never wanted to see another Polaroid camera or picture again. "I was just . . . I thought I saw one in the apartment."

"I don't—" He looked so confused and half-asleep, I almost felt bad for trying to get answers right now. "Shit, I don't know. I haven't seen one. Didn't even know they still existed."

"Maybe Einstein knows." I leaned forward to kiss him quickly. "I have to run an errand, so I'll be back. I'm sorry for waking you, but there's fresh coffee."

He sat there, staring blankly, too out of it to ask where I was going as I hurried out of the room and the apartment.

And I was thankful for it. I'd been worried he'd want to come with me, and I couldn't afford that right now.

A few minutes later, I was pulling up to ARCK Investigations, the private investigating firm Kieran Hayes and his wife had started with another Holloway member after dissolving the gang. The place Einstein worked at when she wasn't working for my brother.

For all the bad I said about Kieran Hayes, I had to be fair when I said he did a lot of good for others.

This business had been started with the intention of helping those who couldn't help themselves. Sure, they did the typical P.I. things, but their main operation was helping women start over if they were trapped in dire situations.

That's where Einstein came in. She could create flawless new identities and fabricate lives for those women and their children in her sleep.

ARCK didn't promote this part of their work, but word still got around to those who needed the help.

Like I told Maxon . . . terrifying to be in the same room with, but he was one of the good ones.

His business partner, Conor, was the best of the best. Sure, he had been Holloway and was just as terrifying, but he was a giant teddy bear. We'd already tried to adopt him and make him and honorary Borello.

I was here to see him.

Because if anyone could and *would* help me with my Polaroid problem without snitching to Dare, it was Conor.

I pushed a calming breath from my lungs and got out of my car.

I breathed a little easier when I glanced around the parking spaces out front and didn't see Einstein's car, but that didn't mean much.

As soon as I stepped into ARCK, a smile crossed my face when I saw the man tapping away at a computer near the back of the room.

Over six and a half feet tall. Terrifying. And a boyish grin on his handsome face when he looked up and saw me walk in.

I stayed pressed against the front door and kept my voice low. "Kieran here?"

Conor's grin faltered. "No."

"Einstein?"

He lifted his hands out and looked around. "It'd be nice if she came in once in a while."

My relief was met with unease. *It'd be nice to know that she wasn't out ruining her life.*

"Anyone here at all?"

"Should I be hurt?" he asked gruffly.

A breath of a laugh left me as I pushed from the door and walked to his desk. I leaned over and gave him a kiss on the forehead, then sat on the corner of his desk. "Don't hate me."

His face fell. "Shit, first you come in here with those questions then follow them up with that?"

I let my amusement fade to show him an ounce of my fear. "I need help, Conor."

He transformed in an instant.

The man sitting in front of me was no longer the massive teddy bear I wanted to make my little brother . . . he was a giant. A mobster who had seen true evil and lost too much—including his own brother. And there was nothing that would stop him from protecting those who needed protection.

"What happened?"

I took the envelopes out of my purse without hesitation. "These were left for me at my apartment over the last few days. One outside, one inside. I need to know if there are any fingerprints on them that aren't mine. DNA . . . I don't know what you can do. Just anything."

Conor's eyes flashed to mine before going back to the envelopes, his stare missing nothing as I took the pictures out and laid them on his desk.

I turned over one of the envelopes and tapped on the printed name to draw his attention to it, then tapped on the picture left for me this morning. "This was taken sometime after I got home from work last night around three and left for me propped against the kitchen faucet."

The muscles in his jaw twitched, but other than that, there was no indication he was bothered by what he saw. I knew he wouldn't show his emotions.

This was now a job, and his focus would be on it one hundred percent until he completed it. Emotions got in the way.

"You slept through someone taking this?"

My expression answered for me. I clearly had, and I was embarrassed for it.

People from our lives shouldn't relax enough to sleep through a stranger in their room—let alone the sound of a Polaroid camera.

But I'd been in my safe place.

Destruction could rise up around me, and I would remain blissfully unaware as long as I was in Maxon's arms.

"What's your boyfriend's name again?"

"Maxon."

Conor dipped his head in a nod. "He didn't take these? Or one of his friends?"

"He'll get over it. He doesn't have a legitimate reason for blaming you."

I ignored the second question, knowing I couldn't answer it honestly.

Knowing I didn't *want* to answer it.

"Maxon didn't even know Polaroid cameras still existed, and he doesn't know about these." I caught Conor's eye and said, "No one else knows. They *can't* know."

He leaned back in his chair and folded his arms over his chest. "Einstein could do this better and faster."

"She'll tell Dare, and if he knows . . ." My shoulders sagged. "He can't know, Conor. No one can."

"Libby, if you were a stranger, I wouldn't blink at that. But this is you. I have to know why. Your family could take care of this before it could become a bigger problem, and from how much the pictures escalated from the first to the second, it *will* become a bigger problem. Kieran and I could take care of this in a heartbeat if you let me tell him."

I shrugged helplessly. "Because everyone except you will tell Dare. If Dare knows, he'll do what he used to whenever there was a massive Holloway threat. He'll put us all in one house until the threat's gone. If that happens, my mom will find out." I choked on the next words that almost broke free, then carefully said, "My mom has always been sure an old enemy was coming. And I need to know if these pictures are in fact from them before I tell anyone. Because they might just be from one of Maxon's jealous fans who thinks they can scare me."

Conor stared at me for a few seconds before asking, "And you don't think you could tell him?"

I swallowed thickly and tried to force the tears away, but soon Conor and the office were blurry. "No. Because if it *is* the enemy my mom worries about, then I need to protect Maxon. If he knows what's happening, he won't let me do that."

"Libby . . . who's your mom worried about?"

"Dare and Mom know. That's more than enough." I let my hand hover over the pictures and said, "I just need your help, Conor. Please . . . please look. Look for anything that could tell me who's doing this. Then we can either put an end to it, or I'll tell you exactly what we need to be worried about."

He growled, "Your brother's gonna fucking kill me."

A soggy laugh left me. "Story of my life."

Twenty-One

Him

GLARED AT MY COUSIN when he came into my office, coffee in hand and tie loosened. "You look hungover. Did you even sleep?"

His lip curled before he took a long drink. "Hard to when I was doing your bullshit errands all weekend. Lucky for me we don't have meetings today."

"Bullshit?" I asked in a deceptively soft tone, challenging him to confirm what he'd just said.

"Bullshit," he repeated without hesitation as he dropped into one of the chairs.

He didn't blink when I took a gun out of my drawer and set it on the desk, barrel facing him.

"This company is just as much mine as it is yours," he said on a low growl. "I don't have time to keep doing this shit for you. Consider checking on her yourself more than once every few years. Then we'll see who's walking in here looking like this."

"I own her, there's no need. And I have people like you to watch her every move."

He rolled his eyes and huffed.

I leaned forward and dropped my tone. "I don't care if you're an equal partner. I'm next in line. I say *fetch*, you say *what*. I tell you *get me information*, you say *yes, sir*."

"Oh, fuck off." He barked out a frustrated laugh. "You and your old man sit on your goddamn thrones giving orders and keeping your hands clean. Our name is revered because of me—because of the rest like me. *We* keep people in line. *We* keep fear in their hearts."

"You're expendable."

"You sure about that?" His tone was cool and unaffected as he set his gun near mine, facing me.

I stared at the firearm for a second and gave a brief nod, then went back to reading over the reports on my new computer screen.

"From what I can tell, this Maxon isn't leaving. He's here to stay."

Rage erupted in my chest instantly, but I didn't let it control me. My fingers paused above the mouse for a few seconds before I resumed scrolling through the report. "For your sake, I hope you have more than that."

"All that I've learned about him, we already knew from the article." He sighed when I shot him a look. "Again, you can check on her yourself."

I was in the process of building my empire. I was preparing to take over a family.

I didn't have time to check on Elizabeth. To dote on her.

I saw her when it was necessary. When I thought she needed to remember what it felt like to belong to me.

Besides, I was trying to prevent a war by staying hidden from her family. And I enjoyed the game we played.

The one where she believed she was free. All the while I was in the shadows, killing off her betrayals and feeding off the memory of her screaming my name like a goddamn drug.

But in all these years, she'd never done this. Never been involved with someone and thrown it in my face like she didn't belong to me.

I considered myself a rational man.

This was pushing me too far.

"I want Maxon James taken and killed immediately."

I thought my cousin was going to choke on his coffee. "What about the timeline? Nine months between when she sleeps with the guy and when we kill him. *Nine months*. Always."

"That timeline is for the random men she fucks," I yelled, slamming my hands on the desk and smashing the mouse. "She has a type. Men who roll into town that she doesn't know. Men she will never see again. This doesn't fit under that category, and I want him gone."

"Then you're gonna have to figure out a damn good way to do it."

"Rock stars overdose all the time. It won't raise suspicions." I looked at the desk and loosed a frustrated sigh. "Get me a damn mouse."

"What was that? You say *do something* and I say *fuck off*?" He grabbed his gun and stood. When he reached the door, he called over his shoulder, "You have an assistant for a reason."

Potential Polaroid Assholes

~~Literally anyone. Ugh.~~ Has access to apartment.

Jared

Mom

Twenty-Two

Libby

ROLLED OVER AS I stretched . . . and kept rolling. There was no warm body to stop me. No strong, tattooed arms wrapped around me. My mouth pulled into a frown when I twisted my neck and found no trace of Maxon in the room.

Fear instantly unfurled in my stomach and spread through my body, threatening to choke me.

My gaze locked on the corner of my room where there should've been a guitar case propped up, and I made myself breathe. If the guitar was gone, Maxon was somewhere making beautiful music.

He was safe.

I rolled over and buried my head in the pillow and released a shuddering breath. Then another and another until my body relaxed.

At least if I'm waking without him, I can be happy I'm waking alone— without *Einstein and her freezing toes.*

Bright side.

Sometimes you have to focus on it.

In a life of fear and corruption and murder, I'd learned early on to do exactly that.

I'd found my bright side and clung hard to it. To him—*Maxon*.

When Henley first left Wake Forest, it nearly broke me.

I hadn't just lost the boy I loved, I lost the boy who grounded and freed me. Who calmed and exhilarated me. Who made me forget the darkness in my world.

But I couldn't let myself break. I couldn't let his absence destroy me.

So I found the silver lining in simple things. Mundane things.

Getting the best coffee of my life after fighting with my mom.

Finding the perfect shoes and shade of red lipstick the morning after Maxon butt-dialed me at the beginning of a hookup.

Finding a twenty in my jeans right before I got the call that Maxon went to jail with Lincoln.

A month passing in between anyone in the family killing someone.

Mundane things . . .

But they were all Band-Aids compared to Maxon.

When he first came home, I worried every day I was dreaming. That I would wake and my bright side would be gone.

Now with the pictures and unknown sender, I was terrified I'd wake to find he'd been taken from me . . .

I knew exactly how brutal the mafia could be when they wanted to send a message.

We'd all learned when Dare's ex had been ripped from their bed and killed in front of him.

Icy fingers trailed up my spine, sending chills across my body as I climbed from the bed and left my room.

My fears melted away and my lips stretched into a smile when I heard the gentle strums of Maxon's acoustic and his low, gravelly voice coming from the living room.

His eyes locked on me when I rounded the corner into the

room, intense and full of some unknown emotion as he watched me lean against the wall.

I bit down on my bottom lip, trying to hide my smile when the song he was singing teased my ears, taking me back to the day he wrote it.

I woke, already giggling and tensing.

"Stop," Maxon said quietly. "Don't move."

"That tickles."

"Libby."

I blinked against the harsh sun coming through the hotel window until I could look at his too-handsome face, scrunched in concentration.

His lips were moving, but nothing was coming out. His caramel-colored eyes were searching my naked body, but there wasn't a hint of the carnal need or passion that had been filling them since he'd come home last night.

They were light, open, excited.

And then he moved his hand over my stomach, and I flinched again.

"Oh my God," I said on a breath of a laugh. "Oh my God, I can't."

The corners of his mouth twitched, his eyes darting up to mine twice before he leaned forward to give me a quick kiss. When he sat back and hunched over my stomach again, he explained, "The only paper in this damn room is a Bible."

I glanced over my arms and chest, then down to my stomach. Every part I could see was covered in Maxon's handwriting. Some places were scratched out, some had arrows leading to other parts.

"And you couldn't use your phone?" I asked teasingly.

He gave me a heated look that made my stomach clench with need and my breaths deepen. "Phones stay off when we're together, Rebel. Even for this."

Maxon whispered the new lyrics when he slid into me minutes later, claiming me again and again with his words and his body and his heart.

The song was about trying to hold on to a girl as wild as they come and knowing the only way to keep her was to free her.

As if I wasn't already his.

As if I hadn't always been his.

"What happens after you free her?" I asked when we finished, our bodies still joined. "What if she doesn't come back?"

Maxon smiled, like he knew a secret I didn't. "Wait for the next album. I'll answer you then."

I waited. I listened to every song—like always—then called and told him he was wrong with a smile in my voice. The next time he came to town, he whispered the words of my answer against my neck as he slowly undressed and teased me until I was writhing between him and a wall.

A song telling a girl to go and pretend she's having fun, and he would do the same.

Saying it wouldn't change that she was his and he was hers.

Claiming he already knew how their story would go—with a house and kids and his ring on her finger.

Promising he would wait until the day her rebel heart found her way home to him.

"That one's always been my favorite," I said, my voice soft as a breath after I blinked away the past.

"I know," he murmured.

I nodded down the hall. "You know . . . it would be really nice waking up next to you."

His fingers never stopped plucking the strings as he shrugged. "Couldn't sleep."

My eyebrows lifted. "So, let's not sleep."

That possessive, predatory look flashed through his eyes. Carnal hunger so unrestrained, my body heated and begged to be filled with him in response.

I pushed away from the wall and lifted my hand, mouthing, "Three minutes."

He just smiled and shifted back on the couch, his voice easily joining his hands in the middle of the song as I headed toward the bathroom.

I had just finished brushing my teeth and was cupping water in my hands to splash on my face when the fingers of my right hand hit something on my left, and I stilled.

I looked at my palms, not able to comprehend the band wrapped around the ring finger of my left hand. Slowly, as if I didn't trust my sight or touch, I turned my hands over.

"What . . ."

A diamond on my finger.

There was a goddamn diamond on my finger.

No, no, no . . .

I wanted to search my apartment.

I wanted to scream for Maxon to run.

But I couldn't move.

I couldn't speak.

That fear from earlier was real.

It was paralyzing me.

The Polaroid pictures could've been anyone. *Anyone.*

But I knew who'd put this on my finger. What this was.

And I needed to get Maxon far away from them.

From *me.*

I didn't realize I was crying until warm, calloused hands slid down my arms and folded over my hands.

"Every lyric I write, I write for you," he whispered.

My chest hitched and my body swayed. Every racing thought halted so suddenly it felt like I ran into a wall.

Then realizations trickled in, slow and perfectly clear.

There was a diamond on my finger.

Maxon was singing my favorite song, and there was a massive diamond on my finger.

Oh my God.

Relief and surprise and excitement rushed through me, overwhelming me until I was trembling and my tears were flowing faster.

A quiet sob tumbled from my lips when he pressed his mouth to the back of my neck.

He wove his fingers through mine as he wrapped his arms loose-ly around me. "I thought of how to do this. I thought of taking you to our field, having something elaborate set up and getting down on one knee." His chest shook with a laugh when my nose scrunched.

I glanced up through my tears to see him watching me in the mirror.

"But that's not you," he continued. "I thought of singing that song on the stage at The Jack and then asking you . . . almost did, actually." He dipped his head to trail his lips along my ear, eyes locked with mine the entire time. "And then I stopped thinking of the romantic gestures and thought of *you* instead."

"You think this isn't romantic?" I asked, my throat tight.

His mouth twitched into a smile. "You crave your freedom and you need to run wild. You command everyone's attention when you walk into a room and feed off excited energy. But when it comes to *us*, you don't want the rest of the world there. You want to hide away so you can finally shed that mask you wear around everyone else . . . and just be."

That he understood that at all—that he knew me so perfectly and could flow with both sides of me so easily—was one of the things I loved most about him.

I wasn't easy to handle. I knew that. I'd *told* him that long before I ever gave him my heart or body.

I needed to be around people and needed time with my family.

But what I needed more than anything was time alone with Maxon where everything else disappeared. And he had always been happy to give me both. Sometimes even knowing when I needed one or the other before I did.

"When *I* think of us . . . I think of loving you to the point of exhaustion," he continued, turning me in his arms and pressing me closer to his body. "I think of lazy hours in bed and watching you walk around in nothing but my shirt. I think of writing lyrics with you next to me and singing them to you before anyone else hears them. I think of repeating the cycle again and again. So here we are. The world gone. Just us as we've always been."

Tears filled my eyes again, but I managed to keep them from falling.

"Marry me, Libby."

My mouth was on his, swallowing the taste of my name on his tongue. "Yes," I whispered through our kiss . . . through the tightening of my throat . . . through my overwhelming joy.

This was real. This was finally happening after years of running. After years of wanting it.

And it was more perfect than I could've ever imagined.

The kiss was rough and hard, but somehow still held a hint of a tease that matched his smile I could feel against my lips. And then he was grabbing my thighs and lifting me onto the vanity.

Weaving my fingers through his hair, I forced him back to look into his eyes. "Yes, I'll marry you. Yes, I want your last name. Yes, I want the future you promised me years ago." I moaned when he slammed his mouth back onto mine, whimpering and begging when he spread my legs and pulled me to the edge of the counter.

Seconds later, he was pressing into me, filling and stretching me.

It wasn't sweet or slow. It didn't have me on the verge of tears again.

It was rough and fast. It was desperate and excited. It was the overwhelming amazement and bliss that this moment was here and needing to know it was real.

We wouldn't last long. Couldn't.

We'd been heading toward this moment for years. There was no way to take our time.

And that was perfect too. It was us. All passion and love and unrestrained need.

Maxon pressed his forehead to mine when I began tightening and vibrating around him, my body strung so tight that I wasn't sure I could take a breath without shattering.

"Come on, Rebel."

He drove into me relentlessly, jaw clenched and muscles straining until I came crashing down around him.

He kissed me hard.

Fierce.

Swallowing my moans and raking his teeth over my bottom lip as he continued to thrust deeper and deeper, prolonging my orgasm until I was trembling.

A growl built low in his chest when he found his release inside me, his body tensed and shuddering as he held me close. His lips brushed mine over and over again. "I love you."

I nodded weakly. "I—"

"There's really only so long you can expect me to—huh." Einstein's voice sounded in the bedroom so suddenly, Maxon and I didn't have time to start scrambling before she added, "Nice ass, Maxon."

"*Einstein.*"

Maxon slammed the bathroom door, his face set in a mask of frustration.

"Well, it's true," she yelled. "Let's eat, I'm hungry."

I gave Maxon a look, but he was now barely holding it together. His mouth mashed tight and eyes shut as his chest shook.

"Does she know?" I whispered. When he nodded, I raised my voice so she would hear me. "Now's not the best time."

"I'm gonna assume you didn't say *no* since I just walked in to see that. Get dressed and come out here so we can celebrate. And clean that damn sink."

Maxon laughed, but I was staring at the door with a dumbfounded expression. "You've got to be kidding me."

Maxon nipped at my neck teasingly, then placed a kiss there. "We need to move. Soon." Humor coated his words as he helped me off the vanity.

"I think she'll move with us and not tell us. We'd come home and she'd be moved in."

"Jesus," he said on a soft laugh. "I know she doesn't have boundaries, but I don't remember her like this."

I wasn't going to get into Einstein's life with Maxon—not right now.

She was hurting and needed help. She'd been shutting people out but clinging to me harder than ever. And at this rate, she might be standing right next to me at that altar, expecting him to marry her too.

Maxon was right . . . Einstein didn't have boundaries, but this was different. This wasn't her.

"That's because she never was." I stared at the door for a moment, then looked at Maxon and gave him a quick kiss. "I love you," I whispered, finishing what I'd been saying when Einstein walked in.

His stare danced over my face, the corner of his mouth twitching into a smile. "I've always loved you."

Twenty-Three

Maxon

AFTER WE SHOWERED AND DRESSED, we joined Einstein in the living room.

"You're officially engaged. And it seems so different than what you were before. Yay. Let's celebrate," she said dully from where she sat on the couch.

She'd brought coffee and a ton of food . . . and didn't touch any of it. Just sat there silently staring out the window while we ate.

It was awkward.

It wasn't until Libby and I started talking about *when* we wanted to get married that Einstein seemed to remember she was in the room with us.

"It'll have to be kept quiet. Anyone who might say something can't know about it. That way, paparazzi can't catch wind and try to get pictures."

"We're the masters of keeping quiet," Einstein murmured as she grabbed her phone and began rapidly tapping on it.

Libby sighed, but agreed. "We can keep it quiet. We wouldn't even have to go to a courthouse."

My brow furrowed in confusion, then smoothed when I realized what she was saying. I shot her a look. "A *legal* marriage would be great, Libby. And what do you mean *courthouse*? Don't you want an actual wedding?"

Einstein laughed. She glanced up a few seconds later and waved us on with her phone. "Continue. Please. I can't wait to see how this plays out."

"Just because illegal things happened within my world doesn't mean there weren't ways to do things legally." She rolled her eyes. "It's common for people in mobs to marry in secret. Don't get me wrong . . . some do huge, extravagant weddings. But others don't want enemies knowing details of their lives. It can be dangerous to have a wedding, because it's like inviting an enemy to attack."

She was talking about enemies attacking and secret weddings the way she talked about a night at work. It was still surreal. "Are you sure I'm going to get used to this?"

Her lips twitched into a smile. "Yes."

I nodded absentmindedly, my gaze traveling to Einstein when I felt her stare on me.

Her thumbs were hovering over the screen of her phone, but her light eyes were boring into me—one eyebrow lifted like she was waiting to see what I was going to do.

"There are ways to keep actual weddings a secret, Libby," I finally said, and looked back to her. "Real weddings, not hidden mob weddings. You can't tell me you don't want that."

"I don't want that," she said immediately, lifting her shoulder in a hint of a shrug. "Dare and Lily got married this way. She was the princess of the Irish-American mob, and he was our boss. Even though they're both *out*, it's hard to ever really be out. Just because *you've* decided you're done doesn't mean other people understand that or care. With their names, they need to keep their lives quiet still."

"She isn't just a Borello by oath, she's a Borello by blood. People know our family. Our name. I dissolved the gang, but enemies don't care. When you put her in the spotlight, you put a blinding target on her back."

I swallowed thickly as Dare's words rang through my mind. "Right. Right, yeah, that makes sense, I guess."

"What is it?" When I glanced at Libby, she said, "You suddenly look like something's wrong. Tell me."

I blew out a slow breath and rubbed my forehead. "Nothing. Just something your brother said."

She leaned against the couch and lifted her eyebrows, letting me know she wasn't going to drop it.

"Might as well spill," Einstein mumbled without ever looking up from her phone.

"He said people know the Borello name. That being in the spotlight with me is dangerous."

Libby opened her mouth, frustration darkening her features. Panic suddenly flashed through her eyes, stopping whatever she was about to say as her face drained of color. After a second, she bit down on her lip and looked away.

"He's right, in a way," she whispered after a moment. "People know the name. But if we can stop them from digging into my past—if your publicists and Einstein watch stories that are printed—"

"Or just me," Einstein said.

"If Einstein watches stories," Libby conceded with a roll of her eyes. "She can make sure my last name never gets out."

"Your last name will be mine," I reminded her.

She looked at me again, a hint of a smile on her lips as she scooted over to curl into my side. "I meant *Borello*." She traced the tips of her fingers over my lips, her stare drifting to the floor. "Considering if anything's ever printed about me, it'll say *Libby James* and not *Elizabeth Borello*, I don't think the spotlight is something we need to worry about."

It was as if she touched me with a live wire the second she said that name.

That goddamn name I'd waited a lifetime to hear from her lips.

I felt hyperaware of every breath she took. Everywhere she touched me. Every second that separated us from making that name a reality . . . and we didn't even have a day in mind.

"Say that again."

Her dark eyes flashed to mine and widened. "What?"

"Say your name."

"Elizabeth Borello." The name left her lips on a shaky breath, like she was suddenly aware of the name she was uttering—afraid of its weight.

"No." I swallowed, the action much more difficult than ever before. "No. The other one."

Her tongue darted out to wet her lips that were now slowly spreading into a smile. "Libby James."

I crushed my mouth to hers, weaving my hand into her hair to deepen the kiss until Einstein loudly cleared her throat.

"Still here. Still feeling like a third wheel. Not that anyone cares."

A rumble sounded deep in my chest, but I only backed away enough to ask, "If we do your version of a wedding, when can it happen?"

"Tonight," she whispered, her breath washing across my lips before she was trying to kiss me again.

My face fell and I leaned farther away to search her excited stare. "Don't tease me, Rebel."

"I'm not. These things have to happen immediately sometimes. But I'd like to have my nails done first."

I wanted to laugh—it was such a Libby thing to say. But there was nothing amusing anymore. Something about this felt wrong. Not marrying Libby . . . but marrying her *this* way.

"You have work . . ."

"Zeke will understand," she said flippantly.

" . . . and I want to give you a wedding, Libby."

"I don't want one."

I knew Libby.

Just like I knew she wouldn't have wanted the grand, romantic proposal. Just like I knew when she needed to hide away from the world. I knew she would regret not having this day be something more than a hidden ceremony.

I glanced at Einstein, but she was tapping furiously at her phone, pretending to be invisible.

Lowering my voice, I asked, "You can honestly tell me you don't want a day you can plan? A day that's all about you? A day you'll look back and remember how amazing it was?"

"I want it to be you and me together at the end of the day. That's all that matters—that's all that *will* matter." Her voice took on a frantic tone, and that panic from earlier was back in her eyes. "Not a big wedding. I'll have a life to look back on with you . . . and that's enough."

I'd never felt more confused.

"I don't—*Libby*," I called when she stood from the couch and headed toward her bedroom.

She turned and held out her arms in frustration. "If you thought there was going to be an actual wedding at some point in our lives, then I'm sorry to disappoint you, Maxon. It's not happening."

I sat there in shock, rooted to the couch, staring in the direction she'd left. "What the fuck just happened?"

"What I was waiting for," Einstein mumbled.

I slowly dragged my stare to her. "You knew that would happen?" When she made a sound of affirmation, I asked, "Care to explain? Because I know she'll regret this one day."

"Oh, no . . . she will." Einstein dropped her phone onto her lap, then gave me a sympathetic look. "I told you, I've rooted for you from the beginning. You're what's best for her. You know her better than anyone—I mean, other than me. Of course. And you don't want to give her what you think she should have. You want to give her what you know *she* wants."

I dropped my head into my hands and gripped my hair. I was too thrown by the drastic change in conversation to understand where Einstein was going with this.

"I don't . . . I don't think I follow you."

"I'll dumb it down," she said with a sigh. "You're right. Libby wants the whole thing. Gorgeous wedding and dress and cake and flowers and blah, blah, blah. But she'll never go for it."

I dropped my hands and twisted my neck to look at her again. "Why? Because she's afraid of something bad happening? Of people attacking, or whatever the hell happens in your world?"

Einstein snorted. "No—" Her brows pinched suddenly. For a long time, she sat there thinking. "Huh. Maybe. But even if she is, that's not the main reason. Unfortunately for you, I can't tell you the main reason."

My gaze drifted to the hall again. "Let me guess . . . Libby won't tell me either."

"Who knows? Now that you know so much about our lives, she might. But it's not really something she likes to think about, so I doubt it."

I nodded as my mind raced, trying to figure out what could keep Libby from wanting a wedding.

"Hey, rock star."

I looked to Einstein, wondering how long she'd been trying to get my attention.

"You know marriage was something she blatantly ran from before. You don't know she always wanted it. Openly admitting what she wanted was huge for her, and then it was a rough time around here. She thought she'd lost you. She thought she'd lost the only guy she wanted to spend her life with."

A mixture of pain and frustration unfurled in my chest at the reminder of my first night back, but I pushed it away.

So much could've been ruined—so much had—but we fixed it.

"If Libby is ever going to marry someone, it's going to be you," she continued. "It doesn't matter what she wants, or what *you know* she wants. She's only going to marry you in a mob-style wedding."

"Einstein . . ." I blew out a rough breath.

"Like she said, at the end of the day, it's you and her together. At the end of the day, that's all that really matters." She picked up her phone and started tapping on it, letting me know she was done.

For half a second, I thought if I held off marrying the girl I'd waited for, I could find a way to change her mind.

And then I remembered this was Libby . . .

She'd figure me out and do things her way.

With an amused huff, I stood from the couch and headed toward her room.

I found her sitting on the bed, playing with the edge of the comforter. "I'm sorry," she whispered when I sat next to her. "I just . . ." She shrugged but didn't continue.

"Next Saturday," I said, the words barely escaping my strained throat. Like even my muscles knew this wasn't right and tried to protest. "Gives me time to do some things for you and gives you time to tell anyone you want there. The guys and Nate are all here, so it won't be hard to get them in the same place."

Her eyes were wide and smile unrestrained when she looked at me. "Really?" When I nodded, she said, "Einstein probably heard you and is already telling Dare, Lily, and the twins. They'll be there no matter when or where."

"What about your mom?"

She laughed harshly and shot me a look like she didn't know why I even mentioned her. "What about her?"

I watched her for a few seconds, not understanding where the sudden hostility came from. "You don't want her there?"

"No. I don't think she would come even if I told her."

I stared at her with open confusion. Waiting.

When she realized I wasn't going to drop it, she sighed and dropped her stare to the comforter. "Let's just say she has other ideas about who I should marry."

My eyebrows rose and tone dropped. "Is that right? Who?" Libby was silent and still for so long, I finally nudged her. "Who, Libby?"

She blinked and cleared her throat, then lifted her head to give me a ghost of a smile. "Not important."

"Right . . . but you think your mom wouldn't want to see you get married because of him?"

"We don't get along, Maxon. You know this," she said on a groan. "We've fought for . . . God, as long as I can remember."

"Yeah. Not that I would know, but I thought it was something that kids and parents do." I gestured to her. "Shit, Libby, you told me it was because the two of you were too alike."

She shrugged helplessly. "Well, that might be true. I wouldn't know. We don't talk much because we're usually fighting about the fact that she doesn't like you."

I stared at her for a few seconds before a stunned huff left me.

"I didn't—I just meant she never wanted us together. Wait, *no* . . . it keeps coming out wrong." She started to reach for me, then stopped and ran her hands over her face instead. "Jesus."

A strangled laugh slid up my throat and died on my tongue when I stood from the bed.

"Where are you going?" she asked, panic coating her words when I walked hesitantly away.

It wasn't until I was at the door that I stopped. I gripped the frame in my hand and turned, jaw clenched and stare on the floor.

"When you said you wanted to settle down, I didn't think past *this is the moment I've waited for* . . ."

It had always been Libby and me, and I'd known it would be us forever.

But for the first time in my life, I wondered why I'd been her safe place.

Why she'd been with me.

Why she wanted to marry me.

For the first time, I was questioning everything that was *us* . . . and it was on the day I'd given her a ring.

"But now I'm forced to think past that," I whispered, then finally looked up at her. "You never wanted to get married or settle down until you thought I was settling down with someone else."

"No. No, no, no, that's not true."

"And I just realized that not only does your family not want you with me, but your mom wants you to *marry* someone else." I forced a pained smile. "And you've always done what everyone told you not to, Libby."

"No." Horror dripped from her tone, amplifying the panic in her voice when she yelled, "Maxon, *no*."

But I was already down the hall.

I could feel Einstein's stare as I snatched Libby's keys off the hook near the door, but I didn't turn. Didn't look as I walked out. But it was impossible to ignore the way Libby's voice cracked and twisted around my name as she begged me to wait.

Begged me not to leave.

Exactly what I'd silently promised her I wouldn't do not even an hour before.

She was there, grabbing my arm as her sob ripped through the morning air. "Maxon, *please*."

I whirled on her, conflicting needs and emotions tearing through me seeing her there, standing in nothing but my Henley shirt and the ring I'd just put on her finger, tears streaming down her cheeks.

My blood pounded with heat but my heart ached at the thoughts flying through my mind.

I wanted to pull her into my arms and hold her. I wanted to take her back into her room and show her what she meant to me.

I wanted her to tell me why she loved me.

"It's always been you for me," I said, my voice rough. "That's it, Libby. Nothing else. No one else."

Another sob tore through her.

"You kept me close but made sure to keep me far enough away to know I could never catch you. And I got it, I did. Because I knew you. And I know I left . . . I fucking know, Libby. But don't act like I didn't ask you to go with me every damn time. Like I didn't *beg* you."

Her head dropped as she nodded, her shoulders shaking.

"*You* said you wouldn't be waiting. *You* wanted to see other people. Like I said in the song, I knew I had to let you go. Every goddamn thing I've ever done has been for you. To give you what you needed. And I did it gladly because I love you. But for the first time, I feel like the biggest fucking idiot."

"What?" Her face fell into a look of horror when I shrugged her off me. "Max—"

"I feel like I've been played so damn perfectly by you. I've been the guy in love with you, giving you everything. Space when you needed it. Attention when you wanted it. All while unknowingly helping you piss off your family. And I've been so blinded by you that I didn't realize what you were doing until now."

"No. No, Maxon, no." When I turned toward the parking lot, she said, "I'll do the big wedding if that's what you want, just please don't leave."

I made a noise between a laugh and a sneer when I turned on her again. "Are you serious? I don't want a big wedding, Libby. I want you to be mine. All I've ever wanted was for you to be mine. Fuck, don't you get that?"

I didn't make it two steps away before she cried out my name.

I stalked toward her, grabbed her, and walked her back until I had her pressed against the building. "I've poured out my goddamn heart to you in every song, Libby. I've never hidden anything from you. I've loved you and worshipped you and been so damn transparent every step of the way." I rested my forehead on hers and lowered my voice, but couldn't hide my dread when I asked, "Can you even tell me why you want to get married? Why you love me?"

Her only response was a strangled cry.

Agony pulsed through me, making it hard to breathe.

I pushed away from the wall and her, a growl wrenching from my throat.

I sank into her car and tore out of the parking lot. Feeling her sobs like knives to my chest the entire time I drove.

Twenty-Four

Libby

DON'T KNOW HOW LONG I'd been outside.

But Dare was suddenly there, pulling me into his arms and murmuring things I couldn't understand as he led me to my apartment.

Once we were inside, I looked around as Dare sat me on the couch, confused to see the twins, Lily, and my six-month-old nephew.

"What are you—"

"What the fuck did he do now?" Dare asked, his tone rough and full of frustration.

"Ah-ah," Einstein cut in from where she sat on the kitchen island. I hadn't even noticed her.

"Did you call everyone?"

She gave me a dull look. "Duh."

"Someone tell me what happened," Dare demanded.

"I can't," Einstein said simply as she lifted her phone. "I only heard bits and pieces. But I will say I think your anger might be directed at the wrong person."

Dare's gaze shot around the room before landing on me. When he spoke again, his voice was gentle. "What happened? Einstein sent out a group message that you and Maxon were getting married next weekend, and three minutes later said, '*Never mind. Wedding's off. Come fast.*'"

My head whipped around to face her again, my eyes filling with tears. "It's *off?*"

"Isn't it?" she challenged without looking at me.

"I don't . . . I don't know. It can't be. We just . . . ." A sob broke through and I crumpled where I sat.

The truth was, I didn't know.

I didn't know where Maxon and I stood.

I didn't know what he wanted—or didn't want anymore.

But how could that be it? One half-finished conversation and he was done?

When I calmed, Dare quietly asked, "What happened?"

I recounted the day and my conversations with Maxon as best I could, leaving out the bathroom sex. When I finished, only Dare and Lily were listening.

Maverick and Einstein were having a quiet argument in the hall.

Diggs was raiding the pantry again.

The baby was crawling around the floor.

And I wanted to sink into the couch and die from the looks my brother and sister-in-law were giving me.

"What?" I finally asked when neither said anything.

Lily cleared her throat after a few seconds. "You had my back when you didn't know me during a situation you knew nothing about. So . . . we'll just say this is me returning the favor."

"That's cheating," Dare said roughly.

She shrugged unapologetically.

Dare ran his hands through his hair and over his face, groaning as he did. "I can't believe I'm gonna say this. But I agree with Maxon."

He shot me a look. "Why *wouldn't* he wonder any of the shit he is? I don't know why he didn't ask if you're actually in love with him."

Lily smacked his stomach. "Dare."

"What? He has a valid reason for looking at their relationship the way he is. It wouldn't surprise me if he's thinking it. Even more now that Libby didn't answer him."

"I couldn't. I was so shocked that it was even happening—that he would even ask me why I loved him—that I couldn't do anything but stand there." My stomach clenched and chin wavered. "But none of what he thought I did was true. I never once played him."

"I know," he said gently.

"I don't understand why you told him you didn't want a real wedding," Lily said. "You gave us so much crap for getting married the way we did."

"Yeah. And the shit about Mom?" Dare shot me a look of confusion and annoyance. A look I mirrored.

"Are you serious right now?" I asked on a laugh. "I know why Lily wouldn't understand . . . but *you're* asking me?"

Dare made a face that said *obviously*.

I leaned forward so my voice wouldn't carry through the apartment. "*Why* hasn't Mom ever wanted me with Maxon? *Why* has she told me for years that I'm not allowed to be with him? *Why* are we always fighting?"

"Fuck if I know. I've told you to get over your bullshit with her."

I stared at my brother blankly for a few seconds and made myself breathe a few times so I wouldn't yell. "Moretti. You fucking idiot."

Dare barked out a laugh, but the amusement quickly drained from his face. "You're trying to tell me that you and Mom have been fighting over Maxon—have been fighting period—because of *Moretti*? This whole blowup between you and Maxon happened because of *Moretti*? I took care of that shit over ten years ago, Libby."

"Is that a kind of pasta?" Lily asked softly.

"Yeah, you *took care of it*. But you're an idiot for thinking it was over. It's like Mom said, we're all naïve if we think we can actually escape the mob."

"I'm gonna guess it's not," Lily whispered to herself and picked up Beckham when he crawled to her.

I laughed bitterly when I thought of the pictures I'd entrusted with Conor. *I'd* been an idiot thinking it was truly over.

"Mom never lets me forget," I continued. "She never stops reminding me. Every time Maxon is mentioned, she loses her mind because I'm 'single-handedly destroying an alliance.'"

"I said I took care of it," Dare seethed.

"But what if you didn't?"

"You think they'd let ten years go by without collecting if I hadn't? It's done. Over. I'll talk to Mom. Jesus Christ, Libby." He roughed a hand through his hair, his movements slowing when he took it out. "Libby." His dark eyes darted to mine, understanding and hesitation lighting them. "Libby . . . is that why you refused to date Maxon all those years?"

I ground my jaw when it shook and lifted my chin. "Mom said they would come."

"Jesus fucking Christ."

"She said it didn't matter what you'd done, and I couldn't put Maxon in that position."

"I can't believe it," Dare said on a breath of a laugh. "I actually feel bad for the guy. You need to tell him."

My head was shaking, but I wasn't sure why. I didn't know if I disagreed with Dare or if it was simply the thought of telling Maxon . . .

What happened in the years before he left—how I would've had to leave him without a word.

Why I both hated my family and owed them my life.

Why I'd kept him at a distance during that time, and in the years after.

That I wouldn't be here if I hadn't loved him so much.

"You say that like I should've told him so long ago," I mumbled.

"No," Dare said immediately. "No, you couldn't. But I took care of it so you could *live*, Libby . . . and you still let them have complete control over your life. He deserves to know now."

Lily was lifting Beckham in the air and making faces as she lowered him again. Her amused expression didn't match her tone. "So now I know the Moretti are a *who* not a *what*, but I'm missing a crucial part of the story if they made you say no to a wedding."

"That's because there was supposed to be a Moretti wedding," Einstein said, suddenly chiming in from the other side of the room. "A big wedding. One that meant ending bad blood and forming an alliance. Libby knows the details since *she* was supposed to be the one getting married."

Twenty-Five

Maxon

"TAKE YOU THIS LONG TO think of an answer, or to find me?"

I didn't look over at her. I didn't need to. I knew she was there.

I drove around for over half an hour before I headed to our field. I wasn't sure how long I'd been out here on the hood of her car. Only knew it was long enough for memories of us at this spot to drown out thoughts of why I'd left at all.

"Took this long for anyone to give me their keys." She slid onto the hood of the car but didn't lie down next to me. Her back shook with a soft laugh when she said, "After I got chewed out, they all thought you needed time alone. No one thought you would listen to me when you were that upset."

I didn't know if they were right or not.

I'd always been the calm one of the two of us. But I'd never been as pissed or as hurt as I was this morning.

"Maxon, I—"

"Just tell me." My voice was rough and bordered on a plea. "I don't want to draw this out if you're gonna tell me that I was just another way to rebel against your family."

She twisted to look at me, her eyes filled with tears. "Is that really what you think?"

"I don't know what to think anymore, Libby." I spread out my arms, then let them fall to my stomach. "I've been sure of us and of what I wanted my entire life. I've been sure of every step I've ever taken—even if it fucking hurt at the time—because I knew where it was leading. And for the first time, I didn't know where I stood with you. And I felt lost because of it."

"Can you really look at me and say I was with you to piss off my family?"

No.

I ran a hand over my face, groaning into it before sitting up beside her. "I've wanted to marry you since that day you first called yourself a rebel." I stared at my hands, a small laugh escaping me at the memory. "I didn't know what love was. I didn't really know what marriage was. I still thought half the girls in school were gross . . . but not you. Never you. And you never wanted to marry me up until a few weeks ago."

"Maxon," she whispered softly. I wasn't sure if she actually said it or I just imagined it.

"Once you did, I didn't question it. I was just so damn happy. We'd already lost so much time and been through so much bullshit that I wanted to make everything happen right then. The house, the wedding, the babies. Only reason I waited this long to ask you was because I didn't want to scare you away again." I shifted my stare to look at her and asked, "Do you even want to marry me?"

A sob wrenched from her body and she seemed to crumple on herself, dropping her head into her hands. "Maxon—" Another sob tore through her, and for a while, she just sat there shaking and crying.

And I braced myself.

Hardened my shredded heart.

Clenched my jaw and steeled myself when it felt like the slightest breeze would knock me over.

She lifted her head, her face stained with tears, and her lips trembling. "I owe you so many apologies and even more explanations. Marrying you—" A strangled cry worked up her throat, and she took a second to breathe. "Marrying you is all I've ever wanted. Being with you—being *yours*—is all I've ever wanted."

I laughed harshly. "I can think of a dozen or more years where that wasn't true."

"It was *always* true."

"You wanted me there, Libby. You didn't want to be *with* me." I lifted my hands only to let them fall. "And like I've said, I got it. It's how you were. You needed your freedom. But now . . ."

What if it wasn't *how you were?*

I couldn't get the words past the knot in my throat.

She nodded slowly, as if she didn't realize she was doing it. "We were fifteen when you first told me that you'd already written your name on my heart, and one day you were gonna make good on that claim." A faint laugh touched her lips, and she glanced at me. "Do you remember?"

I grunted an affirmation.

Did she think I'd forgotten? She kissed me for the first time that night at this spot.

"There'd always been something about you, Maxon. Just . . . something that felt right. But when you said those words, it was like you stopped time and showed me our future. And I knew right then I was going to marry you someday." She twisted her hand to look at the ring on her finger, a smile briefly lighting her face before they both fell. "I'd been waiting so long for you to do something. Kiss me. Hold my hand. *Something* . . . but there was never anything until you went way past handholding and announced you already owned my heart."

"The thought of kissing you was fucking terrifying."

"And telling me you were going to claim my heart wasn't?"

I shrugged. "It was true." My mouth twitched into a smile when she dropped her head back and laughed. "You were already so unattainable. So far out of reach."

"You were my best friend. You were my everything—even then."

"You've always been like a wild horse. One wrong move, and you would've run. And I would've been left there, waiting for you to come back."

"Never said I was easy to handle," she whispered, repeating words she'd said to me most our lives.

But she was. I'd understood her so well.

At least, I thought . . .

We fell back into silence for a while before she turned to face me. "My dad was killed two months later."

"I remember."

Libby's head shook quickly, like I wasn't understanding. "My dad never approved of our friendship."

"Jesus, this again." I roughed a hand through my hair and stared at the field ahead as she continued talking.

"He always told me I shouldn't have friends outside our *family*. That it would be best to cut ties with you before one or both of us wanted something we couldn't have. When he realized things were changing between us, he was livid. Told me I wasn't allowed to see you—told me it would only hurt *you* in the end." My eyes flashed to her, and she held up her hands. "I know what you're thinking, but I wasn't friends with you because he told me not to be. I didn't see you because he told me to stay away from you. Maxon . . . I loved you. There was no way they could've kept me from you. But they could keep me from *being* with you."

My brow furrowed. "I don't understand."

She swallowed, the motion seeming difficult. "About a week

after he died, I came home and there were these strange men at our house. They were talking with Dare, Johnny, Mom, and my dad's advisor. As soon as I walked into the room they were in, the old one pointed at me and everyone started yelling at each other. Dare told me to go to my room, but our mom demanded I stay. I left," she said with a shrug. "Dare and Mom came to my room about an hour later, just *screaming* at each other about me and those men."

"Who were they?"

"The old one was Vince Moretti—Boss of a gang in Chicago. The other guy was his advisor. They were there to make sure a former arrangement would still be honored with Dare as our boss. The arrangement was the only thing holding our alliance together." Her jaw trembled and she gave me a pleading look, like she was begging me to understand. "An alliance that was desperately needed. We were already at war with Holloway."

My gut twisted and chest constricted. "What was the arrangement, Libby?"

"My dad gave me to the Moretti family when I was thirteen. I had to marry Vince's grandson by my twenty-first birthday."

My mind raced in the seconds before she started talking again.

Thinking about how she'd always kept me close, but at a distance—until just recently.

Thinking of how I'd left . . . but not until after she should've gotten married.

I would've known. *She didn't want a wedding.*

"Dare found a way to take care of it," she hurried to explain. "Vince died when I was twenty, and Dare threw everything he had at the Moretti family. Weapons, information we had on other families and political parties. Anything he could get them, he gave it freely as long as they altered the arrangement."

My head shook as I tried to process what she was giving me. "But that . . . Libby, that was eleven years ago. That doesn't explain why you continued to keep us in the same place we'd always been."

"I told you, my family couldn't keep me from you, but they could keep me from being with you. You were in danger for loving me when I belonged to the Moretti family. I put you in even more by loving you, and I'm sorry for that. But by the time I found out about the arrangement, I couldn't . . . I didn't know how to live without you, even then." Her dark eyes found and searched mine. "Dare knew . . . he knew how much you meant to me. That's why he fought so hard to free me from the contract. But my mom lost it, said I was destroying an alliance. Said in their eyes, I would always belong to them. And one day they'd come to take what was theirs."

"You believed her."

"I was scared," she whispered. "I was terrified of what they'd do to you. So I didn't let myself have you. Then years continued to pass, and I started doubting they were coming." A strained laugh sounded in her throat and her wrecked eyes met mine. "By then you were living your dream, and my life would continue putting yours at risk. I knew you needed to find someone and forget about me, but I couldn't let you go. You're mine, Maxon."

My chest lurched when her voice cracked over the claim.

I wanted to grab her. I wanted to hold her. But I couldn't move as I listened.

"That was what made these months so much worse. For years, that was what I wanted for you, but agonized over. Then I finally got to a point where I stopped worrying that the Moretti family would come, and I had to accept that I might've kept you at a distance for too long. Then everything surfaced about you and Ava expecting a baby, and it just—it destroyed me. I knew I'd finally lost you and had no one else to blame but myself. Well . . ." She huffed. "I liked trying to blame you. Especially when I thought she was a groupie."

Despite the heaviness, I laughed.

Some of the tension between us eased when Libby joined in, but soon we quieted again.

The silence that surrounded us then wasn't uncomfortable like before. It was calm, the way it usually was between us.

I had a dozen questions begging to be voiced, but I knew Libby wasn't done.

When tears filled her eyes, I grabbed her hand and waited until she was ready.

"What happened between us today . . . what you thought. Maxon." Tears slipped down her cheeks when she slowly shook her head. "It kills me that you would ever think that. What makes it worse is knowing I've given you every reason to have those thoughts and doubts. But I was keeping you safe the only way I knew how. This wasn't something I could tell you before. Honestly, if you hadn't told me that you'd figured out what we were on your own, I still wouldn't be able to tell you."

"Even though it's over?"

She didn't respond and her hand tensed in mine.

"Is this why you wouldn't go to California with me?"

"No." She hesitated, then amended, "I guess it's part of it. I could've been followed there to you, but leaving was never an option. Up until a year ago, my family was in the middle of a big situation. One that involved clearing out the Holloway Estate." She shot me a wry smile. "I needed to be here to help even though Dare knew I wanted to stay out of it as much as possible. But he'd already done so much for me. And despite everything, this *is* where I want to be. And I want to be here with you . . ."

I looked at her curiously. "But . . ."

"Only if that's what you want." Before I could respond, she said, "I love you and want to marry you because you're my home. You're my calm. I would do anything to be with you—even if it meant keeping us apart."

Funny how everything had turned without me realizing.

"And you would do the same," she whispered. "You would let me go to give me freedom. You would let me go in the hopes that I would come back to you. The first thing you've ever done for yourself was leave with the guys. I can't expect or ask you to relocate—to change your life—because of me."

"I told you . . . everything I've done has been because I knew we'd be here one day. It doesn't matter where *here* is. As long as it's you and me."

"Even if it's you and me in a mob-style wedding?" she asked hopefully.

My chest heaved with the beginnings of a laugh but stopped suddenly when everything finally made sense.

Libby's insistence on the secret wedding.

Einstein's anticipation of Libby's blowup over the idea of a real wedding.

Einstein knowing something I didn't . . .

"You're still afraid. That's why you don't want a wedding."

"No." Even though she answered immediately, her voice was unsure and her stare seemed far away.

"Libby, you're allowed to be afraid. Especially if it's of fucking mobsters."

The corners of her mouth twitched up into a brief, pained smile. "Who knew I could be afraid of so much, huh? But that's not, uh, that's not why I don't want the wedding." She tried to speak before finally exhaling roughly. "I want that—I do. But whenever I think of a wedding, I get lightheaded and nauseous. I was supposed to have an extravagant wedding, and I had no control over the outcome. Moretti sent someone to the house to size me for a custom dress. And then they sent me these dresses—these gorgeous dresses—and told me to choose. Then bouquets of flowers showed up one day, and they told me to choose."

"Did you?"

Her head shook subtly. "I couldn't. That wedding meant losing you, and every reminder and every year that brought me closer to it ruined something inside me. After spending five years getting physically sick and devastated every time I thought of a wedding . . . it's hard to change that reaction. Even if the person I'm marrying is you."

I nodded and tried to relax my hands.

But I'd never once known Libby was going through this. For *five* years she thought she was going to be forced to marry someone else, and I hadn't had a damn clue.

"Did you ever meet him? The guy you were supposed to marry?"

"No, I don't even know his name." When my brows pulled tight, she said, "Really. Don't you think he would've disappeared if we *had* known his name?"

I would've laughed. Except I knew she was serious.

"Vince ran his family . . . different than other families. His wife was kept secret, and no one knew her name. No one even knew they had children until he and my dad made this arrangement. Even then, he only told Dare it was his oldest child's son I would marry. No one knew names until one of them became their new boss. We still don't know how many there are or the rest of their names. But secret family or not, everyone knows the Moretti family owns Chicago. They're merciless. And they aren't someone you want as an enemy."

"And your mom thinks by not going through with the wedding . . . you are," I assumed.

"More or less. She's still terrified. We fight over it—over you—nearly every time we see each other. She thinks I should go to Chicago and offer myself to them to prevent whatever fallout she's sure is coming."

"Yeah, that's not gonna happen." I blew out a heavy breath and reached for her left hand, running my thumb over the ring a few times before looking at her. "Okay, Rebel. No big wedding."

The corners of her mouth twitched into a sad smile. "I'm sorry."

"All I want is you." I forced out a laugh. "I wanted to hold off for at least a week so I could get some things together and surprise you—cake, flowers, a dress . . ." A fuller laugh left me when she made a face. "Now that I won't be doing that, just tell me when and where so I can mob-marry you."

"Even if it's tonight?"

"Even if it's right now." I gripped her chin in my fingers and dipped my head toward hers, but stopped just before our lips met. "Promise me one thing first."

"Anything," she whispered, her breath washing over me.

"No more secrets between us. No more hiding anything."

Her eyes flashed with something dark as they searched mine. "What if it keeps you safe?"

"Keeping me safe kept us apart for too long. No more." I pressed my mouth firmly to hers when she echoed my last words.

"I hate champagne and white cakes," she said against my lips. "And getting flowers."

I smiled and kissed her harder. "Noted."

"And dresses. I hate them all, but especially if they're white."

I pulled back to study her flushed face. "Tell me everything Moretti sent you so I can know what not to give you."

"That was it. I threw it all away as it came." Her lips twitched into a coy smile. "Einstein and I burned the dresses when Dare worked out the new deal with them."

"Jesus," I said on a laugh and leaned in to kiss her again, but paused. "Did they send you rings?"

Her smile grew. "Nope."

"Thank God." My lips had just brushed hers when I stopped again. "When you say *disappeared* . . ."

She let her head fall back, her smile wide and not matching the groan sliding up her throat. "He would've found himself not . . . around . . . anymore. In Chicago. Or the United States. Possibly the world."

Again, I wanted to laugh because her tone was so carefree. But I knew she was serious.

"I feel like I should actually be afraid of you and your family."

Instead of laughing or brushing off my comment, she wrapped her arms loosely around my neck and pulled me close. "You haven't seen or heard anything yet."

Twenty-Six

Libby

"I'M HUNGRY," EINSTEIN SAID FROM where she stood beside me, tapping rapidly on her phone. "If I ate all the pastries in that case, how much weight would I gain? Don't answer that, I already know."

I rolled my eyes. "I think you've been hanging out with Maverick and Diggs too much. You've been whining about food since you finished breakfast."

Hence the reason for the coffee and food run.

Her thumbs stilled over the screen for a few seconds before slowly resuming whatever she'd been doing. By the time she spoke, they were flying at full speed again. "Haven't really seen either of them."

I made a sound of indifference in my throat. "Not even Maverick?"

"Your hearing is perfect. I don't need to repeat myself."

We moved forward a spot in line at our favorite coffee house before I said, "You've been gone a lot, just figured you would've been with him."

"And I figured you'd have better things to do—like Maxon—than to care about whether or not I've been hanging out with Maverick."

"Well, that's rude."

"Someone's nosey," she mocked in the same tone.

"What are you, twelve?"

"Actually, yes. How'd you know?"

I gritted my teeth to keep from saying something I'd regret—like Dare had a point in saying she'd turned into a different person in the year and a half since Johnny died.

"Just be careful," I whispered instead.

"I'm safer when I'm not in the apartment."

I cut her a look and opened my mouth to ask what that meant, when my phone rang.

I tensed when Conor's name lit up my screen, and only took a second to think about what to do. Not answering would be too suspicious for Einstein to let go. Not something I could afford right now.

"Hey, we're still getting coffee."

There was a pause before Conor spoke, his voice low when he said, "You can't talk."

"Right."

"Okay, there's nothing," he said quickly and quietly. "Literally nothing other than your prints."

I wanted to beg him to tell me he was joking. I wanted to ask him to repeat himself just in case I'd heard him wrong. But Einstein was standing right next to me, listening to every word.

So I feigned indifference and said, "Okay. Be back soon."

As soon as I hung up, Einstein mumbled, "See, I'm not the only one who's hungry."

Conor's disheartening news, Einstein's digs at our life, and the loud music in the shop were suddenly too much.

I turned on her and snapped, "If you're that damn hungry, go to Brooks Street and pick up the order so we can be done that much faster."

Einstein's eyes widened and shifted to me.

"Jesus, I'm sorry. I just—*shit*." I groaned and dropped my head into my hands when she turned and walked out of the coffee shop.

Part of me wanted to follow her and apologize, but I needed a second to breathe. I needed to come to terms with the fact that whoever was taking the pictures and leaving them for me was doing it without a trace.

I needed to wrap my head around the fact that Einstein was staying with someone—somewhere—and not telling me. Not only that, she was throwing it in my face that it was safer there than our apartment.

What the hell did that even mean?

I still needed to get coffee for everyone, and Einstein and I drove together. There wasn't a point in getting out of the line when we'd have time to talk after I calmed down.

I called Conor after I ordered and was thankful he answered right away. "There's really nothing?"

"Not a thing. No partials, no nothing. Only your prints." He sighed heavily. "Does this mean it's whoever your mom was worried about?"

"I have no idea," I answered honestly. "I was hoping for proof of someone. This just makes it more disturbing."

Terrifying. It made it *terrifying*.

People pulling pranks rarely covered their tracks.

"Yeah. Have there been any more?"

"No, I would've told you." I turned at the sound of the barista calling my name and walked over to where there were two trays of drinks waiting. "Hey, Conor, I have to . . . oh God. No, no, no."

The coffee shop. The barista talking to me. Conor.

Everything disappeared.

I wasn't sure if I was breathing or how much time passed.

There, peeking out from beneath one of the trays, on the corner of an envelope, printed neatly, was my name.

I nearly dropped the phone.

"*Libby*," Conor shouted.

"There's one here," I whispered, my voice wavering. "It's right in front of me. It's right—"

"Where are you?"

I turned to look at the people in the shop with me. I searched their faces and hoped someone would be watching me to give themselves away, while also praying no one would be.

"I'm getting coffee."

"Don't open it," he yelled. "Take it and put it somewhere. You have your bag?"

"Yes."

"Put it in there. Just pick it up and put it in there like it's nothing, Libby. Otherwise they're going to know they're scaring you. Can you bring it to me?"

I hated that I was shaking. I hated that I wanted to face the people in the coffee house and scream, "*What do you want?*"

"No," I whispered. "Einstein was next to me when you called earlier. She's my ride back to the apartment."

"Okay," he said, his voice calmer now. "Probably wouldn't make a difference. If there was nothing on the first two, I doubt there'll be anything on that one."

"I have to hang up to carry the coffee. I'll open it when I can and send you a picture."

"Okay. If you can, try to see if there's anyone in there watching you."

"Of course." I left out that I already had.

I left out that I wanted this to be over.

I left out that I was scared.

After we hung up, I texted Einstein that I was done and dropped my phone in my bag next to the offending envelope, then grabbed the drink trays.

I made myself look straight ahead. Only allowing my gaze to touch the people in my natural line of sight when all I wanted was to look wildly around the entire shop.

When I got to the door, I turned to open it with my back, allowing myself a quick sweep of everyone inside.

No one was looking at me.

I knew every single one of them.

And not one of them seemed like someone who would break into my apartment and take a picture of Maxon and me while we were sleeping.

Well, there were some girls who might go a little crazy if they knew the Henley boys were sleeping in my apartment while waiting to close on the Holloway mansion. But not crazy of this magnitude. And not directed at me.

Einstein and I didn't talk the entire way to the apartment.

I didn't realize it until we were walking to our door. I'd meant to spend the time apologizing to her, but I was too distracted.

It was eating me alive knowing I had a new envelope on me but not knowing what it contained.

As soon as we were in the apartment, I pushed the drink trays into Maxon's hands and pressed a hurried kiss to his lips, praying that would keep him from worrying about any wild expression that might be on my face.

"I'll be right back."

I rushed into my room and then into my bathroom—just in case anyone followed me—then dug into my purse for the envelope.

The second it was in my hands, everything came rushing back again.

The deafening silence.

The shards of ice pushing through my veins.

The unsteady legs and uneasy stomach.

I made myself take a few breaths before flipping it over to open it. The room still spun when I saw the printed name on the bottom corner.

I had the flap open and the Polaroid out in no time.

Too fast.

I needed more time to prepare.

But unlike the last two times, I knew exactly what I was seeing.

Maybe because I'd already suspected and had been hoping I was wrong.

It was of me, standing in line at the coffee house, with my head in my hands.

Right after Einstein had walked out.

At the bottom of the picture, in Sharpie, were the words:

I own you.

I stumbled back against the wall just before my legs gave out beneath me.

I pressed my hand to my mouth to mute the cry that wrenched from deep within me and struggled to drag in air.

I couldn't break now. I needed to pull myself together. I needed to be strong. I needed to send this to Conor.

I needed to calm down.

But this person had been so close to me.

I leaned forward and snatched my purse off the counter and quickly searched through it until I found my phone. My movements were shaky as I dropped the picture on the ground and took a picture of it to send to Conor.

ME: *This was taken right after you called today.*

Less than a minute later, he responded.

CONOR: *Shit.*

CONOR: *People at the shop?*

ME: *I knew everyone. No one was watching me.*

CONOR: *Well. What do you think . . . mom's fear or Maxon fan trying to scare you?*

I glanced at the Polaroid, at the written words, and recalled the people in the coffee shop in my head again.

I own you.

ME: *I'm afraid it's the first. Still praying it's the second.*

Twenty-Seven

Maxon

SET MY SHOT GLASS on the kitchen island and welcomed the burn sliding down my throat and into my chest.

Ledger let out a roar and spread his arms wide.

The girls standing on the opposite side of the bar cheered in response—fuck if I knew why.

I dropped my head to hide the involuntary eye-roll when their cheers faded into high-pitched giggles.

"What did I say?" Ledger yelled, his glassy eyes straining to focus on us. "No better way to say *welcome home.*"

The girls cheered again.

Jared booed.

Jesus.

I poured another shot and slammed it back, then clapped Jared's shoulder. When he looked at me, I held up two fingers and mouthed that I was done.

As soon as he nodded, I turned and forced my way through the tightly-packed kitchen, in search of the only person that mattered.

When I finally found her, I would've laughed if it weren't for her expression.

Dare had been so sure my lifestyle would be bad for her. He'd been positive I wouldn't be able to keep her from this.

Partying wasn't my scene, but tonight was an exception and I wanted Libby with me. It was Henley's Welcome Home Party in none other than the guys' new home—the Holloway Estate.

Well, they wanted to change it to the Henley Estate. I didn't think they'd be able to pull it off.

The only time I planned to take her to a party, and she was leaning against a wall with a dazed look like she didn't even know there were other people around her.

I ducked in beside her and pressed a kiss to her neck. "You gonna be all right?"

Her neck vibrated with a moan, but it was delayed. So were the rest of her reactions and movements.

She'd been that way ever since she and Einstein returned from getting lunch that afternoon.

She lifted her eyebrows and forced a smile. "Hmm?"

"With being in this place." I let my gaze dart across the massive open front room.

"Oh." Her face pinched as she took in the surroundings, like she just realized where we were.

As though we hadn't been there for over an hour.

"I don't know. It's weird. I got chills as soon as we walked in. Like even the walls knew a Borello had set foot inside and were angry." A whisper of a laugh left her. "My dad has to be rolling in his grave."

I cleared my throat and looked at the wall I'd just leaned against. "Right. Well, let's move from the walls before they start talking."

My mouth twitched into a smile when she dropped her head back and laughed.

Wild. Free. Fucking beautiful.

That was my Libby.

My Rebel.

"Did you have your two obligatory shots?" she asked as she slipped her hand into mine.

I huffed and glanced over my shoulder to where Ledger and Jared were still entertaining the crowd of women. "Be glad you missed it."

She shot me an amused look and pressed closer to my side. "Does that mean we can leave?"

I blew out a slow breath and pulled my phone from my pocket. "Little over fifteen minutes."

"Fifteen minutes of girls trying to crawl all over you and asking you to put a baby in them? Yes, please."

I choked on a laugh. "That hasn't happened."

"Oh, it hasn't?" She drove her hands into her long, dark hair and her expression turned frenzied—a look I'd come to know too well over the years. "Oh God. Maxon James, put a baby in me," she pretended to scream. She gave me a dull look and nodded toward the front door. "Two girls when we were trying to get in the door tonight."

"That's disturbing."

Her brows lifted in agreement.

"The only woman who will ever carry my child is you, and for the love of God, don't ever ask me to put a baby in you."

Her head fell back for another full laugh, and I stood there, absorbing my favorite part of the woman I loved.

As the laugh ended, I bent down and drove my shoulder into her stomach, lifting as I went.

"*Maxon.*"

I didn't respond, and I didn't return any of the looks from the other people at the party.

"Maxon, what the hell are you doing?" Libby yelled when I finally made it to one of the halls leading to the bedrooms.

"I'm gonna put a baby in you."

She made a choking sound. "No. No, that's even more disturbing."

My laugh was loud and unrestrained.

I quickly backed out of the first two rooms I came across when I realized they weren't empty, then went into the third and kicked the door shut behind us.

"Caveman."

"Something like that." I smirked and twisted the lock, then slid her down my body and pressed her against the adjoining wall.

Her face was flushed and her eyes were bright with excitement, offsetting her next words. "You can't honestly think I'm turned on now."

I shrugged and curled my hand against her cheek. "Doesn't matter. Fifteen minutes before we can leave, and I got us away from the party."

She relaxed against the wall and my hand, her lips curling into a soft smile. "Thank you."

"Anything for you."

"So, fifteen minutes . . ." Her dark eyes flashed to mine, hidden under her thick lashes. The look all seduction and need.

I fought a smile and dipped my head to press my mouth just under her ear. "Not turned on though, right?" I asked in a low tone.

"I lied."

I raked my teeth across her skin and groaned when she trembled. "You want to make these walls angry, Rebel?"

She sucked in a sharp breath and tightened her hands around my forearms, the sound going straight to my hardening cock. "Yes."

I trailed the tips of my fingers down her curves until I hit the top of her shorts. Slowly curling my fingers inside the band, I eased my fingers in deeper while working the button and zipper until her breaths were rough and uneven in my ear. Until she was arching off the wall and breathing hushed pleas, as I pushed her clothing to the floor and spread her legs.

Her hands were on my stomach, slipping under my shirt and clawing at my stomach when I slid my hand between her thighs and teased where she was already wet.

"Maxon." A whimper caught in her throat when I pressed a finger deep inside. "God, yes."

I hooked another finger inside her and teased the seam of her lips with my tongue, swallowing her moans and pushing harder and deeper until she was trembling. I angled her head back farther, demanding more of the kiss and more of her as I slowly removed my fingers.

My chest expanded with pride when a stuttered cry tore through her.

I knew that cry. I owned that cry.

I'd known its beginning, and I would know its end.

It didn't matter what had happened in between.

Her rebel heart had always belonged to me.

I stepped away and reached for my clothes, watching as her eyes devoured every movement I made while I undressed.

After so long together, her expressions still mesmerized me.

Dazed and adorable when she woke.

Possessive and entranced when I bared myself to her. Like it was the first time she was seeing me.

Erotic and calm when she came.

I wanted to be mesmerized by her forever.

I closed the distance between us again and curled my hand around her neck, my thumb tracing faint patterns until her head tilted back and she hummed contentedly.

I dipped my head and pressed a soft kiss on her jaw. "Turn around. Hands on the wall."

Her stare flashed to mine and her teeth sank into her bottom lip, but she turned without a word. With one last glance over her shoulder at me, she shifted her legs farther apart and slid her hands down the wall until her ass was pressed against me.

I gripped her hips in my hands and bent to place kisses along her spine and over the rounded cheeks of her ass as I knelt behind her, spreading her legs wider and baring her to me. I ran my thumbs through her sex, spreading her and teasing her before leaning forward to taste her.

Her body shook and legs nearly buckled before she caught herself.

"Oh God," she whispered when I teased her again and again. Her next plea got lost in her moan when I flattened my tongue and devoured her in a way I knew drove her crazy.

There wasn't a thing about this girl I didn't know.

I knew when she'd push against me in a silent plea for more.

Knew the exact pitch of her whimper when tremors started rolling through her body.

Knew she shied away just before she came because she didn't like the free fall—the feeling of losing control just before waves of pleasure surged through her body.

I knew her like the back of my hand . . . and yet, I never wanted to stop *knowing* her.

Never wanted to stop making her cry my name.

Never wanted to stop being the cause of her ecstasy.

I sucked her clit and rolled it between my teeth when she pressed closer to the wall, that slight, instinctive withdrawal, and continued through her orgasm when she cried out and pushed back against me.

When she struggled to stand and catch her breath, I placed a slow kiss to her sex and smirked when she trembled in response.

I took my time standing, kissing and leaving teasing bites over her ass and up her back until I was gripping her hip and pressing my length against her.

I fisted myself in my hand and pumped slowly, sliding against her sex and groaning when I teased her entrance.

"Maxon," she whimpered and flattened her hands on the wall, using them to arch against me. "Oh God, please."

She sucked in a stuttered breath, and her head dropped between her shoulders when I pushed in inch by inch until I was fully seated.

Home.

Everything about the wild girl in my hands screamed home.

"How I ever lived without this . . ." My words were nothing more than a rumble in my chest and sent goosebumps across her skin.

Never again.

I dug my fingers against her hips and finally moved.

Slow and controlled.

Then faster and unyielding.

Each roll of my hips more powerful than the last until she was pressing against me and clawing at the wall, my name mixed with her breathless pleas and moans.

I grabbed her hair, making her arch back as I pushed into her harder. Rougher.

A whimper and full-body tremor.

Her name built like a growl in my chest.

A faint twist and hesitant retreat.

Her name ripped from my throat when she shattered, forcing me into my own release.

I pumped into her slowly as my release pulsed from me, relishing in the hushed whimpers and moans with each slow movement.

When I was spent, I wrapped my arm around her stomach and curled over her shuddering body, intertwining my hand with hers where they clutched the wall.

Dropping my forehead to her back, I gently passed my mouth across her skin. "If these walls were mad before . . ."

Her body shook with a laugh, and she slowly rolled her hips against me. "Wonder what else we can make mad in here."

A breath of a laugh left me. "Rebel . . ."

She eased to standing. "Well, if you're not up for it."

She was on her back and I was sliding into her again in seconds, her wild, beautiful laughter still ringing through the room.

I TRAILED MY hand up to rest between her breasts some time later. When I felt the familiar *thrum thrum thrum*, I took a deep breath and let my eyes slide shut.

"Your heartbeat will always be my favorite song," I murmured and smiled when I felt her pace go wild.

"I love you." She wove her fingers through my hair and pulled me close to kiss me.

I nipped at her lips teasingly. "I love you. Let me take you home where there isn't a chance of an audience."

Her face pinched uneasily. "Einstein."

I dropped my head to her stomach.

"We need our own place."

My chest moved with a silent laugh. "As soon as you mean that, we will."

I felt her tense. "What—what do you mean?"

I swallowed thickly and shifted to rest my chin on her so I could watch her reaction. "The second you say you want a place of our own and it isn't a lie, I'll make it happen. But you don't want to leave that apartment."

She opened her mouth to respond—to deny it, from the look in her eyes—but the words never came.

"The last thing I want is to push you, Libby. I know this has been a lifetime coming, but I also know you need your freedom. You need things to go at your pace."

"That's not . . ." She let out a groan and covered her face with her hands. After nearly a minute, she let them fall to the bed and studied my face. "It has nothing to do with my freedom or pacing. Maxon, I want to be with you. I want *our* freedom. But I'll take you however I can get you—even if that's in an apartment filled with the band and Einstein." She wove her fingers through my hair when my laugh danced across her skin. "Hear me when I say I *do* want a place of our own."

My amusement faded, because it was there, lingering unspoken at the end of her sentence. "But . . . ?"

"But I think a part of me feels like I'd be abandoning Einstein when she needs me most, and that's the hesitation you hear." Her dark eyes searched mine. "She's set on pushing the good out of her life to protect it, and it's destroying them. It's destroying *her* and turning her into this unpredictable, unreliable person none of us recognize."

"Sounds familiar."

She started to cut me a dry look, but her expression suddenly turned reflective. "Yeah, well. It might just come from being in this life and knowing the costs."

"There are always costs, Rebel."

"Not like this."

"What, crazy mobsters? Maybe not. But I have fans who think they're in relationships with me because of the way I smiled in a picture." I lifted a brow when she dropped her head back and laughed.

"Oh God, how could I forget?"

"Two of them somehow found Ava's address when the pregnancy thing blew up. One showed up at Ava's house and screamed that she was a home-wrecking whore until the cops came. The other had sent half a dozen crazed letters by the time we made the statement the next day that it wasn't my baby." Libby's face sobered instantly. "You would've known that if you'd answered your phone."

"Maxon . . ." She shook her head. "What happened?"

"Not enough. They aren't allowed to contact her or me in any way or go near us, but they'd stopped caring about Ava by then because the statement had already gone out." I dipped my head and pressed my mouth to her stomach. "But what if they stalk you when our relationship goes public? They're not in mobs, but some of them are literally psychotic. That makes them dangerous too."

Libby's eyes had gotten a faraway look while I spoke. Just before I said her name to get her attention, she cleared her throat and looked away. "I would take care of it."

"Hey—"

"But Einstein," she said quickly, pulling the conversation back. "She was all over the place when Johnny died, but she was still *Einstein*. She still clung to us. She and Maverick were still . . ." She shrugged faintly. "Then one day, something happened and she flipped. She never told me. Or if she tried, I wasn't there for her because I saw the announcement about your 'fatherhood' a couple days later."

Einstein and Maverick . . .

My mind raced after Libby paired them together, thinking back to all the times I'd seen them around each other. It made sense, but I'd never caught on to them before.

Then again, I doubted anyone was supposed to.

If Johnny would've noticed, Maverick would be six feet under with him.

"Some days she's normal—well, as normal as she ever gets. Others, every word and reaction is unlike anything I've ever seen from her. And the way she's been disappearing lately . . . she's never done that." Her eyes brimmed with tears and she gave me a pleading glance. "I know you and I need our own life. Einstein needs her own life. But she's been there for me through everything, same as you. And I wasn't there for her the only time she needed me."

I nodded, then pushed up on my hands and left a line of kisses up her chest to her mouth.

Guilt radiated through me for ever thinking that she'd used me to get back at her family.

I knew Libby . . . I knew her personality. But I'd been wrong about her.

So damn wrong.

When she'd pushed me away all those years, I'd been sure my

wild girl had needed her freedom and time to move at her pace. And she'd been protecting me. Protecting *us*.

And moving out of the apartment? Again, it was more about Einstein than us.

Selfless. Libby was so damn selfless for every move she'd made.

"When you're ready, say the word," I mumbled against her lips before pressing one last kiss there.

I pulled her up with me and off the bed, then helped her find her clothes before grabbing my own.

"Hey," she said hesitantly when we finished dressing. "Are you planning to do what the guys did for this house?" She let her eyes drift to the bed we'd just left. "Buying all new things so you can keep your other stuff in the LA house and go back and forth between them?"

A hint of a laugh left me.

"What?"

"Forever." When she looked like she was waiting for me to continue, I said, "I've been waiting forever for this. For us. You think I'm gonna live half my life across the country without you?"

Her brows pinched in confusion but her mouth was pulling into a cautious smile. She looked fucking adorable. "I didn't think we had a choice."

"I'm just waiting for my car to get here in a couple days. Everything else is already at the house."

Her eyebrows pulled tighter. "This house?" When I shook my head, her entire body seemed to go slack. "You actually bought a house? You have a house?"

"*We* have a house." I barked out a laugh when she looked at me like I'd kept something huge from her—you know, like being in the mafia. "I told you at Brooks Street. Two stories, four bedrooms, three baths. Big trees and a backyard, wraparound porch, and—"

"Shutters on the windows," she murmured. "You were serious? That's ours?"

"Rebel . . . yeah."

I barely had time to react and catch her when she launched herself at me. She pressed her mouth to mine for a quick, heated kiss. When she pulled away, her eyes were bright with excitement. "Can we go see it?"

"No."

Her excitement faded immediately.

I let her slide to the floor and curled my hands around her cheeks, forcing her to look at me. "You just told me why you're not ready to leave your apartment. I don't want a house to change your mind."

"Einstein can figure out her life by herself, I'm sure."

My mouth twitched into a smile and I pressed a faint kiss to her lips. "The second you're ready."

"Don't be reasonable right now. Pretend I never said anything."

I gave her a mischievous grin and pulled her to the door. "Like Einstein and Maverick?"

"What—no, that's not—" Libby looked at me like I'd lost my mind. "Wait, did you not know?" When I only continued walking, she asked, "How? How did *no one* know? It was the most obvious and devastating love story of the decade. Besides ours."

"A certain rebel kept me distracted whenever I came home." I shot her a wink when she flushed red and opened the door for us. "Speaking of distractions, safe to say it's been fifteen minutes."

"And it was such a good distraction, Mr. James. Feel free to do it—" She swore when she tripped over something, taking me with her.

"The fuck is that?" I said under my breath and bent to pick up the dark object that had been outside the door. "What is this?"

I turned it over in my hands and pushed one of the buttons, blinking rapidly when a flash went off in the dimly lit hallway. I held it out when it started making an odd noise and laughed when I noticed what was coming out of it.

"Holy shit, weren't you asking about these?" I pulled the picture out of the camera and murmured, "I don't remember them looking like this."

When there wasn't a response, I looked to my side, then behind me. Libby was staring in horror at the camera in my hands.

"Libby?" I grabbed her shoulder and shook her when she didn't respond. *"Libby."*

"Why was that there?" she asked, her tone dead and eyes not leaving my hands.

"I don't . . ." My chest pitched with a bemused huff. "I don't know. Didn't you just ask me about—"

"We need to go."

"What?"

Her eyes were wild when she focused on me. "We need to leave. Now."

"Libby, what's—what the fuck?" I snapped when she smacked the camera out of my hand, then turned and stormed off.

She didn't try to explain. She didn't say anything at all.

No matter how much I begged for her to say something when I caught up to her. No matter how much I yelled for her to have some kind of reaction on the drive home.

As soon as we set foot in the apartment, she turned to go to Einstein's room without a backward glance.

"Libby, fucking talk to me," I yelled, and growled in frustration when she walked through the apartment, headed to our room.

Eyes straight ahead.

I reached for her and stared at her in shock when she yanked her arm from my grasp.

"What the hell, Libby? We were fine—better than fine. We were great. And then, Jesus, I don't know. You freaked out over a damn camera."

"We needed to leave," she said simply.

"We needed to leave," I said dully. "That's it? That's all you're going to say after I've been begging you to explain what happened?"

I spread my arms wide, my voice raising and echoing in the apartment. "Everything that's happened since we left that room has been because of something other than us needing to leave. Tell me what I'm missing."

She turned without a word.

"Libby—"

She whirled on me. "Maxon, *stop*."

I searched her face for a few moments. "Tell me what's going on."

"What's going on is I wanted to leave and you had a problem with that."

"A problem?" I laughed harshly. "There was no problem. But you can't expect me not to ask questions when you want me to leave somewhere the way we just did."

"We left, Maxon. There's no reason behind it. No matter how many times you ask, my answer won't change." Her stare fell to the floor. For the first time since we'd left the bedroom in Holloway, there was something other than horror or frustration lingering there. "I'm going to bed."

"No more secrets. No more hiding anything," I reminded her. "Even if you think you're protecting me. You promised me that."

Emotion swirled in her eyes when they met mine. "I know I did."

Before I could beg her to give me something—*anything*—she went to our room.

Leaving me confused.

Drained.

Feeling like the high I'd just been riding from our time together had been ripped away.

Over a fucking camera.

What the hell is going on?

Potential Polaroid Assholes

~~Literally anyone. Ugh. Has access to apartment.~~

Jared

Mom

Moretti

Psycho fan

Literally fucking anyone

Twenty-Eight

Libby

'D NEVER REALIZED HOW UTTERLY lonely being alone was until the last two days.

Sounds self-explanatory.

It really wasn't, not in my life anyway.

I grew up surrounded by others. Always.

My family. Extended family. Extended family we weren't actually related to and I wanted nothing to do with. The older generation of Borello members . . . and the younger—mine.

Our house constantly swarmed with activity that was impossible to get away from. In part, it was normal because it was what I'd grown up with. It was also something I wanted to get away from.

I thrived off chaos. But I needed calm.

The rare moments when no one was around were dominated by fear. Because there was only one logical reason for everyone else to be gone. They were all dead.

Maxon provided the calm I always craved but could never

achieve, and it was always when he was right beside me.

Now he was out of state working.

Einstein was MIA.

I was truly alone—simply alone. And I hated it.

I reached for my phone when it chimed and felt my disappointment like a living thing when I saw Conor's name instead of Maxon's.

Not that I could've allowed myself to respond to Maxon.

Not that I could tell him I hated myself for what I was doing to him. To us.

Because I would do it all again if it kept him safe.

CONOR: *You busy?*

I sighed and looked around the stupid, empty apartment as I sank deeper into the couch cushions.

ME: *No.*

CONOR: *Gotta get to the bottom of these pics.*

CONOR: *Just got to your mom's. Meet me there.*

I lurched forward and shouted, "No."

I hurried to respond, praying he was joking.

But my fingers were moving so fast and I was shaking at the mere thought of my mom knowing about the pictures—of anyone else knowing about the Moretti family—that none of the words came out correctly.

ME: *Wht?! Whu?! Ni!*

ME: *Ni . . . wht.*

ME: *Duck it.*

ME: *Duck mu life!*

I nearly threw my phone across the room but called him instead as I ran to my bedroom to put on a clean shirt and to grab my bag and shoes.

Even if this was a prank, I was leaving the apartment to kill Conor for nearly giving me a heart attack.

When he answered, all that came through the phone was his laughter.

"Please tell me you are joking," I yelled. *"Conor."*

"What?" he asked, his voice light.

I stood at my door, my hand on the knob and eyes shut tight. "Where are you?"

"I told you."

I hissed a curse and ran out the door. "Why . . . *why* are you doing this to me?"

"We need to know what's happening, Libby."

"That doesn't mean involving my mom."

"She's the only one who might know who it is."

I tore out of the parking lot, screaming into my phone the whole way. "I have a list of people it might be. That's a hell of a lot more than she has."

"Who?" he demanded, his words now dripping with wrath.

I hesitated. "Well, I have to keep crossing names off . . . so, let's hold off on the list. But it could be someone I don't know at all. It could still be one of Maxon's fans."

There was a pause before he spoke. When he did, his tone was skeptical. "Do you think it is?"

"It would make it easier."

"No," he said, answering his own question.

"No," I agreed.

"I don't like how closely they're watching you," he said after nearly a minute of silence. "I took another look at the pictures after you told me about the camera at the party. There's nothing. Whoever's doing this knows what they're doing."

"I know." The words were a whisper, but they hung in the air like the aftermath of a bomb. "I'm a couple streets away. I'll see you soon. Do not go into that house without me."

"Yep."

Conor was waiting outside his truck when I pulled up, arms

folded over his massive chest and expression set in stone.

And then he smiled.

All boyish dimples and ready to sweep any girl off her feet.

I was so adopting him into the family.

Speaking of . . .

"This is a waste of time. Trust me. My mom won't be helpful at all."

"You said it was *her* fear, so she'll know it better than anyone." His blue eyes darted to my car then rested on me. "Where's the boyfriend?"

"Fiancé." I showed him my hand for a second before mirroring his stance and folding my arms across my chest. "Henley's in California for a few days. Radio interviews."

Conor searched my face. "You know, I don't know much about this shit, but Jessica practically tackled me in excitement when she and Kieran got engaged. You look—"

"I've received a third picture and camera since then. It's been rough."

Understatement.

"Uh-huh."

I didn't need this. I didn't want this.

"I'm clearly still in my pajamas. I don't have makeup on, and my hair is a wreck. I don't need you talking about how I look."

He rubbed at the back of his neck. "Not what I meant."

I rolled my eyes and started for the house, but Conor caught my arm and turned me toward him.

"Really, Libby. Not what I meant." He looked around, like he was struggling to find the words, then shrugged helplessly. "Just figured you'd be more excited."

My shoulders sagged. "I am," I whispered, praying he couldn't hear the waver in my voice. "But if there's one thing I know about these pictures, the person behind them doesn't want Maxon and me together. And in trying to keep him a safe distance away from all this bullshit, it's putting a strain on us."

I waited for it.

For him to tell me what I was doing was wrong—that I should tell Maxon.

But he gave me a sad smile and slanted his head in the faintest of nods, like he understood.

He pressed something against my arm when we were almost to the door. "Here. I've done all I can."

I knew what was in the small manila envelope without having to ask. I took it from him slowly, my movements shaky. "Is it weird I'm glad to have those back . . . and also never want to see them again?"

Conor gave me a curious look.

"If I have them, I know I'm not crazy." I swallowed thickly and pushed the envelope into Conor's hand. "Keep these."

"I can't do anything with them. I've tried."

"I know. But like you said, they know what they're doing. They've been in my bedroom, Conor. If they decide to suddenly take the pictures back, I'll have nothing to show for what's happening. So keep those. The third picture is in my car. I'll give it to you before we leave." I stared straight ahead and reached for the door. "Waste of time," I whispered.

I had the door open and was about to call out for my mom when it felt like the air was knocked from me.

Einstein was sitting in the living room, laptop open, and tablet in hand.

"What the hell are you doing?"

"Working," she responded in a dull tone. "I've been known to do it."

I dragged my eyes from her for a second to look at Conor. "Did you know she was here?"

"She barely comes in lately."

"Einstein, why are you *here*?" I asked when I rounded one of the chairs to stand in front of her. "Why aren't you at our place?

Or ARCK?"

"Einstein's allowed here whenever she wants, as long as she wants," my mom said gently as she entered the room. "All of you are."

I whirled on Einstein. *"This* is where you've been hiding? This is your safe place?"

Einstein stopped tapping on her tablet long enough to give me a dry look. "Someone's running a little slow lately. Wonder why?" She glanced back down, fingers flying over the screen. "If you'd taken more than a second to think about what I was saying, you would've known where I was."

I started to ask *how* but stopped.

This wasn't just my childhood home; it was the Borello gang house. It was where meetings had been held and decisions had been made.

It was also where we all gathered to wait out enemies—like the Holloways. That way when they found us, we wouldn't be easy to pick off.

The location might be known to enemies, but it was still our safe house.

This house was exactly why I hadn't told Dare about the pictures . . . because I was afraid he'd make us all come here and wait out whoever was behind the Polaroids.

Einstein was right. I should've known.

I sat next to her on the couch. "Why do you need a safe place, Einstein? Just talk to me, I know you're having a rough time, but I'll help you through it."

"That would be your answer."

"What is my answer?"

"I don't want your help. I don't want anyone's help." Her fingers paused over the screen and her eyes drifted toward me. "I can't let what happened before happen again. I need a safe place from me."

I was so at a loss that I sat there for a minute staring at her.

This went far beyond what I'd already known was happening . . . and I didn't know how to help her.

I looked to Conor, but he seemed just as lost as I was.

When I turned to Einstein again, she was completely absorbed in her work.

I hated how she could switch off all emotions so instantly.

During those painful months when I thought I'd lost Maxon, I'd envied her.

I slowly stood from the couch and stepped away, leaning toward Conor to ask what we should do when I saw it.

Across the room, near the back doors, was a black Polaroid camera.

Exactly like the first one.

"Conor." His name was only a breath leaving my lips, but he must've heard and followed my line of sight, because he was at the camera before I even moved.

"Einstein, is this yours?" he asked, his tone holding no room for discussion.

I looked back in time to see Einstein peer at Conor for a few seconds, her brow furrowing. "Yes. Because you've seen me with a camera so many times before."

Conor's expression morphed into frustration, and I jumped when my mom slipped silently beside me.

"Is this yours?" The question came out harsher than I meant it to, but then again, I rarely spoke to her calmly.

She eyed it with disdain. "I've never seen it. Maybe Lily left it here." She moved closer and lowered her voice. "First you turn your back on an alliance and the family who will be our ruin, and then you do it with a Holloway. What are you doing to our family?"

Conor looked up, his eyes round with surprise.

"Clearly sabotaging it, like you've always said, Mom. And I'm not with Conor, Jesus. Maxon and I are engaged, by the way. I'm sure you wanted to know."

She looked at me with all the disappointment a mother could possess. "What will it take for you to see the threat that's right in front of you? Everyone you love in the ground?"

I rolled my eyes and nodded toward the camera in Conor's hands. "I told you this was a waste of time. Bring that with you."

Thankfully he came with me without objecting.

"You're rushing into a marriage with that James boy to keep him from leaving you again," my mom said when we were almost to the door. "For everyone's safety, you should let him go."

Conor hesitated and looked back at her for a few seconds, then said to me, "I need to know who she's talking about. Who you could be up against."

"It's been talked about enough in my life that I know most, if not everything, she does. If it's that important, I'll tell you."

He held up the camera. "Libby . . . it's starting to look pretty damn important."

I sucked in a shaky breath and nodded, then leaned close. "But what I tell you doesn't leave the conversation."

Conor's eyes darted over my face before he murmured, "Understood."

I knew that look.

I'd seen Dare give it.

I'd used it so many times with Maxon.

The agreement only went so far as to ensure the other was still safe. If safety was compromised, all bets were off.

Twenty-Nine

Maxon

WAS IN A DAZE.

This was the fourth radio interview we'd done, and we still had one more to do.

They were all the same.

Some of the questions got a little more personal than others. Some of the hosts were funnier than others.

But they were all the same. Talk about the tour that just ended. Ask about any upcoming albums.

And then . . .

"So, we're gonna cut to it. If you didn't see it, you missed out. If your friends didn't save it and send it to you—you've been living under a rock, because social media has been going crazy over the disappearing pictures of Maxon James kissing that girl. Reports were all over the place with who she is to Henley's bassist. Girlfriend. Friend. Just some girl he met on the road. And the most popular, a girl he's known his entire life. Cue the awws. We have to know,

Maxon, who is she?"

Then I tried to laugh and play it like I wasn't sure whether or not I should tell them—giving *that* station the inside scoop.

But there was a knot in my chest that had been there since Libby and I left the party at Holloway Estate a few nights ago, and it had only grown. And it was making it hard to do anything at all.

She hadn't spoken to me when I'd crawled into bed behind her that night, and we'd barely said more than a few sentences to each other the next two days until the guys and I left.

She was working when we landed.

We were practicing when she called back the next day.

I'd sent her one text since. There hadn't been a response.

This went beyond a drastic mood swing and not wanting to talk. She was keeping shit from me. I knew it. I could feel it.

I wanted to be there for her, to help her through whatever it was—the way I'd always done.

But she was letting it get to her. Letting it control her and twist her thoughts until she seemed fine one second and then shut me out the next.

And I couldn't keep up.

"We have to know, Maxon, who is she?"

I glanced up and made a sound that resembled a laugh.

Lincoln and Ledger laughed for me, probably because they knew this was coming and had made a bet.

Jared cut me a frustrated look.

I knew he still struggled with living in Wake Forest over LA, and I knew a part of him still blamed Libby for it.

It wasn't her fault the guys decided to stay.

It wasn't her fault I fell in love with her long ago and didn't want to continue living without her.

"That girl . . ." I huffed and ran my hand over my face. I shrugged and spoke simply and truthfully. "She's every lyric I've ever written."

Thirty

Him

"**J**ESUS, WHAT?" THE WORDS WRENCHED from my chest, ragged and gravelly.

They were storming into my office again, uninvited, and it could only mean one thing . . .

Someone was about to lose his life.

I shot a cold look at my cousin before letting it settle on my assistant. "We have phones for a reason. You call. I tell you I'm busy. You don't bother me until I want you to."

He was shaking when he rounded my desk, his hands hovering in the air like he wasn't sure what to do with them next. "Yes, sir. I know, sir, but this is . . . it's well—" He cleared his throat and turned toward my computer. "I'm going to touch this now."

"No shit."

"Give the guy a break," my cousin said from where he was leaning back in one of the chairs opposite me, his feet resting casually on my desk. "You'd just make him pull up what he's about to tell you anyway. He's skipping steps."

I leaned forward and shoved his feet off my desk. "We don't skip steps around here."

He smirked. "No. Just bury the illegal ones."

I shrugged and looked to my computer when my assistant moved away. "Tell me what I'm seeing."

"Radio interview with that Henley band," he answered quickly. "They have video of it here, but this . . ." He moved forward to scroll down the page and stepped back again.

My eyes darted over the summary of the interview.

Where they asked Maxon James who the mystery girl in the pictures was.

"James kept quiet on a name, but the depth of emotion was undeniable when he answered, 'She's every lyric I've ever written.'"

I stared at the words until I no longer saw the screen.

Only red.

My jaw ached from the pressure by the time I pushed away from my desk and slowly looked at my assistant.

"I checked. Nearly all their songs were written by him." He looked warily to my cousin then his stare fell to the floor. "I'm sure they could be about anyone."

I laughed darkly. "You're not stupid enough to suggest that to me."

"No, of course not," he mumbled quickly while taking another trembling step away.

"I want these lyrics. Now—" I stilled when my cousin threw a stack of papers on my desk.

"You're not stupid enough to think I don't know you."

"Watch yourself." The words were a clear warning—one that didn't faze him.

One that should.

He dipped his head toward the papers. "Those are all the songs he wrote that have to do with a girl. Not that you would, but don't bother thanking me. Your assistant is the one who pulled them all. I suggested he *skip a step* and print them."

I looked at him with disdain then flipped through the first ten songs before dropping the papers on my desk.

There was no need to continue.

I already knew more than enough.

In every song, he laid claim on a girl who wasn't his to claim.

"It's time he knows that she belongs to me."

"Because we haven't done anything toward that," my cousin said dryly. "If she hasn't told him yet, I doubt she'll tell him about any other *brilliant* threats you plan."

I stared at my cousin for a few seconds, my mouth twisted in a cruel grin that he easily matched. "Thinking of putting a bullet in your head gets me through the day."

He barked out a laugh. "Funny. I've always had to pull the trigger for you." He stood and leaned over the desk, his eyes taunting. "If the day ever comes when you take the throne, you'll be the first boss who came to be with no blood on his hands."

My eyes narrowed into slits.

"Are you listening?" He paused, his head listing like he was waiting for something. "The whispers and rumors are rolling in about you. I'll be here to fuel them."

My hands fisted.

"What is it you want us to do this time?" my assistant asked once my cousin left.

It only took a moment for a plan to form. Excitement pulsed through me. My blood raced. "This one's all mine."

Thirty-One

Libby

MY HEAVY EYELIDS PARTIALLY OPENED to my dark bedroom; confusion clouded my mind and sleep beckoned me.

I opened them again, not sure when they had closed, and tried to figure out what had woken me. Before I could find my way out of that place between sleep and awake, my body relaxed when an arm curled around my waist and pulled me close.

"You're back," I mumbled.

His nose gently trailed along my neck before his lips followed the path.

Somewhere in the recesses of my mind, I felt tension pressing down on us. It was dark and heavy and . . . wrong.

With the way we'd left things, and then hardly talking for three days, I wanted nothing more than to curl into his arms and never leave.

I wanted to clear the suffocating air between us.

But something in my gut twisted whenever I considered telling

Maxon the truth. As if voicing the words would bring our relationship to an end.

Because I knew he wouldn't let this be taken care of the way it needed to be. He would try to protect me, which would solidify him as the target.

I refused to let him face an execution for me.

And the frustrating thing of all this was, he already knew about the Moretti family. I'd told him before I ever honestly thought the family was behind the pictures.

Just like I'd told him about being a rebel without realizing what I was doing.

But there was a second camera now. Conor knew about the Moretti family, and he was positive they were behind the Polaroid shitstorm. No one else made as much sense to him, and I was struggling to find reasons anyone else would bother.

But why now? After all this time?

And they'd been so close to me in each photo, yet I hadn't seen anyone I didn't know.

They'd been in my apartment.

My bedroom.

Unless . . . unless someone was betraying my family. Betraying me.

Then Maxon was easier to get to . . .

Jesus.

I placed my hand on his and was turned to face him.

"I'm so tired," I murmured groggily, unsure if my words were even audible, and moaned into his mouth when he kissed me.

Rough. Demanding.

Unyielding.

I sucked in a stuttered breath when he moved, kissing and biting down my throat until he reached my breasts, his hand easily slipping between my thighs to tease me.

"Oh God," I moaned, my eyes fluttering open to reveal my headboard before they slammed shut again when he slid his hand into my underwear and eased a finger inside me. "No. No, Max—Maxon, stop."

I had lost my mind.

I was both arching into his touch and twisting away from him.

The half of me still in sleep's embrace was begging to let him continue.

The half of me toeing the line of consciousness was screaming that I needed to continue distancing myself.

I needed to do whatever it took.

Sacrifice our relationship.

Break my heart.

Shred my soul.

I rolled to my back and dropped my hands over my face, fighting with myself and wanting to let him make me forget about the looming threat—just for a little while.

My breaths were uneven when I finally managed to whisper, "Sleep. Please, just sleep."

He murmured something that sounded like an assent, then slowly—so slowly—removed his finger and rolled me onto my side so he could slip behind me again.

"Maxon," I murmured carefully when his mouth met my shoulder and he ground his erection against my butt, only covered by the thin material of my underwear. "Sleep."

"I am." The words were so soft and low, and muffled by my skin, that I wasn't sure I heard them at all.

I tried to remember the kiss—tried to remember if I'd tasted liquor on his tongue—but my mind was too hazy and sleep was wrapping me tight, pulling me under.

The last thing I remember was that tension, still covering us like a cocoon.

Dark.

Heavy.

Wrong.

Potential Polaroid Assholes

~~Literally anyone. Ugh. Has access to apartment.~~

~~Jared~~

Mom

Moretti

~~Psycho fan~~

Literally fucking anyone

Thirty-Two

Libby

WALKED INTO THE LIVING room after using the bathroom, my eye-brows pulled low and face set in frustration when I found the apartment empty.

I don't know why I even bothered checking Einstein's room.

Habit, I guess.

With a quick glance in the kitchen to see there was no fresh coffee or food, I started walking back to my room—sure I had missed something—when a key sounded in the lock.

I stopped, eyes wide and heart racing as I waited to see who was there.

When the door propped open and Maxon's voice sounded, relief and frustration rushed through me.

"You know, just once it would be nice to wake up with you beside me." The words were out before I could stop them.

Before I could remember my imperative role.

The door slowly fell open, revealing Maxon. Wide-eyed, phone tucked between his ear and shoulder, and a duffle bag in hand.

His chest pitched with a frustrated laugh as he let the bag fall to the floor.

"Nate, I just got back. I gotta go."

I went still.

I couldn't look away from the duffle bag. Maxon's words were playing through my head repeatedly.

"I just got back."

"I just got back."

"I just got back."

I shook my head roughly, trying to push the words from my mind.

I was going to shatter.

No, no, that couldn't be right, because he'd been there the night before.

He'd been there.

I'd talked to him.

I'd felt him.

Oh God, no. No, no . . .

Maxon lifted his hands to his sides and let them fall. "Welcome home, right?" His words were all sarcasm and venom.

"Where were you?" I wheezed, my hysterics making me nearly hyperventilate.

"Are you kidding?" He barked out a dull laugh. "Jesus, Libby, I had interviews in California. You knew this—we talked about—"

"No. *No.*" I drove my hands into my hair, already wild from sleep. "Where were you just now? Where were you when I woke?"

He looked confused and so, so lost. Before he responded, that confusion morphed to frustration. "Considering we haven't talked, I can't answer that. I don't know when you woke up, Libby. I don't know what you've been doing because you haven't fucking talked to me."

I stumbled back, one of my hands falling to my souring stomach.

A mouth on mine.

A tongue coaxing my lips open, demanding a kiss that was rough and possessive.

Teeth and lips on my skin and over a shirt.

A finger teasing and pushing—Oh God. Oh God, oh God.

"Oh God."

Maxon was saying something, but I wasn't hearing a word.

I wasn't seeing anything in that room.

I was reliving last night over and over like a never-ending nightmare.

I ran for my room, intent on looking for something I prayed wasn't there, and rushed for my bathroom at the last second. I only made it to the sink by the time my stomach lurched, ridding my body of bile.

"Libby . . ."

A sob wrenched from my chest. I stumbled back to the wall and lowered myself to the floor.

Maxon settled next to me, his face a mask of worry and confusion. "Libby, what—what the hell's going on? Are you okay?"

I nodded weakly.

It was all I could do.

I was the furthest thing from okay, but I couldn't tell him the truth.

Conor was right. Mom was right.

Deep down I think I'd known all along. From the very first picture. But I'd wanted it to be anything else—anyone else.

Any real threat could be twisted into a prank when that's what you wish for it to be.

After so many years of denying myself—denying *us*—I would've dismissed any threat to our relationship.

Because that's what this was.

It wasn't a simple claiming. It was an open threat to the man I loved.

It was a dark blanket on the happiness I only found with him.

It was mocking the future I wanted.

I'd worried over what might happen to Maxon and me if I told him.

Now, I knew that ending was inevitable. The one I'd agonized over.

Until we put an end to the Morettis, I couldn't see a way to continue living with Maxon without risking his life.

We'd dealt with enemies before—faced assassins silent as the night.

But the Moretti weren't silent. They were fucking ghosts.

"Talk to me," Maxon pleaded. "Are you—" He shifted closer and curled his hand around my neck. "Libby, are you pregnant?"

I jerked against the wall, my head snapped up and eyes widened. "What? *No.*"

His face fell a fraction. "Don't look so disturbed by the idea."

"I'm not. I just—" I didn't know how to respond in any way that would make sense. My head had been so filled with thoughts of what the Moretti family would do to Maxon that it stunned and terrified me when thoughts shifted to what they would do if I had Maxon's baby inside me. "It caught me off guard. Why would you even ask that?"

"Caught *you* off guard. Are you . . . Jesus." The tips of his fingers grazed his forehead before he flung his hand out toward the door. "And why wouldn't I ask? I come home after being gone for days, and you're yelling at me before I get inside. Next thing I know, you're running in here to throw up."

"Because you should know it doesn't work that way. You can't move home and expect me to be miraculously pregnant and having morning sickness two weeks later."

His mouth formed a hard line. "Month."

"What?"

"I've been back almost a month."

My mind raced as I tried to put everything that had happened in that timeframe.

It had felt like the longest days and weeks of my life—and yet, I couldn't believe any time had passed at all.

My chest wrenched when I focused on Maxon and saw the pain on his face, but when I reached for him, he stood.

"Maxon—"

"I'll get you something to drink."

I dropped my head into my hands when he left and tried to mute the sob that betrayed me.

But as his footfalls faded, the memory of why I'd come running in here in the first place came jarring back, and I scrambled to stand.

I opened every drawer and cabinet in the bathroom before rushing into my bedroom and looking wildly around. When I didn't immediately find what I was searching for, I ran for the dresser drawers, opening and shutting each drawer quickly when there was still nothing there.

Just when I started for my closet, an image from the night before flashed through my mind, making my stomach roll and halting my feet.

I turned, staring at my bed with revulsion and disdain . . . and the slightest bit of fool's hope that it had all been a horrible nightmare.

My legs felt like weights trying to walk toward the bed, and my arms wouldn't move fast enough as I ripped back the comforter and sheet. When the pillows on Maxon's side were on the floor, my fear started to ease.

I rolled my eyes and huffed, frustrated my mind conjured a dream so vivid—and that it had created such a horrible start to the day. I grabbed my pillows to take the cases off them, but they slipped from my hands and I sank heavily to the mattress.

I reached for the envelope and lifted it from the spot where my head had rested just an hour before. My hand was trembling so violently, it was as though my entire body feared touching it.

But before I could open the lip, I heard Maxon coming down the hall. I hurried off the bed and back to my dresser, fumbling with a drawer to stash the envelope in there.

When Maxon rounded the corner into my room, his brow was furrowed and his eyes were darting around my room.

"What were you doing in here?"

My chest heaved when I finally released the pent-up breath. I glanced around the room, then gestured to the bedding and pillows on the floor. "I need to wash the sheets."

One of his brows ticked up. "It sounded like you were hitting the wall."

"I was looking for extra sheets," I said quickly, surprising myself with the lie that came so easily. "But they're in the hall closet."

He started to nod but stopped. "I'll, uh . . . I'll get them."

"No, I've got it."

He stopped mid-turn, his whiskey eyes searching me. After a minute, he sent me a bemused look and reached out to hand me the water. "We left for the airport at four this morning. I'm gonna shower then crash."

I tapped my fingers on the glass, anxious to know what that envelope held. "All right. Well, I work tonight, so if I'm gone when you wake up, that's where I am."

Maxon's eyes widened, filling with shock and hurt as he slowly nodded. "Right . . ." A frustrated laugh burst from him, the action seeming to take all his strength and light and life. "Right. Fuck."

Oh God. Maxon . . . I'm sorry, I'm sorry, I'm sorry.

I hated this.

I hated that I was causing him so much confusion and pain.

He doesn't deserve this.

I dropped my stare to the floor, unable to watch a man—who had always walked so tall—walk away from me looking like he was crumpling.

"I know what you're doing."

I glanced up at his whispered words. He stood in the doorway separating the bedroom from the bathroom, his hands curled around the doorframe.

He turned to face me, his pained eyes meeting and holding mine. "You know, I was asked about you in every interview. Everyone wanted to know who you were. Everyone wanted to know details about us." His head shook slowly and his hands lifted before falling. "I only told them one thing."

I lifted my chin in defiance.

Praying he couldn't see the pain raging through my soul.

Praying he didn't notice the slight waver in my stance or tremble around my mouth.

"I told them the only truth I could give them—that you are every lyric I've ever written." He laughed sadly. "Not because of your name and who you are—because you can't be in the spotlight. I didn't tell them about you, because no one knows you the way I do, Libby. And I've spent half my life with your eyes begging me to chase you and one of your hands pressed to my chest, keeping me from catching you."

I wanted to say that wasn't true.

I wanted to defend every time I'd ever put any distance between us.

But I couldn't.

"No one knows exactly how it feels to be pushed away by you. To be loved by you," he whispered. "But fuck, I do. You've never loved *or* pushed as hard as you have during the last month."

Fresh tears pricked the backs of my eyes, threatening to betray my façade.

"Keeping me in the dark, pushing me away . . . it's slowly ripping my heart out of my chest. You've given me the greatest gift laced with the cruelest pain, because I know . . . damn it, I know any day you're about to take it away. So why would I tell them about you—tell them your name—when I know I'm about to lose you all over again?"

My chest wrenched open and I stumbled forward when he turned from me.

I pressed my hands over my mouth to hold in the words begging to be freed.

"Please understand none of this would be happening if there were any other way."

"Please know I need to keep you safe."

He glanced over his shoulder and murmured, "I love you, Rebel."

My soul cried out when he left, sending me to my knees.

My heart ached so fiercely I thought it would shatter, but all I managed was a soundless sob.

Because his words weren't a claim.

They were a reminder. A plea.

I love you. I love you. I love you.

But I can't let you die.

Thirty-Three

Maxon

'D BARELY SLEPT.

When I'd finished showering, the bed was still a wreck, and Libby was in the living room, sitting on the couch, staring at a spot on the floor.

She hadn't noticed me standing there watching her and hadn't reacted when I called her name.

I woke up an hour later to some guy changing the locks.

I lost my goddamn mind.

Yelling and threatening him until he shoved the order in my face.

There, on the bottom, was Libby's signature.

Her credit card information.

And a note quickly scrawled on there asking to leave the keys with her boyfriend.

"Apparently I'm just her boyfriend now," I said numbly and handed the clipboard back to him. "Sorry for earli—"

The look he gave me brought me up short.

Like he was uneasy.

Like he was in a situation he didn't want to be in.

Like he was afraid of how I would react.

He cleared his throat and dropped in front of the door. He eyed me quickly then looked past me. "I'll, uh." He cleared his throat again. "I'll be done here in no time and y'all can sort it out."

I turned, expecting to find Libby behind me, and tensed.

Eyes locked on me and filled with rage. Hands clenched into fists.

How hadn't I seen him sitting there?

Like he *belonged* here.

"Who the hell are you?" I asked with all the venom I possessed.

"I was just wondering the same thing."

He stood, slowly unfurling to his full height.

The guy was tall. Fucking massive. Built like a damn brick wall.

"And what do you think you're doing here?" he continued. "I'll give you three seconds before or I suggest you run."

"No, man. That's not how this works. I live here. And the last thing you're gonna do is scare me out of here with a bullshit threat."

He stared at me with open amusement before his face lit with recognition. "Fuck me . . . you're the guy. Uh . . . shit, I can't remember. But the rock star. Right?"

My hands fisted when he slowly stalked toward me.

"See, I'm the guy who was here while you were out playing rock star." He stopped in front of me and stared down at me. "I'm the guy who took care of Libby when you couldn't be bothered to."

My chest pitched with ragged breaths. "That right?"

"And I'm the guy she's choosing over you." He cut a look at the locksmith and flashed a grin. "Clearly."

"See, I'm gonna call bullshit on everything you just said." I stepped closer and tried to get in his face. "I know Libby. She tells me shit. I've also been here nearly every day for the last month, and you haven't been around."

His grin widened. "You sure about that?" When I didn't

immediately respond, he laughed and walked over to the waiting locksmith. "Thanks. We appreciate it."

I hurried over, trying to take the keys from them. "No. I don't know who the hell you think you are. But you need to go."

The locksmith held the keys away from me. "I'm sorry, sir. Ms. Borello told me to leave them with him."

My stomach dropped when I watched the keys drop into the stranger's hand.

I was too stunned to react.

"See, you might not know me. But I know everything about you."

I blinked slowly and looked away from the open door. I clenched my teeth and demanded, "Who the fuck are you?"

He shrugged. "I'm every hesitation you've noticed. I'm every inch of space between you and Libby."

"Bullshit."

"Do cameras mean anything to you?" he asked with a snide grin. "Because they mean something to us."

My head slowly lifted as images rushed through my mind: Libby asking if I had a Polaroid camera . . . Libby finding one at the party.

She'd been horrified when we found it. *Cold.*

I knew she had.

"Leave before I make you," I growled. "Come near my girl again, we won't be talking."

He looked me over and huffed a laugh. "You're gonna make me?"

I didn't care that he had half a foot on me. And probably a hundred pounds of muscle.

I didn't care if he was in the goddamn mob.

If he was the reason behind the changes in Libby lately, I would go round for round with him until I won.

He pulled his phone from his pocket and tapped on the screen a few times. A few seconds later, Libby's voice came through the speaker, soft and familiar. "Hey."

"Locks are changed. There's a guy here wanting my spot in your life."

"Seriously, who the fuck do you think you are?" I demanded.

"Shit." She sighed heavily. "Just . . . just give him a key and leave him there. He has stuff he needs to move out."

"Libby," I barked.

"Maxon, don't be like this. I'll have someone get the key from you later."

"*Libby.*"

The guy murmured something and ended the call, but I was too stunned to listen.

"Just give him a key and leave him there."

"What did you do to her?" I asked when he tried handing me a key. "What the fuck did you do to her?"

"Apparently what you didn't." He let the key fall to the floor when I didn't reach for it and leaned close. "You try to pull any shit in here or with Libby, I'll find you."

"He has stuff he needs to move out."

This wasn't happening.

Something was wrong.

She'd been acting differently. She'd been distant. But *this?*

"Maxon, don't be like this. I'll have someone get the key from you later."

"The ring you gave her?" the guy said as he stepped outside. I looked up in time to see the condescending look. "It was a nice effort."

I don't remember the door shutting.

Moving.

Or time passing.

But I was now lying on the floor of the living room, strumming my acoustic and murmuring words that meant everything and nothing, trying to get my head around what the fuck had happened.

Words about a girl with hair dark as night and teasing eyes.

A girl who warned me long ago that I couldn't keep her.

But loving her had been the only thing that made sense in my world.

I'd been sure this was our time. We'd waited long enough for this.

What had I missed? What *was* I missing?

Because there wasn't a chance in hell *another guy* was it.

I thought back over the last month, trying to find the day where it all started changing, and kept coming back to the hours after I asked her to marry me.

She'd pushed me away even then . . . but I'd ignored it because she was fighting to keep me just as hard.

My fingers stilled, then slowly resumed when I remembered walking out—the fight I was sure had ended us. And it had changed everything. I learned more about her through that fight—more about why she'd always pushed me away—than I had in a lifetime of trying to figure her out.

"No more secrets between us. No more hiding anything."

Something dark flashed in her eyes. *"What if it keeps you safe?"*

I sat up and dropped the guitar to the floor beside me.

My mind raced, thinking of the days leading up to then, and all the days after.

"I love you and want to marry you because you're my home. You're my calm. I would do anything to be with you—even if it meant keeping us apart."

I looked to the side so quickly I thought I'd get whiplash.

Because I knew in my gut that every answer was waiting at the end of that hall.

There'd been days lately where I'd felt I didn't know her at all. On those days, she always ran for her bedroom and tried to keep me from it. Even today, she'd been banging around in there and had stripped her bed . . . then left all the sheets and pillows on the floor.

Before my thoughts had fully formed, I found myself running to her room and trying to recreate the sounds I'd heard that morning.

I opened every drawer in the room, searched her closet, stripped the bed I'd made, and flipped the mattress. But in the end, I was more pissed off than before.

I dropped to the mattress and hung my head for a few moments, then lifted it slowly and looked around the room.

"No more secrets between us. No more hiding anything."

"What if it keeps you safe?"

"What are you hiding from me, Libby?"

I looked at the dresser in front of me, then glanced behind me to the bathroom.

Every drawer and door had been open in the bathroom when I'd walked in to take a shower.

The dresser drawers had been shut and she'd been standing next to it when I'd come in.

I stood slowly and walked toward it.

I wanted to jerk the drawers open again, but my movements were agonizingly slow as I opened the drawers and searched through all her clothes methodically.

My blood ran cold when I grabbed a pair of jeans and an envelope fell out of them.

I didn't need to know what was in it to know *this* was what she'd been hiding—*this* was what she'd been trying to protect me from.

I bent to pick it up, my movements faltering when I saw her name printed on the back and pictures spilling out.

Polaroids.

My pulse quickened and my heart thundered.

"Do cameras mean anything to you? Because they mean something to us."

"Shit."

I stood with the envelope and pictures and dropped them onto the top of the dresser so I could study them.

When I realized what I was seeing, what was on there, I started shaking.

There was a picture of Libby in the shower.

. . . but you've always belonged to me. was written on the bottom.

I quickly looked to the second Polaroid. It was a picture of a picture . . . of *me*. My face was crossed out in red, and below was the note:

You're every lyric he's written . . .

"Jesus Christ."

I wanted to find that guy and beat the shit out of him.

I wanted to find her. Tell her I wouldn't let her do this to us.

All I could do was stand there, staring at the pictures, and wonder what the hell I was actually going to do.

Potential Polaroid Assholes

~~Literally anyone. Ugh. Has access to apartment.~~

~~Jared~~

~~Mom~~

Moretti . . . now who the hell are they??

~~Psycho fan~~

~~Literally fucking anyone~~

Thirty-Four

Libby

JOLTED WHEN FINGERS BRUSHED my arm, pulling me back to the present, and looked up into bright blue eyes.

It took me a second to recognize who I was looking at, to realize where I was standing. I shook my head when all sense came flooding back. Conor was standing directly in front of me, on the other side of the bar, with a mixture of frustration and worry on his face.

"Hey. Hi, how did it . . . Is he okay?"

He studied me for a second. "Are *you* okay?"

"Of course." My reply was weak and quick. Too quick.

I was wrecked.

Broken.

I'd spent every moment of the last two hours consumed by grief.

After the phone call from Conor, I'd laid in the back seat of my car and sobbed until the pain became too much.

Conor nodded slowly. I knew from his expression he didn't

believe me for a second. Just like I knew he wouldn't push me.

"Libby, I care about you a lot. After all the shit our gangs went through, it means everything that you guys took me into the family." He rested his hands on the bar top and leaned close. "But if you ever ask me to do that again . . ."

I glanced at him and ground my jaw to stop it from wavering.

"I've done bad things without a thought. We all have. We had to. But I *hated* myself earlier. Maxon was gonna try to take me on. *Me*, Libby. For you. That guy fucking loves you. And I had to stand there and pretend like I was enjoying crushing him. Don't ever make me do that shit again."

"You think any of this is easy for me?" I bit out. "It's necessary, Conor. It's the only chance I have of making him leave."

"No, I get that it's necessary. But I can't help you break him the way I did today. Fuck, if he would've swung, I would've let him. And I wouldn't have fought back, because I hated what I was doing to him." He reached into his pocket and slid three keys over to me. "I'll do anything else you need for this case, Libby. Not that."

I stared at the keys until I was no longer in The Jack again, and all I was seeing was Maxon's broken expression.

"I love you, Rebel."

Over and over.

I cleared my throat and worked one of the keys off the ring before handing it back to Conor. "Can you switch out Einstein's key without her noticing?"

He blew out a harsh breath and twirled the key between his fingers. "Fuck," he murmured, drawing out the word. "I can try."

"I need you to."

Conor's expression shifted into frustration. "This is what Kieran and Jessica do. They sneak in and out of places undetected. Einstein hacks and creates fake identities. I protect people. You're having me do everyone else's job, Libby. There's a reason I *don't*."

I leaned over the bar and dropped my voice so it could barely be heard over the other voices in The Jack. "Consider this part of protecting me—protecting *Einstein*. I need you to switch out those keys."

He looked like he was going to argue, but continued to stare me down for a few moments before clenching his teeth. "And if she catches me?"

I wanted to tell him not to get caught.

I wanted to tell him to lie.

I wanted to tell him so many things so long as it kept Einstein in the dark.

"Then tell her the truth." The words were out before I could begin to take them back. I lifted my hand to point at him. "*Only* if she catches you."

He dipped his head in understanding, but relief rolled from him in waves.

I looked down the bar, trying to distract myself with the very few customers we had at the early hour of the evening, but felt the question pulling me toward Conor. Ripping from me. Begging to be freed.

"Do you think he'll be okay?" I asked quickly without looking at him.

"I don't know," he answered after a pause. "He was sure I was lying until I called you. He looked blindsided."

The air rushed from my body, escaping me on a near-silent cry before I was able to cover my mouth.

"Libby . . ."

I shook my head . . . slowly at first, then quickly. "I'm fine," I said thickly, then looked to him. "I'm fine. I just . . . I need you to replace Einstein's key. Please."

"What about everyone else? Dare and the twins?"

"What about them?"

"Don't you all have keys to each other's places?"

I shrugged. "It's taken care of. Dare gave me his when I told him I lost mine, and the twins won't go there when Maverick and Einstein are fighting the way they are."

Conor looked at me warily. "For how much you're going through to prevent anyone from finding out something's wrong, you're banking a lot on that guess."

I offered him a mocking smile. "I could always have you go steal their keys . . ."

He rolled his eyes and pushed away from the bar, but I called his name before he could take a step away.

"I'm sorry. For today . . . what you had to do. For all of this."

He dipped his head in a nod and turned to head out of The Jack.

I busied my mind and my hands with prepping for when the rush came flooding in, thankful I only had to make it through a short shift before I could break down at home.

Not five minutes later, a massive shadow towered over me.

"Libby." His tone was pure grit and steel. As always.

"Zeke."

"Do it again, I'm keeping your tips for a week."

I stopped slicing the lime and slowly looked over my shoulder in time to see my boss chuck a cardboard box near me.

"What—"

"This ain't your house," he said, stalking off.

I glanced at the box for only a second before the knife clattered to the cutting board.

I shakily tore into the gently taped box. My gaze went to Zeke's back . . . to the other bartenders . . . to the few people drinking throughout the bar.

No one was watching me. No one seemed suspect.

There wasn't a soul in the bar radiating malicious energy or twitching anxiously. There weren't eyes casting eager glances in my direction or carefully ignoring my stare.

But there was a box in my hands addressed to Elizabeth Borello, without a return address or single barcode . . .

And inside was a black Polaroid camera.

Thirty-Five

Maxon

I WAS SITTING ON THE edge of the coffee table when she came home that night.

When she came *back*.

I roughed my hands through my hair and heaved out a breath that shook my body when I heard the key in the lock.

I'd gone over it all dozens of times.

The change in Libby.

Everything the guy said earlier.

The pictures.

I'd even convinced myself to leave at one point . . . I knew it was what she wanted.

But something still wasn't adding up.

So I was the idiot. Waiting to get my heart ripped out all over again.

I glanced up in time to see her stumble when she noticed me. Her eyes widened and her body shifted like she wasn't sure if she wanted to continue walking in or walk back out the door.

"Maxon," she said, my name just above a breath. "You're here."

Her eyes darted everywhere before settling on the floor not far from where she stood.

A pained laugh forced from my chest. "I'm sure that's a shock considering what I woke to."

"I'm sorry. I . . . I don't know what else to say. I'm sorry." Her voice was thick with emotion and I could see she was trembling.

She started to speak again, but stopped and pushed from the door, her long legs taking her to her room.

"Tell me what's going on," I begged in a hopeless, last-ditch effort.

"I'm going to my room."

I clenched my teeth. "With us."

"Thought it was obvious."

If it weren't for the slight hitch in her voice, I might've believed her careless tone.

My gaze caught on the small cardboard box in her hands she was trying to keep hidden, and my mind instantly went to the pictures I found earlier.

"You gonna add that to your jeans drawer?"

She stopped so suddenly I thought she'd fall forward.

For a few seconds, she stood staring straight ahead before turning to look at me. "What?"

"What's in the box, Libby? More pictures?"

Her face paled and her legs gave.

Terror flashed through her eyes . . . and then it was gone.

All of it.

She was standing tall. Steady. Staring at me, horrified.

I wasn't sure if I'd blinked or imagined it.

"You went through my stuff?" she demanded.

I'm losing my fucking mind.

"You were supposed to grab your stuff and go, not search my things."

I huffed and reached behind me for the envelope. I threw it in her direction and said, "I want you to tell me who took those."

"Maxon . . . I'm sorry you found out the way you—"

"No. No, fuck that. That guy? I'm not buying it for a second."

"It doesn't matter if you buy it, Maxon. You can deny that the sun rises, but it will still rise every morning. I'm sorry I let us get to this place, but it has to end."

The air rushed from my lungs on a pained wheeze. I clenched my teeth tight and demanded, "Who, Libby?"

When she looked up at me, a mixture of anger and devastation raged in her eyes. "What do you want from me?"

I stood from the table and yelled, "I want you to tell me who took the fucking pictures." I spread my arms wide when she didn't respond. "That guy earlier? I know it's not him. Took a while, but I finally realized he messed up."

She watched me carefully, not giving anything away.

"He knew *of* me . . . but didn't know what I looked like." I gestured to the envelope on the floor. "One of those is of me."

There was nothing.

Not a sound.

Not a flinch.

No reaction at all.

She was too still.

"Stop shutting me out and pushing me away, and tell me. Is it that family you were supposed to marry into? Was he one of them?"

I'd considered it a handful of times since finding the pictures.

I'd agonized over the thought of being near one of them and doing nothing.

A bitter laugh fell from her lips. "If he had been a Moretti, he would've killed you without a thought."

I raked my hands through my hair.

My thoughts had been clearer before she'd come home.

I was sure she'd been scared. Sure the guy in the apartment had been lying—had possibly been part of that Moretti family.

Now . . .

"Libby, I . . . fuck, I'm missing something. I know I am. Things aren't adding up. I've seen your fear lately. I saw his confusion when he saw—"

"I was afraid you would find the pictures. Find out about him," she nearly yelled. "And did you ever think maybe he was messing with you?" She clenched her jaw tight and gestured to the hall leading to our bedroom.

Her bedroom.

"He knew you were asleep when I left. He's *known* who you are. And you're Maxon James. You're famous. After what I've put him through, apparently he wanted to take a dig at you by pretending not to know you."

"What you put him through . . ." I laughed, stunned. "*Him?*"

She rubbed at her forehead and sighed. "Both of you. But I . . . I was with him before you came back. I told him I was ending things with you for good, then I let things get out of hand. I got caught up in everything because for the first time, you said you would stay. And the next thing I knew, we were engaged—"

"Wait, what? Are you—are you kidding? That wasn't you getting caught up. I—" My chest pitched with a pained huff. "Fuck, Libby. *No.*"

"I'm sorry. I'm so sorry for letting it go on this long. For doing this to you." Tears filled her dark eyes and quickly slipped down her cheeks. "I love you, Maxon. God, I love you. But you leave. It's what you do. And no matter what you say or promise, I can't trust that you won't leave me again."

I stared at her as a pit of devastation formed in my stomach and slowly spread through my body.

I felt destroyed.

Raw.

"Libby . . ."

She reached for the ring I'd given her and slowly slid it off her finger, a sob wrenching from her chest when she held it out to me. "It had to end sometime."

I stumbled back when my knees buckled and gripped at my hair, praying for this nightmare to end. "No. No, no. Libby, don't."

"Take it," she begged as she stepped forward.

"I don't want the fucking ring."

"And I don't want to continue living a lie," she cried out. "Don't make this harder than it is. It's over, Maxon. This has to be goodbye."

This wasn't happening.

"I love you and want to marry you because you're my home."

This wasn't fucking happening.

"You're my calm."

She was tearing herself from me. Exactly as I'd worried she'd do.

I turned for the door and had almost made it there when my steps slowed. I twisted to face her and looked at the girl I'd spent my life loving.

Sobbing. Broken.

" . . . living a lie . . ."

Her pain . . . that wasn't a lie.

I staggered over to her and pulled her close. I slowly trailed my fingers up her throat and over her jaw to cradle her cheek, and let every memory with her shred me piece by piece, then bent to kiss her.

Her lips parted easily, her tongue moving with mine in a slow dance we'd perfected over the years.

She tasted like rebellions and freedom and sorrow.

It was perfect.

It was pain.

It was the last piece of her I would ever claim.

I pulled away and searched her glassy eyes until the tears in my own made it too hard to see.

My mouth twitched into a sad smile as I traced my thumb over her lips. "Your lies have never tasted so true."

I left the apartment listening to her sobs fade behind me.

And I broke.

Heart ripped from my chest.

Unable to catch a breath.

Struggling to move.

Thirty-Six

Libby

"SURPRISED TO SEE YOU ALONE."

I tensed at the voice but didn't react otherwise.

I wasn't sure I could.

Not after what I'd been through the last two days.

I hadn't slept.

I'd barely eaten.

The night Maxon left, I'd lain on the floor sobbing and clawing at the empty space in my chest until tears stopped falling.

Tonight, I had to pretend.

Pretend I hadn't obliterated my heart.

Pretend I hadn't ruined the best thing in my life.

Pretend I wasn't seeing Maxon's broken expression—his tears—on an uninterrupted loop.

My mom slid into the Brooks Street booth opposite me, her brows slightly raised. "You always look so provocative."

I looked down at my full cup of coffee that had cooled long

ago. "I have work soon."

"How nice to work at a place that requires you to dress that way." When I didn't respond, she asked, "Shouldn't you be surrounded by a group of irresponsible men? Or at least *one*?"

I rolled my eyes in an attempt to relieve the stinging of fresh tears and let them settle on the mug again.

"It's one thing to act and behave the way you do. It's another to surround yourself with people like those boys in a childish attempt at rebellion."

I bit back my frustration and sat in stunned silence before twisting to slide out of the booth. "Always a pleasure seeing you, Mom."

"You've had your rebellion," she said before I could leave. "It led to destruction in case you forgot."

I slanted a glare at her. "You know . . . if you took half a second to learn anything about Maxon, you would know that he's good for me. He's the kind of guy moms would want their 'rebellious' daughters with. He calms me. He's always made me stop and consider what I was about to do."

If she heard the hitch in my voice, she ignored it.

Her expression screamed she doubted every word.

I sank back into the seat. "And in case *you* forgot . . . he and his friends are rock stars. Of course they're a little wild for your taste, Mom. Hell, I said no to an arranged marriage and you thought I ended the world with my brazenness."

"You certainly tried."

I bit down on my tongue to stop my automatic response.

She spoke with such conviction and sadness, as if it pained her that I didn't understand the impact of my actions, because she knew one day I *would*.

It was the first time I'd seen some emotion from her rather than her frustration.

"Why do you hate me?"

Her face softened. "I couldn't if I tried, Elizabeth."

A shudder rolled through me at the sound of my name, but I pushed the panicked feeling that accompanied it away.

"It's frustrating as a mother to watch your children blatantly make the wrong choices and then throw them in your face."

"Wrong choice for who?" A weak laugh caught in my throat. "Not me. Not Dare—who was boss at the time, so it was ultimately his decision." I lifted my hands to stop her when she opened her mouth and conceded. "I get it . . . Dad made this deal to keep peace. But part of it was selling me to a family that our ancestors rebelled from—fought and fled from. For crying out loud, our symbol is a representation of when we got away from them. Neither of you could've expected that marriage to go well."

She gave me a patronizing look. "That was so long ago."

"Well, apparently you think they won't let it go that I refused to marry one of them. So why would they let it go that we tried to kill off their entire bloodline only a couple generations ago?"

"You're being dramatic again. Things change, deals are made to keep peace. And you took the most important deal of all and spat on it."

"Because you tried to sell me like a piece of property," I cried out. "And your biggest worry throughout it all was the greater good of the family . . . the *ceasefire*. Not *my* life. Not *my* well-being."

Her mouth formed a tight line indicating she wouldn't object.

I shook my head and looked across Brooks Street Café as my mind bounced from subject to subject.

Maxon.

Dare and Lily.

Deals made in blood.

Maxon.

White envelopes with a too-formal name.

Polaroid pictures that invaded and destroyed every piece of my life. My home. My relationship. My sense of security.

Maxon, Maxon, Maxon . . .

"I just wanted to live my own life," I whispered after some time had passed. "That choice should've been given to me—not taken away." I looked at her again and forced a smile even though my chest was aching from the guilt that flooded me. "When Gia was murdered, I was sure Dare would never love anyone again."

Mom's eyes slid shut on a shaky exhale and didn't open until I started speaking again.

"When he found Lily . . ." My head shook subtly. "I couldn't believe he was so captivated with her, let alone falling in love with her. But I was happy. God, I was so happy for him. But if I would've known who she was from the beginning, I would've been against their relationship. One hundred percent."

She knew where I was going with this. I could see it in the way the pain from Gia's memory faded and her mouth and eyes tightened.

I leaned over the table to hold her glare. "I want you to look me in the eye and tell me if you'd known Lily was the Holloway Princess before we all fell in love with her, you would've fought Dare on their relationship the way you fight my relationship with Maxon."

Her eyes drifted. "Different circumstances—"

"Look me in the eye and tell me."

"You can't compare the two, Elizab—"

"Look me in the eye, Mom!"

She slammed her hand on the table and leaned close. "What do you want me to say? Those are two completely different situations. A boss and a princess from rival gangs? It's unheard of. Her father murdered your father. He murdered Gia. Of course I would've been against it—but I also would've learned shortly after how trapped that girl was in that prison. Your relationship with Maxon is not only preventing you from your duties and keeping you from your family, it's putting you both in unfathomable danger." She lifted a hand to silence my next words. "Not to mention, your brother was and will remain Boss until his death. You are simply a member. I am simply his mother. I cannot tell him what to do any more than you can."

"You can," I said when she sat back in the booth. "You just choose not to."

"Have some respect for our family for once."

"Respect me for once," I nearly shouted. "You care so deeply for everyone in this family, blood or not. Why can't you extend that care to me? You've only ever viewed me as a pawn you couldn't control."

"That is not true, Elizabeth."

I just lifted my brows in response.

In denial.

"You have to know that's not true," she said.

"I don't have to know anything you haven't shown me."

I dropped my stare, ignoring the hurt covering her face, and slowly turned the mug between my hands.

I'd shown Maxon how much I loved him . . . until I couldn't.

Until his life was at risk.

The woman in front of me had always been the loving, caring mother figure to every Borello member . . . except me.

"Maxon and I broke up," I whispered suddenly and looked up to see the excitement lying below her surprise. I spread my hands across the table exaggeratedly. "Which would be why I'm alone—especially considering my roommate would rather stay with you."

She ignored the Einstein comment. "For how long this time?"

"For as long as is necessary."

Not forever.

It can't be forever.

"While I'm sorry for the hurt I know you're hiding . . . I won't pretend I'm not glad. This is what's best. He would've been a casualty one day, and you know it."

"It can't be what's best when it feels like I'm missing my heart." Tears welled in my eyes and tightened my throat. "I want to be with him. I *need* to be with him. I've never doubted who I'm supposed to live my life with, but his life is at stake."

Her eyes rolled and she delicately gestured toward the front door of the café. "If you're so worried, Elizabeth, then go to Chicago. Offer yourself to the Morettis. Apologize. You won't have to live your life worrying and looking over your shoulder, wondering when they'll come."

My head was shaking so quickly I wasn't sure if it was intentional, or if my entire body was trembling. "Mom . . . they're already here."

Her eyebrows slowly lifted, her expression full of concern.

"Do you think I would've destroyed Maxon's heart if they weren't? Do you think I would've destroyed *mine*?" A pained laugh caught in my throat. "His life is at stake. They're watching me. They're threatening him. They're *here*."

She roughly sank back into the booth. "Oh God."

For once, I didn't hold anything back.

There was no reason to now.

Our worst nightmares had become reality.

I leaned close, lowered my voice, and told her everything.

About the pictures and cameras—where I'd found them and when, and what they contained.

About the night I thought I'd woken to Maxon coming home—only for him to arrive the next morning.

How when I went to pay the locksmith, I found my purse emptied of everything it usually contained except my license and credit cards, and the Polaroid of a note saying, "Give you one guess how to get it all back."

The more I spoke, the paler my mom's face became.

When I got to the night of the third camera's delivery and breaking up with Maxon, she was staring vacantly and had a shaking hand resting over her mouth.

"Why didn't you say something to me before this?" she asked nearly a minute after I finished explaining.

I shrugged helplessly. "I kept doubting everything. I thought it was someone playing a prank or trying to scare me—one of our friends or a fan of Maxon's. About a week ago, I thought it might be them . . . but by the time I'd eliminated everyone else, I didn't know what else to do. Conor's been trying to pull fingerprints off what I've found, but there's been nothing."

"That's why he was at the house with you?" Realization lit her face. "Others know?"

"Just Conor. I thought he would be the only one able to keep it to himself." When her brow furrowed, I said, "I was worried if anyone found out, they'd tell Dare. If Dare knew, he'd make us bunker down at your house until the threat was gone—the way he always has. This all happened in the last two weeks. I wasn't even sure who was behind it until a few days ago." I rubbed my temples and groaned. "Maybe I shouldn't be sure. Maybe I just want it to be them."

"Nothing else makes sense."

I laughed faintly. I'd said the same thing to Conor.

I cast her a look and warily asked, "Should I have told Dare?"

She considered for a few moments before giving me a helpless look. "It's like you said. If you had, he would've had every member protecting you. If the family's protecting you, they're seen as threats to the Moretti family. Unaware of the situation, they aren't." She leveled me with a hard look. "That doesn't mean they don't deserve to be warned of the danger in town. Find a way to warn the other members without tipping them off to the danger."

"Right. Easiest thing in the world."

I let the *member* part slide.

Mom would never let the mafia part of our family die.

She didn't know how. This life was all she knew.

She'd been born to a prominent mafia family, then married into the Borellos over thirty years ago. Was *given* to them. All for an alliance and traded secrets.

Just as I had been given to the Moretti family.

My dad fell hard and fast for his new bride. His heart softened and ruthless ways shifted. Mom had fallen in love with the notorious, young Boss long before I was born.

They'd been lucky, and I was sure my mom anticipated the same for me. Knew she expected me to give my life to the mafia as she had hers.

But I'd always wanted my life to be my own.

I glanced at my phone and started sliding out of the booth. "I have to get to work."

"If Moretti are here and watching you, you need to let them know you're not going to fight them."

I stood and froze, my lips curled in a sneer. "And what . . . hand myself over? Fuck that. I'm not you, Mom. I still have a life I want. I fought them then, I plan on fighting them now."

Her gaze slowly lifted, her eyes filled with sadness. "Then you'll lose."

The hollow in my chest was screaming that I'd already lost the only thing that mattered.

Thirty-Seven

Libby

"LIBBY," ZEKE CALLED OUT AS he made his way toward me. "This is a bar. This is where you're employed, in case you forgot."

My brow furrowed as I poured the mixed drink into the glasses, garnished them, and pushed them forward. "Uh . . . I didn't."

He stopped beside me but didn't speak again until after the customer had paid and turned. The entire time, her eyes were darting back and forth between us, like she was waiting for something to happen.

Like Zeke to fire me.

Not happening.

"We've never had a problem before, and I don't want one now. I'm only gonna say this once: I don't pay you to get deliveries and love notes here," Zeke said gruffly. "Do we understand each other?"

"I have no idea what you're—" I stopped cold when he shoved a plain white envelope at me, back side up, full name typed neatly on the bottom right corner.

My stomach swirled with inky dread and icy fear.

"Where—when—Zeke, who gave that to you?"

He leaned close and rumbled, "I'm your boss, kid. Not your messenger."

"Oh, for fuck's sake, you're ten years older than me. Tell me who gave you this." When he started backing away, I grabbed his arm and begged, "*Zeke.*"

His eyes rolled and he blew out a pent-up breath. "A homeless guy."

"Homeless," I stated dully. "In Wake Forest."

Zeke rubbed at the back of his neck before gesturing toward the front of the bar. "He came up asking for free drinks, so I told him to get out. He dropped the envelope on the bar and said he was on a mission to deliver this to you and was owed drinks for completing it. I made him leave after that."

If there had been any food in my stomach, it would've ended up on Zeke.

"No more, Libby," Zeke said in warning.

I nodded weakly. "I'll uh . . . I'll—yeah. No more."

When Zeke turned to go back to the other side of the bar, I let my gaze slowly move through the crowded bar while my thumb worked under the lip of the envelope. Once I had it opened, I pulled out the Polaroid waiting inside and sucked in a frail breath.

With one last look around, I dropped my head to look at the picture.

It was instant. The feeling like someone had punched me—stolen every last ounce of air in my lungs. The way tears built and my chest tightened from trying to keep them at bay.

But I didn't let myself react. I couldn't.

If I did, they would know they were affecting me—frightening me.

And I knew with one hundred percent certainty that was exactly what they wanted. Just as I knew they were watching.

The picture was of me working the bar from just a few stools away—tonight, if my hair and *provocative* top were any indication. On the bottom, written with a Sharpie, was one simple word.

Boo.

I glanced up and whispered under a shaky breath, "Fuck you," to the crowd and the people sitting at the bar. I put the picture back in the envelope and ducked down to shove it in the cabinet on top of my purse.

"No one owns you. No one controls you. Nothing scares you," I chanted to myself. "They can't touch you. You're Libby Borello, damn it."

With a steadying breath, I fixed a *fuck off* look on my face and straightened in time to see Gabe making his way into The Jack with another man.

I grabbed two tumblers and a bottle of whiskey, and was finishing his drinks when he stepped up to the bar with a crooked smile that quickly turned bemused when he glanced down.

He reached for the barstool. "Someone lost . . ." He held up a thick, plain, white envelope, his brows pulling tight when he flipped it over to look at either side. "Uh, this."

The bottle of whiskey almost slipped out of my hand.

"Maybe Elizabeth Borello will come back for it. Yeah?" he asked as he tossed it onto the bar top.

I stared at the envelope.

I've been right here. I would've seen someone leave it . . . right?

Knuckles rapping on the bar top snagged my attention, making me look at Gabe.

"I'm Elizabeth Borello," I said automatically, the words sounding like a horrified confession.

Gabe shot me one of those piercing looks. "Thought your name was Libby?"

"It is," I whispered and slowly reached for the envelope.

This one was different. This one was stuffed so full the flap barely closed.

"Are those for me?" Gabe asked carefully when I didn't offer anything more, his eyes now searching me. "You okay?"

"Of course," I said quickly. "Of course, I'm sorry. Yes. These are for you." I cleared my throat and tried to push every worry from my mind. "Only two of you tonight?"

He studied my face for a few more seconds before nodding. By the time he slid his credit card over to me, he was already looking around the bar with that frustrated yet content expression he somehow pulled off.

"See you around, Libby," he murmured softly before stepping away.

I didn't realize I hadn't responded until I was already another handful of customers in and replaying everything from when Zeke walked over to when Gabe left.

I'd never been more anxious or more scared to open an envelope.

I'd known they were in The Jack. I'd known.

But to know they'd been right in front of me had chills dancing along my skin like a taunt.

Or could it have been the girl I last served . . .

Zeke said a homeless man brought in an envelope. Literally anyone could be leaving them for me.

"Screw it." I fell to a squat to grab the latest one from where I'd tossed it inside the cabinet next to my purse.

I didn't need to ease the flap open. I barely touched it and it popped from being so tightly packed.

My hands were shaking so badly I nearly dropped half the pictures while pulling them out.

I stilled for a few seconds before quickly pressing the stack of pictures to my chest when I realized what I was seeing in the first one. I looked wildly around to make sure none of the other bartenders were watching me, then dropped my hands again.

It was a man in a chair. He was dead.

Not just dead—murdered.

There was a date on the bottom of the card written with a Sharpie.

I flipped to the next picture. Another man, another date. The next picture had two dates. Before I could flip to the fourth picture, a cold sweat broke out over my body when I took a closer look at the man in the chair.

I knew that man.

I'd had sex with that man . . .

I fumbled with the pictures as I struggled to look at the previous two and couldn't stop the cry that left my lips when I realized how I knew them. I'd had sex with them too.

"Oh God, oh God, oh God."

I flipped to the fourth picture and couldn't stop the tears of relief when the picture was of a note rather than a man.

You belong to me.

The following pictures were more of the same. Pictures of notes.

I own you.

This is what happens to men who touch what's mine.

This is a few who have dared.

Who will be next?

"Shit. Shit, shit, shit." Another sob burst from my chest as I sloppily shoved the pictures into the envelope and threw it into my purse. My movements seemed slow and my fingers weren't cooperating as I frantically searched for my phone in my large purse. I nearly cried in relief when I finally found it.

My calls to Maxon went unanswered every time.

I shouldn't have expected anything else.

I called Einstein and started screaming into the phone as soon as she answered. "Where's Maxon?"

"Holy shit," she yelled back. "Tone it down, how would I know?"

"I need to know where he is right now. He bought a house. Find it. Track him."

"So much for privacy."

"*Einstein*."

There was a pause. "Did fans find him?"

"This isn't a joke, Einstein," I cried out. "Get Dare and the twins and stay with Maxon. He's in danger."

"Got it. Done."

I threw my phone into my bag and hurried out from behind the bar . . . not thinking to tell anyone I was leaving.

All I could focus on was finding Maxon alive.

I tried to sidestep a couple and ran into the back of a man standing at one of the high-top tables.

"The hell?"

"I'm sorry." My breaths were rough and mind frenzied as I tried to steady myself. "I'm so—"

"Libby?"

I glanced up just as I was about to push away from the man I'd run into, and saw Gabe peering around him.

His eyes were wild as they took me in. "Christ, are you okay?"

I couldn't imagine what I looked like.

I could hardly catch a breath. I could barely see past my relentless tears.

I was fucking terrified.

"I have to go." I glanced at the man Gabe was with and breathed another apology before pushing through the crowd and bolting out of the entrance.

I ran, barely noticing the humid night air pressing down on my lungs. Never once thinking this was probably their plan all along.

That they figured I would leave. That they might be waiting for me outside.

No, I was so focused on Maxon that I didn't think of anything else until I got into my car and nothing happened.

No light turned on. No sound came from the engine.

My body trembled violently.

My stuttered breath sounded like a scream splitting the air.

I slowly leaned over to the glove box and popped it open. My eyes shut and a muted sob lingered on my lips when I reached inside and couldn't find what should've been there.

What was *always* there.

My head dropped as I closed the glove box. I opened my eyes to see my tears splashing on the steering wheel like tiny devastations.

"Fuck you." The curse was nothing more than a breath. "Fuck you." Another breath ripped through me and I screamed, *"Fuck you."*

I jumped when my phone blared from the passenger seat and scrambled to pull it out of my purse. My fingers couldn't move fast enough to answer when I saw Einstein's name and face on the screen.

"Where is he?" I demanded.

"At Holloway."

Relief tore through me so fast that a sob sounded deep in my chest.

Multiple voices murmured words of shock before Dare spoke in a tone I hadn't heard in years. "We're headed there now. Tell me why. Tell me *everything.*"

"I don't have time," I said through the knot in my throat. "Moretti. Dare, it's Moretti. They're here—they've been stalking me. They've killed guys I've slept with."

He swore loudly.

"They were at the bar with me tonight. They did something to my car. My gun's gone."

"Where are you?" he yelled, the car accelerating nearly drowned him out.

"My car."

"Lib—*fuck.* Are you kidding me? Get back in the goddamn bar. We're coming to get you."

"I have *nothing.*"

"Damn it, Libby," he roared. "Run. Run to the bar. Now."

I grabbed my purse and was running as soon as my stiletto-covered feet touched the pavement.

The few people in the parking lot and hanging outside The Jack looked at me like I was insane. I didn't care.

They'd never understand what it meant to live in our world.

I reached for the double doors just as one swung open, sending me stumbling back and nearly knocking me on my ass.

I swore and shot my hand out to the side, reaching blindly for the building and losing my footing.

A large hand latched onto my bicep and pulled me upright. A harsh "Christ" met my ears at the same time my gaze landed on a dark, familiar stare.

"*Gabe.*"

He looked stunned and confused. "Rough night?"

I could hear my name being yelled from far away, and quickly lifted my phone to my ear. "I'm here."

"What the hell happened?" Dare growled.

"I-I fell."

The man Gabe had been drinking with was suddenly there beside us. I hadn't even noticed him until then.

He murmured something into his phone, then smacked Gabe's shoulder. "We going?"

Gabe looked from him to me, his expression darkening with worry by the second. "Are you okay?"

"Of course. I'm—"

Dare was talking, but I didn't hear anything he said.

I felt lightheaded and nauseous.

The pictures were flashing through my mind, the words on the notes screaming jarringly.

This is what happens to men who touch what's mine.

This is a few who have dared.

Who will be next?

My thoughts had instantly turned to Maxon . . . why wouldn't they?

But there was one right in front of me.

My stomach rolled. "Oh God, Gabe."

His eyebrows pulled tight. "What?"

I lifted a hand to my forehead and spun in a slow circle to look at my surroundings.

At the street. At the people around me.

"Meet me at Holloway," I said shakily into the phone.

Everyone began yelling, but I hung up.

I turned again to look at Gabe, who was still watching me warily. "I need you to take me somewhere. Now."

He laughed hesitantly. One of those crooked smiles lit his face for a brief second before disappearing. "Uh . . ."

"We don't have time to stand here. We have to leave."

The frantic edge of my voice didn't go unnoticed, and after a quick glance at his friend, he stepped closer. "Libby, what's going on?"

"I'll explain later, but we have to leave. Now. Right now. And my car—" I swallowed thickly and looked in the direction of my car. "We need to use your car." When he only stood there staring at me in bemusement, I gripped his arm and begged, "Gabe, *please.*"

His eyes searched mine for a second before he nodded. "Okay. Okay, yeah."

After a quick word with his friend, he placed his hand on the small of my back and led me across the street.

"What about—"

"He has another car." He shot me a look when we reached his truck, his features no longer pinched with worry and confusion. "You gonna tell me what's going on?"

"When we're driving." We needed to get away from The Jack as fast as possible.

Gabe didn't respond, only rubbed at his jaw and gave a single nod as he opened the door.

"There's a lot I can't tell you, and I'm sorry for that," I mumbled once we were off the main street. With a sobering breath, I turned to face him in my seat and told him the truth. "I know this is going to sound crazy, but the bottom line is, there are people stalking me, and they're killing people I've slept with."

Gabe barked out a laugh, then glanced over at me. "Funny." When I didn't respond or waver, his face fell.

I had to catch myself on the dashboard when he slammed on the brakes.

"Are you fucking kidding me?" he yelled.

"No, and I'm so sorry. But that's why I needed you to leave with me. And that's why we need to go where we're going now."

"People are literally killing guys you fucked?" he asked when he started driving again, his tone incredulous. "*Why?*"

"I don't—take a left up here—I don't know. It's this group that's been trying to control me for half my life because they're insane. But I swear nothing will happen to you if you just do what I ask you to."

"Christ." He loosened his tie until he could slip it over his head, then threw it into the back seat.

"Left. Gabe, *left.*"

I looked over my shoulder in the direction we should've gone when he turned right and kept going—taking us out of town—and froze.

Panic gripped me, slowly squeezing tighter and tighter until I could no longer breathe.

"Insane." He huffed. "I wouldn't call us insane. Well, not all of us anyway."

There on the back seat was a long, rectangular box filled with my nightmares. Blank white envelopes, a box of disposable gloves, Polaroid cartridges, and a Polaroid camera.

"We're passionate about keeping what belongs to us . . ."

I slowly lifted my gaze in time to see him smile at me.

"And you've always belonged to us, Libby."

The last thing I remember was lunging for him and the steering wheel before blinding pain exploded across my skull.

And then everything went dark.

Thirty-Eight

Maxon

TWO DAYS.

I hadn't known until now that two days could feel like a goddamn eternity.

Minutes felt like hours. Hours like days.

I'd gone months without her—even a year. But it'd never been like this.

Because it'd never been over. I'd never been the one ignoring the calls.

Throughout it all, I felt like I was endlessly breaking.

My body unwillingly putting itself together just to experience the pain all over again.

I thought I'd moved throughout the house. I thought I'd eaten. Maybe even showered and changed into someone else's clothes.

Whatever I'd done had been forced movements from the guys.

I didn't know where I was now. Only knew my guitar was resting in my hands and my phone was beside me.

She'd called. A few times.

Like she wanted to remind me she was still there, still holding my shattered heart in her hands.

As if I wasn't acutely aware.

Every minute that passed in the past two days had been spent physically keeping myself from going back to where I'd left it with her.

I looked up when someone hit my shoulder.

"Food's here," Lincoln said gently. "Let's go, you need to eat something today."

Maybe I hadn't eaten.

"I haven't eaten?" I asked when I stood, leaving my guitar and phone, and followed him across the main room toward the kitchen.

Huh. I don't remember coming to the main room.

"No, you have. Just thought it would be the fastest way to get you up."

Before I could respond, my attention drifted when the front door flung open and loud voices poured in.

"Hey," Einstein said loudly, drawing the word out. "There's our favorite rock star. Safe and sound."

Dare, Lily, and the twins followed her in.

I froze.

Waited for her.

Because she was always with them . . . except tonight.

A ragged breath wrenched from my chest, painful and exposing every bleeding scar.

"Food," one of the twins yelled and turned for the kitchen.

"What are you doing here?"

"We go where we're sent, rock star," Einstein said with a wry grin.

"Have you talked to Libby?" Dare asked, his voice gruff.

I looked between them and wondered if they knew what had happened. "Not for a couple days."

My answer brought them up short. Even Einstein seemed surprised.

"Want to tell me why you're here and not talking to my sister?" Dare asked in a low tone.

"You think I want to be here?" I bit out a harsh laugh. "I want to be with her. I want to still be engaged to her."

Dare and Einstein shared a look.

Another laugh scraped up my throat, baring my pain. "Your sister changed the locks on me, then tried to give me my ring back. Apparently there's some other guy who won't leave her for California like I do."

"Right," Einstein murmured, slowly bringing her tablet up to tap on it. "That would explain the zombie dark circles under your eyes. Don't worry. It's all part of the life."

"The hell does that—"

"Dare, get Libby on the phone," she continued. "Rock star boys, get me a workstation."

"Wait, what are you all doing here?"

"Apparently helping your maybe-maybe not fiancée protect you from some bad people. Sit down. We'll tell you all about it."

Pain and anger were replaced with every suspicion I'd had just days ago.

"What'd you just say?"

Einstein shot me a look. "There are bad people here. People who want Libby and therefore want you out of the picture. I *would* say I'm guessing, but I'm me, so I *know*, that you went through a breakup so she could protect you from them."

I'd known.

I'd fucking known . . . and she'd still managed to convince me. To push me away.

Goddamn it.

"You mean Moretti?" I asked numbly. "The pictures are from them, aren't they?"

Every Borello member stilled.

Einstein stopped tapping on her tablet. "What pictures?"

"It keeps going straight to voicemail," Dare said before I could respond.

Einstein bit out a curse. "Rock star boys . . . workstation. Now."

I turned in time to see the guys all staring at Einstein with confused looks.

"Computers. Tablets. Anything," Dare barked, and began clearing things off the bar.

I followed the others to the kitchen and watched Einstein tap furiously on her tablet while she set up at the bar. "Someone seemed to think I would've found you at the house you just bought," she murmured without slowing while laptops were set in front of her.

"Me?" I asked slowly, watching in fascination and slight worry as she opened all three laptops and logged into them without asking for the passwords.

As soon as she was in, the twin who wasn't eating started pulling up windows while Einstein went back to the tablet.

"Not talking to anyone else, rock star."

Considering people surrounded her, how was I supposed to know that?

"I bought that house for Libby and me. I don't want to be there without her."

"Fair enough—shit," she hissed. "Problem."

Dare shoved me out of the way, reaching for her tablet. "Is this the last one?"

"What are they doing?" Ledger asked.

I looked at the guys, still staring in stunned confusion.

But I didn't know what to say. I knew what this group of people really were, what they did—to a small extent—and I was just as confused.

I didn't know how all of them knew what to do—how they could hand things off to each other and pick up where the other left off.

And I had no fucking clue what was happening.

"Fuck," Dare yelled, throwing the tablet on the bar.

Einstein picked it up without a word and went back to tapping on it between typing on the laptops.

"What's going on?"

Dare turned on me, expression fierce and chest heaving with rough breaths. "Moretti were at The Jack. Tonight."

Ice splintered in my veins.

The floor fell out beneath me.

He tossed his hand in the direction of Einstein's tablet. "Libby's phone's off. Last tower it pinged off has her headed out of town."

Everything stopped.

Dare's words.

Time.

And in that eternal moment, I wanted to go back.

Back to when she was safe.

Back to when I made her smile and laugh.

Back to when I kissed her whenever I wanted.

Just *back*.

Time came rushing back, nearly knocking me to my knees when Dare spoke.

"They have her."

Thirty-Nine

Libby

MY HEAD WAS POUNDING. THE agonizing beat was made worse when I tried to lurch to my feet, Gabe's name ripping from my throat like a curse.

I cried out when I was jerked back to the floor. The rattling of chains sounded like trains crashing and reverberating in my skull.

I slowly lifted my hands to cradle my head and flinched when I heard movement in front of me.

I looked up and found aspirin and water next to my feet, and Gabe standing half a dozen feet from me, face hard and impassive as he watched me.

I ignored the first and tried to glare at the second.

The pain had my eyes slipping closed and my head falling back.

I wanted to scream.

I wanted to say his name.

I wanted to stand up and face off with him instead of sitting there like a weak, crumpled girl.

All I could do was whisper incoherently. "You can't . . . no. You're not a . . . Name is Gabe Anthony. Seen your credit ca—and business card. God, who're you?"

"Gabriel Anthony Moretti," he responded smoothly.

No, no, no.

Years of fear and heartache slammed into me, flooding my senses and leaving me lightheaded. Or maybe that was a response from the intense ache.

I dropped my head into my arms.

When he spoke again, there was a bite to his words. "Can't say I expected to see your hand weighed down with a diamond from a guy who just came back a few weeks ago."

I stilled.

I hadn't put my ring back on since the night Maxon left.

It had all been part of making the Moretti family think we were over.

I started to wonder how closely Gabe had been watching me and nearly laughed at the thought.

Everywhere. He'd been *everywhere.*

Including my apartment. My room. My bed. My damn bathroom.

Of course he'd known we were engaged.

"I've been with him all my life."

An amused huff came from him. "You told me. The rock star who was out getting his dick sucked on the road."

I looked up and snarled, "You know *nothing* about him."

"If you say so." His expression turned challenging. "You realize you and I had as much of a relationship as you had with him."

I ground my jaw. "We didn't have a relationship."

He slowly walked closer and dropped to a crouch in front of me, placing his hands on the wall behind me so he caged me in. "I've been in you until you screamed. We went our separate ways only to come together again. How's that any different than the two of you?"

"Fuck you."

He slanted his head and that crooked smile pulled at his mouth. "I have been." He dipped closer to whisper, "Only difference is, I was here. He wasn't." He pushed away from the wall and paced a few steps before turning on me again. "You made a mistake choosing him."

My mouth was open to say the only mistake I'd made was sleeping with the man in front of me, but I slowly shut it.

I tried to live without regrets, even if my actions cost me ten years away from the man I loved.

Maxon could never be a mistake, but I regretted bringing him into this—deeply.

Mom was right. He would be a casualty, defending him would ensure that.

And there had already been so many . . .

"You were so convincing," I whispered. "I was worried you'd end up like one of the guys in those pictures. I felt terrible that you were linked to me at all." I glanced at him and let him see how betrayed I felt. "I wanted to protect you. Then to find out you're the man I've hated all along."

Gabe cleared his throat and let his gaze fall to the concrete floor.

I'd spent a decade worrying over the Moretti family and praying I'd gotten away from them. And one of them had been there the whole time.

He'd been inside me.

Oh God.

My stomach churned with acid and my chin wavered. "You killed . . . How many men have you killed because of me?"

Gabe's mouth twitched in frustration. "You really want to know?"

I was afraid I already knew . . . but I had to be sure.

I had to know what I caused.

When I dipped my head in a nod, he said, "All but one."

A cry clawed out of the recesses of my chest and my head fell into my hands.

"I had to . . ."

"You had to what?" I yelled. "Kill innocent men? Stalk me? *What?*"

He sent me a placating look then reached for his phone when it chimed. With a frustrated grimace, he glanced around the large room then bent to push the aspirin and water toward me. "I'm sorry about your head. I couldn't let you know where we were going, and I couldn't bring you in here conscious."

"You should've brought me in here dead. I will never belong to you."

"Oh, Libby . . ." A smile broke free, haunting and threatening. "You can't belong to me if we've never met."

Stunned confusion momentarily replaced my grief and fury.

"You think *I* ordered the deaths of the men you fucked?" His dark laugh sent chills up my spine.

"What . . . I don't—" I tried to press into the wall when he leaned in so his mouth was at my ear, but I couldn't move anywhere he wasn't.

"You don't know me, but I know everything about you. Soon, you'll understand why." His mouth ghosted across my jaw when he pushed away. His gaze searched me, devouring me in a way that felt more intimate than we had ever been.

As though suddenly some shared nights that had been the epitome of a casual hookup meant more to him.

I suddenly meant more to him.

Like he had a claim on me from nights where we'd remained emotionally detached.

Just before he turned, his mouth twitched, the sight making me choke on my breath. "See you around, Libby."

The stare, the smirk, the challenge—they said so many things.

For years, he'd been biding his time . . . and now he was done.

He was the hunter staring at his prize.

A predator stalking his prey.

A man ready to fight.

And I'd had the fight all wrong.

I stared in the direction he'd gone for countless seconds before frantically searching the surrounding space for something—*any-thing*—to help free me.

But there was nothing.

The lengths of chain securing my hands and feet to the wall were long—a couple feet at least. But the cuffs around each wrist and ankle were so tight they bordered on painful.

One gave the illusion of freedom. One mocked there was no escape.

I grasped the other ends of the cuffs where they were secured to a pipe in the wall and prayed for a weak spot. But before I could test them, a door opened.

I dropped the chains and twisted so my back was to the wall and I was facing the sound of confident footfalls.

Gabe's parting words had stunned me . . . the man walking toward me floored me.

I'd spent two separate nights with him, and the last one had been years ago. But he wasn't the kind of guy you forgot. A little dangerous, a lot mysterious.

Same with his name . . . it was unforgettable because it was such an oxymoron for the man himself. He exuded darkness in everything—including the bedroom.

I knew from experience he was the kind of guy you told yourself you would only sleep with once, then years later somehow found yourself slipping away from his extravagant hotel room again.

"What are you—"

I sucked in a sharp breath.

No.

No, no, no.

"Christian." His name was a breath. A denial. A plea for this not to be happening.

Tension pressed around me like a cocoon. The vaguely familiar sensation prodded at my mind.

Dark.

Heavy.

Wrong.

I risked a quick glance to the other side of the room, where Gabe left through, to see if he had come back. But there was no one.

I looked at Christian when he stopped in front of me. Dread filled my stomach like bricks.

His expression was a mixture of rage and need. "Elizabeth."

Oh God.

"Always wanted to see you chained and waiting for me."

A cold sweat broke out across my body.

The dread morphed until I felt like I would either faint or scream until the rage pumping through my veins burned out.

My breaths turned ragged. "You . . ."

His head listed, making him look so much like Gabe that it made me falter until he opened his mouth. "You shouldn't look surprised. After all, you belong to me."

I stood up and was thrashing against the chains as soon as the last word left his tongue, trying to get to him and screaming indecipherably.

My head was suddenly heavy and dropped. I stumbled forward, the chains nearly yanking my legs out from under me.

Christian steadied me and walked me to the wall so I could sit, not reacting to my heavy-tongued curses or the way I was attempting to get away from him.

The throbbing was back and worse than when I'd woken, and tears pricked at my eyes as I cradled my head again.

"Why are you doing this?" I finally asked when I no longer felt like I was going to pass out.

"Haven't you gotten the message yet? You belong to me."

I slowly lifted my head and tried to focus on him. "I will never belong to you."

His eyes widened before narrowing. There was so much anger and hatred burning there, making him look unhinged.

Christian suddenly lunged forward and roughly hauled me from the floor. My cry filled the space when he yanked me closer and something in my arm popped.

"You belong to me." His eyes raked over me as he pressed his body close to mine. "Funny thing about deals . . . they have to be honored. Especially when they're bound in blood."

"Fuck your deal," I cried out.

Using my arm, he slammed me back against the wall and reached for his back pocket.

I made myself stand tall.

Made myself lock my jaw and hold my head high.

But my body nearly crumpled with relief when he pulled out rolled-up papers and threw them at me.

I let them fall to the floor.

"My deal?" he asked in a deceptively soft tone and nodded to the discarded papers. "It's our deal, Elizabeth. And did you really think some guns and information would be a fair trade?"

My mind whirled to eleven years ago—to what Dare had done to get me out of the deal. The pain racing through my arm had tears flowing freely down my cheeks, but my words were laced with venom. "I'm not something to be traded. I'm not property to be given away."

"Your old man didn't feel the same way."

The jab would've had me stumbling backward if I hadn't already been pressed to the wall.

"When your brother tried to change the contract, my family wanted to come down here and obliterate the Borello name and take you with us when we left. But I urged them to give it time, positive you would still make the right choice. When you didn't come on your own, I allowed your indiscretions since you already belonged to me. But now it's time you appreciate what you've been given. Me."

I laughed bitterly. "Appreciate someone who kills innocent men?"

"They touched what belongs to me," he growled.

"I don't want to *appreciate* you. I don't want a life with you. I don't want anything from a piece-of-shit Moretti."

His face fell into a calm so terrifying. "Watch yourself."

"I'm not afraid of you."

"Good." He stepped forward and angled his head so his mouth was just above mine. "Wouldn't want you afraid of your husband."

I wanted to scoff at the absurdity of his words.

Remind him the deal had changed.

But I couldn't move.

I forgot how to breathe.

It was there in his tone. He'd been waiting for this exact moment, to tease me with the secret he'd been sitting on for years and watch my reaction.

His lips brushed against mine when he said, "Let's educate you."

Forty

Maxon

"**E**INSTEIN, I NEED SOMETHING," DARE bit out.

"You say that like I'm not trying." Einstein swore under her breath. "If I had my computers, this would be going so much faster."

"Not wasting time getting them."

Einstein already had three laptops in front of her. Multiple, different windows were opened on each, and she was tapping furiously on her tablet.

She hadn't looked away from a screen since that first call to Libby had gone straight to voicemail.

I'd been calling her nearly every minute since, but nothing had changed.

"I'm just fucking sitting here," Dare growled from where he was pacing.

"We're all sitting here," I yelled.

"That's my sister they—"

"She's my goddamn fiancée." I ended the next call to her and got in Dare's face, my jaw aching from how much pressure I was putting on it. "You're the one who demanded we stay put until we have a lead. There's no lead, so we're all still fucking here."

"I can't lose her."

I dropped my head, my tone lowering with it. "If you think for one damn minute that I *can*—"

"You've left before."

I shoved him. "You think I wanted that?" He stepped up and tried to steady himself when I shoved him again. "You think every day wasn't agony? I did what she needed."

"Bullshit. You left for you." He threw out his arms and looked around. "Looks like you're good at it too."

I lunged at him but my fist only met air as I was dragged back by Lincoln and Jared.

One of the twins was in front of Dare with a hand to his chest, whispering harshly.

"She held me at arm's length for years because of the Moretti shit, but she's always meant everything to me. I'll do anything to find her. Fucking anything."

"You left when she pushed you. Then she was taken." His lip curled in a sneer. "She would still be here if you'd stayed."

"This is on *me*?" I huffed and shrugged the guys off me when Dare turned away. "You dealt with these Morettis so she could have a life with me, then ignored her worries about them a week and a half ago." I beat my hand on my chest and yelled, "I'm the one who noticed something was happening. I'm the one who tried to help her. She did everything to convince me it wasn't them—to make me believe we were over. I never would've left otherwise."

"I didn't deal with them for you." He looked over his shoulder, his mouth twisted in disgust. "I did it so she could have a life *she* wanted."

"Someone do something useful and call Conor and Kieran."

Everyone shouted they were calling Conor within a second of Einstein's request.

"I've already got it," one of the twins said. "Call Kieran."

The other twin looked to Dare, his face white with horror. "Come on . . ."

"Fuck you if you think Lily's calling him," he said on a growl, then spoke into his phone. "Mom, tell me everything you know about Moretti."

"Son of a bitch." The second twin started pacing and slowly brought his phone to his ear, then glared at Lily. "If Kieran kills me, you owe me so much food."

"Yeah, of course, Diggs," Lily murmured. "Only the biggest sandwiches for you."

Diggs smiled and fist-bumped Lily. "Hell yeah, nerd."

The entire exchange went down in about twenty seconds.

I glanced at my bandmates. Their confusion had continued to grow since the Borellos arrived. I shrugged. "I've heard Kieran's a scary motherfucker."

Lincoln nodded, then looked to the other two. "Do you feel like we're missing something?"

Jared made a grunting noise.

"Oh yeah," Ledger said. "Why does that guy get sandwiches?"

I rolled my eyes and walked over to Dare when he hung up and stepped close to Einstein and Lily.

"Mom's on her way here. She's pissed that she's going to set foot on Holloway land."

"The fuck?" I hissed. "Your mom's worried about where we are and not what's happening to her own fucking daughter? What the hell is wrong with—"

"Their mom knows Dare will get her back, rock star." Einstein sighed, her attention never wavering from the computer when she mumbled, "She probably said their dad was rolling in his grave too."

Dare gave a confirming nod.

Despite the weight pressing on my chest, my mouth twitched into a brief smile.

Libby had said nearly those exact words the night the guys threw their first party here.

"Diggs," Dare called out. "Kieran?"

From the smile on the twin's face, Kieran hadn't answered.

Diggs shrugged. "Straight to voicemail."

"He's working," Lily whispered.

The other twin, Maverick, tapped on the counter and nodded in agreement with what Lily said. "Yeah. Yeah, send it." He cleared his throat and glanced around. "We're at Holloway, man. Yeah, I know."

"What?" Dare demanded as soon as Maverick hung up.

Einstein sat straighter, her fingers flying even faster over one of the laptops.

"Conor's coming. He's not happy about where we are."

"None of us are," Dare ground out.

"Hey," Ledger and Lincoln called out resentfully.

"Did he know something?" Dare asked over them.

Maverick sucked in a sharp breath, like he was preparing to give bad news. "He's known about the stalking. Was helping Libby with it."

I don't know who had a worse reaction. Dare or me.

Dare's frustrated curses filled the kitchen.

Rage overshadowed everything else, and soon I didn't see the kitchen or the house at all.

All I could see was Libby pushing me away.

All I could hear were her lies.

All I knew was the frustration of the last week.

And she really *had* been going to someone else.

I didn't know I'd grabbed a barstool and thrown it across the living room until Lincoln grabbed my shoulders and shook me, yelling at me to calm down.

"Mom knows?" Dare roared. "She fucking knew and didn't say

a word?"

I turned in time to see Maverick give Dare an unsure look. "That's what he said."

"Doesn't matter who did or didn't know, we need to be glad someone did," Einstein cut in, her voice an orchestrated calm. "Conor did some of my work for me. Jesus Christ, Dare, you knew all this was in here?"

"All what?"

We all crowded behind her to read the scanned document she was scrolling through, but as soon as we got behind her, she was moving onto another window.

"Maxon, what were those pictures of?"

I gripped the back of my neck. "Libby and uh . . . Libby and me. They had notes on the bottom. Like, 'You've always belonged to me.' Shit like that."

"Okay, think we can safely say it's one of the grandsons," she murmured.

"Vince's grandsons?" Dare asked, dropping low to look at the pictures of the men on her screen. "Like one of the ones Libby was supposed to marry?"

Einstein made an affirmative tone in her throat. "After Vince died, the family didn't keep themselves as hidden as before. Conor got a list of all the men in the family, which shows them actively living in Chicago . . ."

"You don't think they are," I guessed from the way her voice trailed off.

"After reading the contract . . . no."

"You read the contract?" Dare asked, shock coating his words.

Einstein started to glance at Dare over her shoulder before focusing on the screens again. It was the closest she'd come to looking away from them. "You say that like you haven't."

"I haven't," he said roughly. "They refused to let me see it."

"Think that's something you should've demanded to see," she

whispered.

"I've seen him," I said quickly, interrupting whatever Dare started to say.

Everyone stilled.

No one spoke for a few seconds until Einstein finally asked, "You have?"

I stared at the guy on the screen, trying to put a memory with the face. "I don't know where, but I've seen him. Recently."

"This is good and bad."

I drove my hands into my hair. "How is this good?"

Einstein pressed her fingers to her eyes and let out a quick breath, then went back to one of the other laptops, leaving the picture of the man up there. "Because it means she *was* taken by a Moretti." Before any of us could react, she said, "They won't hurt her, but . . ."

I looked to Dare and Lily when she didn't continue.

"*Einstein,*" Dare yelled.

"We're also safe," she said distractedly, then cleared her throat. "Borellos. Maxon isn't because of who he is to Libby."

"But what, Einstein?" I begged.

She finally glanced away from the screens long enough to look at us. "That guy? Gabe. He's a regular at the bar."

Recognition hit. "That's where I saw him."

She looked at me warily then squared her shoulders, like she was about to deliver bad news. "I hate to do this to you, but it's not like you didn't know it was happening anyway. I'm also positive they slept together when you were gone. And when I say positive, I mean they did."

My hands slowly slid from my hair and fell heavily to my sides. I stumbled back a step.

Einstein noticed the look on my face and rolled her eyes. "I meant when you were living in California and touring. Not last week."

I'd known.

But knowing and someone telling me were two different things.

Seeing one of the men talking with Libby was something I never thought I'd have to do.

"And if Libby slept with him," Einstein continued, "then this went from bad to *shit*." She switched windows on one of the laptops, bringing up the contract, and turned the laptop toward us. "You should read this."

Under the arrangement agreed upon by Vincent Moretti and Lucas Borello, the following must be complied:

The Moretti and Borello families will refrain from violence against one another immediately following the signing of this contract.

The Moretti and Borello families will come to each other's aid during times of distress. Including, but not limited to: Outside threats, financial struggles, emotional grief, and work crises.

The Moretti family will discontinue retaliation and forgive any wrongdoing made by the Borello family in the past. Including, but not limited to: rebelling against, and withdrawing from, the Willow Gang under unsavory terms.

The Borello family will offer their daughter, Elizabeth Borello, to the Moretti family as a guarantee of peace and unity between the two families. Guidelines as follows:

Elizabeth Borello, hereinafter referred to as "Elizabeth", has until the day she turns twenty-one to join the Moretti family on her own terms. By joining the Moretti family, Elizabeth will marry a grandson of Vincent Moretti's, whose name will be kept from this contract and the Borello family until the wedding for his own safety.

If Elizabeth fails to do as instructed, in order to retain the peace between the two signed parties, she will be transferred to the Moretti Family by a person of the Moretti family's choosing.

In the unfortunate occurrence of the above paragraph, the Moretti/Borello union will still be seen as lawful in the eyes of the State the day following Elizabeth's twenty-first birthday. At that time, a lawyer of the Moretti family's choosing will sign this contract.

The Moretti/Borello union will be seen as lawful in the eyes of God when the two parties subjected to the arrangement willingly consummate their marriage. At that time, a priest of the Moretti family's choosing will sign and finalize this contract.

The terms stated above are effective immediately upon signing by both parties. The terms are bound once the contract is finalized. This is a blood-binding contract. If death should occur to either of the signed parties, the contract will remain intact through the next blood relative.

This contract is void only upon the death of one or both parties subjected to the arrangement. If the contract is broken beforehand by either family, it will be considered an act of war.

Below were all four signatures.

I fell onto one of the barstools. "Fuck."

Forty-One

Libby

"I DON'T CARE," I SHOUTED when Christian finished reading the contract out loud. "I don't care what it says. We changed the terms. That one is void."

"Doesn't work that way." Christian laughed darkly. "Whatever you thought your brother did, I assure you he didn't. You belong to me."

"No. No, I don't—I never. You can't do this to me," I cried out. "You can't claim me and then decide how the rest of my life is going to play out because you think you *own* me. That stupid piece of paper means *nothing* to me."

He pulled me closer and yelled, "That was a contract signed in blood, Elizabeth. You and I are the only things binding our families—the only things keeping them from fighting."

"That's not entirely true," Gabe whispered as he emerged from the shadows.

"Screw you and your fucked-up family," I yelled at him.

Gabe's mouth twitched into a crooked smirk.

My next scream was nearly as piercing as the sound of the gunshot tearing through the warehouse.

Christian stumbled back, roaring in pain and clutching his shoulder.

What . . .

What the hell?

I couldn't process what was happening.

There had been so many shocks tonight that I couldn't grasp this new one. It was as if my mind was trying to protect me by filling itself with mundane things instead.

The only thing I could think in that moment was Dare would give me so much shit if he found out I'd screamed . . .

"The hell are you doing?" Christian snarled.

Gabe rounded on him, his smirk growing broader. "To answer your questions from earlier, *Elizabeth*, yes, I had to stalk you and kill innocent men. But I'm not the man you've hated all along. That award goes to this man here." He lifted his arm and shot again.

I barely flinched, and only cast Christian a quick glance to see him bleeding from both shoulders and struggling to stay upright.

"Cousin. My partner at the firm. Underboss of Willow Gang," Gabe continued dryly. "He ordered every picture to be taken and delivered to you. Ordered the deaths of the men you slept with. And he snuck into your bed a few nights ago."

"Oh God . . ."

Gabe smirked. "I had to hear about it. In detail."

My stomach rolled violently.

The box in Gabe's truck. The film, camera, and envelopes . . . it hadn't occurred to me someone else might be behind any part of it.

I should've known.

The presence Christian exuded—so dark and heavy and wrong—it'd been in my room that night.

I'd felt it. *Dismissed* it.

A growl built from deep within Christian's chest when Gabe stood before him.

"You don't deserve to be next in line. You also don't deserve to be the one in the contract."

"You don't get to decide—"

"Don't I?" Gabe slowly advanced, making Christian stagger back. "It said a grandson, which I am. It said they had to consummate the marriage." Gabe smiled wide, making him look feral. His stare dragged to me for a few seconds. "Which we did. Over and over. After all, you had me watching her for years."

Christian lunged just as another gunshot rang through the warehouse.

He stopped suddenly, clutching at his chest and staring wide-eyed before dropping to his knees.

A wet cough worked up his throat, spraying blood from his mouth.

Gabe stepped directly in front of him, all cruel smiles and greedy stares. "That fourth signature? I made the call for it." Gabe shrugged slightly. "We already had the contract signed and delivered back to us before you decided it was worth your time to meet her. We've just been waiting for you to make a move desperate enough to warrant being taken out. For example . . . your decisions the last couple weeks."

"I'll kill you," Christian choked out.

Gabe laughed, short and mocking. "Thought we already covered that you have clean hands." He bent his head closer and said, "I'll take care of the family better than you ever could."

Christian's face twisted in rage and pain, his mouth opened to retaliate, when Gabe put a bullet through his forehead.

I jolted when Gabe suddenly appeared in front of me, brow furrowed and eyes searching me.

"You look like you're going into shock."

Did I?

It wasn't the first murder to happen in front of me.

Not by a long shot.

But I'd felt blindsided tonight. Repeatedly.

"I was unaware you two were related. And Moretti." My eyebrows slowly lifted and a breath of a laugh escaped my lips. "Then you started picking each other off in front of me. And somewhere in the middle of that, I found out I was married to a goddamn psychopath."

Gabe looked to where I'd gestured to Christian, then back to me. That crooked smile I used to beg to see making an appearance. "Not."

"Not what?"

"Weren't you listening? You were always married to me."

I stumbled back into the wall, my head spinning as I tried to remember what was said. "No. No, no . . . oh—*shit*." I flinched when he palmed my waist and tried to move away, but he crowded me in place.

"I won't hurt you."

A maniacal laugh burst from my chest. "Excuse me for not believing you."

Anger briefly flashed across his face. "I never hurt you before tonight."

"You lied to me," I bit out. "You let me think I was free for *eleven years*."

"There are prices to pay for trying to back out on a blood oath, Libby. Freedom is usually one of them."

"We didn't back out. Dare—"

"I'm aware of the cataclysm your brother was at fault for."

I blinked quickly. "What? He . . . what? He didn't do anything."

"He almost started a war because he was too young and careless to think about the consequences of his actions." He shrugged, the movement jerky with frustration and bringing him closer when his body relaxed. "But he was the only blood male, so what he said went."

"What is that supposed to mean?"

Gabe stared at me for a moment, stunned that I clearly didn't know yet another thing. Leaning forward, he growled in my ear, "There's a reason your brother was made boss at thirteen. Didn't any of you think someone else would better fit the job?"

I looked past him, denial and confusion warring within me.

"Blood *had* to fill the position to keep our contracts and alliances alive. Dare was the only blood male. No one else was allowed to take the position. The older gens knew that."

"No . . . no, that's not—"

"Read the damn contract, Libby."

"Dare would've told me," I yelled at him, pushing him away.

He spread his arms wide, gun still hanging from one of his hands. "You sure about that?"

"Fuck you."

"If he knew," he said calmly, conceding. "Vince came back *livid* after his visit when your old man died. Kept yelling about your brother and how he was going to try to break the contract."

"Of course he wanted to break the contract. For *me*."

Gabe looked at me like I'd lost my mind. "It's a blood contract, Libby. Do you know what breaking one means? Did you read the last line?" He stepped closer and lowered his tone. "War, Libby. Death."

I blinked slowly when I realized what he was saying—what his family had done.

"He was thirteen," Gabe continued. "Not hard to think he might not have been told by the older gen why he became boss. That no one else was allowed to. But before Vince could remind your brother how serious our arrangement was, he stopped fighting Vince on it."

"And then Vince died," I said through gritted teeth. "And your uncle let Dare break the contract. He knew Dare had no idea what he was doing and he *welcomed* it. Your uncle wanted Dare to start a war."

"Do you see a war going on between us?" he asked in a dangerously low tone. "Are Borellos disappearing? Do you see them dropping all around you? There *is* no war because we figured your brother didn't have a fucking clue what was really going on."

I stared blankly at Gabe when he turned and holstered his gun as he started pacing. His long legs easily eating up the space. "I don't . . . I don't understand." I shook my head, trying to sort through the chaos swirling around inside. "Why not tell him? Why not retaliate after he did it—or after I didn't go to Chicago?"

He stopped suddenly.

For a long time, he stayed like that. Back to me, body still, barely showing even a hint that he was breathing.

"It was obvious he would've done anything to have you taken out of the contract . . . and that's not something *anyone* can do. We knew he would've taken it to a point we didn't want it to go, so my uncle let him think he could have it his way." He turned to face me and folded his arms over his chest. "Dare gave us information and weapons. Helping each other is in the contract—not that we needed the help—but he wasn't offering anything that we didn't already have a right to."

I lifted my chin. "And me?"

The corner of his mouth lifted into that crooked smile. "You?" A breath of a laugh left him. "Jesus, Libby . . . Moretti almost went to war against each other over you."

"I'm sorry you didn't."

He shot me a cold glare. "Nearly half of us wanted to send someone after you. To bring you to Chicago and keep you locked away until you broke. Until you *begged* to be allowed into the family."

"I would've fought my way out, killing as many of you as I could."

"I don't doubt it." For a split second, amusement and pride flashed through his eyes. "The other half was sure it would have the younger generation of Borellos coming after us. Once again, starting a war."

"And which side were you on?" I asked, my tone part challenge, part taunt.

"The contract said if you didn't come to us, you would be transferred to us by a person of our choosing." He held out his arms. "I've been here . . . and you're still here."

I tried to hide the horror now pulsing through me as everything began clicking in place. "Wait, you? What about Christian?"

Rage burned in his eyes. "He's the only son of Vince's oldest son. He's next in line by birth . . . but no one thought he deserved it—including his old man. It's been in place for me to take over since the contract was written. You learn a lot about yourself and your limits when you're forced to watch your wife fuck other men for years."

"I am not your *wife*."

Gabe was suddenly there, in my space with his face directly in front of my own. Body pressed to mine and hands on the wall, caging me in. "We have an arrangement bound in blood. And it says you're mine."

"*No*," I yelled, my voice getting louder and higher when I continued. "Why didn't Vince or your uncle tell Dare what the contract was? If he would've seen it, he wouldn't have done what he did. If *I* would've seen it, I wouldn't have thought all these years—" A sob wrenched from my chest.

That I could've had a future with Maxon.

That I'd really escaped the whole thing.

"Thought what?" he asked, goading. "That you weren't married? That you weren't already fucking your husband? That you weren't *finalizing* the contract the first night you slept with me?"

My stomach rolled and my head felt light.

I'd *tried* to live life without regrets. Who knew the tall, dark, handsome strangers in my bar would end up being the biggest regrets of my life?

"I hate you," I breathed.

"Dare never saw the contract because we didn't have it at the time," he mumbled after a few moments. "The lawyer did. He'd had it from the day it was written. When you turned twenty-one, I got a call that he signed it. He told me to let him know when the next step was completed, and he would take care of getting the priest's signature."

I slapped him.

He looked stunned before his eyes set in anger.

His hand shot out to catch mine before it could connect with his face a second time.

"You tricked me into sleeping with you to get a fucking signature," I yelled and tried to wrench my hand free.

"Is that right?" He dipped his head close, his mouth grazing my jaw when he whispered, "I seem to remember it going a little differently. You flirted relentlessly. You gave me your number. You asked if I was going to take you back to my place."

"Stop."

His knee pressed between my thighs. "You *begged*."

"*Stop.*"

"And that was just the first time."

"*Shut up.*" I thrashed against him and finally got my hand free enough to push him away.

Instead of the amused or taunting look I'd been expecting, he looked furious. "And the entire damn time, you just wanted placeholders until some guy came back. But *I* tricked *you*."

A harsh laugh left me. "I never said I wanted anything from you other than what we had. It was sex. Nothing more." I waved a hand at him and curled my lip. "And don't act so hurt now. You never pretended it meant anything to you. You never pretended I did. Not until now."

His face fell. Again, he looked at me like he didn't know how I couldn't understand the situation. "I was trying to figure out how

to get to know *my wife* when she had no idea we were married,"
he yelled. "I was trying to figure out how to gain her trust and
get her to fall for me, all the while knowing how she would react
when she found out my name. I was fucking pissed off that I had
to watch my wife flirt with other men—and know that I couldn't
do anything about it without telling her everything."

"Years. You were there for years and you never said anything."

"Would it have changed anything?"

"In your favor?" I wanted to laugh in his face. I wanted to tell
him he was delusional. But the genuine curiosity and want pooling
in his eyes stopped me. "Gabe, you've been stalking me. You've
been scaring me and killing guys I knew for one night." I held his
hardened stare and clenched my teeth. "A *night*. You married me
without my consent. You've lied to me about who you are. And you
have me chained to a wall." My chest pitched with a ragged breath.
"The guy I used to beg to smile? I have no idea who that is. I don't
know who you are. But even if all that was taken away . . . there's
still Maxon."

He nodded slowly and started to turn but stopped to look at me
again. "I didn't say anything because after a while, I had to come to
terms with the fact that you'd hate me when you found out. And
I lived for Friday nights. They were the only nights I could let you
see me. The only time I could talk to you. I *craved* the nights I took
you back to my place. And I knew those would be gone when you
found out. It would go one of two ways after that . . . I'd drag you
back to Chicago kicking and screaming, and you'd hate me. Or
the war I'd been trying to prevent all along would finally happen."

"So what now?" I asked when he started slowly pacing again.
"If you keep me here, my family will find me. If you take me
anywhere else, I'll spend every waking minute thinking of how
to escape until I finally get the chance. Either way, you will never
own any part of me."

"I've never wanted to *own* you, but that doesn't mean you don't belong to me. And like I said, we *are* passionate about keeping what belongs to us." He stopped a few feet from me and faced me. "This is the one time I agree with my cousin's methods."

My brows pulled tight and stomach knotted when he pulled out his phone and tapped on it.

"Alive, Maxon will always be in the way, Libby." He flashed me a quick smile. "I appreciate you telling me where he is."

The room tilted. *"No."*

Gabe held the phone to his ear, his expression settling into stone as he waited.

"Gabe, *no*. Please . . . please, I'll do anything. I'll go to Chicago. I won't run. Just don't do this."

His eyes locked on me. "Kill him."

Forty-Two

Maxon

"**I**'VE GOT SOMETHING," EINSTEIN MURMURED.

I looked up, my movements slow as I tried to process what I'd read in the contract—what it possibly meant for Libby. For us.

"There's nothing for Moretti, but Christian Daniel and Gabe Anthony—both partial names of a couple of our Moretti boys—have a firm in Raleigh. They also have apartments, and Christian has a warehouse on the way there in a very secluded place. Not sketchy at all."

"We're hitting that first," Dare said as they all moved into action. When I stood, he put a hand to my shoulder. "We'll get her."

"Get your fucking hand off me."

His stare hardened. "I can't lose another part of my family. You'll get in the way and guarantee that."

Before I could respond, Einstein said, "Sloppy, sloppy, sloppy . . . not even checking the property first." She clicked her tongue, her eyes glued to the screen and fingers unnaturally still where they rested on the keyboard. "Someone's trying to sneak up on us, Dare."

Dare stepped up behind her, looking at the live feed she was watching.

"One of ours?"

"No. Looks like he was sent to keep us here. Walked on too. Guess he didn't want us to hear the car or see headlights."

Dare looked over his shoulder at me and the guys. "Are you expecting anyone?" When we didn't respond fast enough, he ticked off, "Food, friends, manager. Anyone."

"No," we all murmured.

He looked back at the screens. "Maverick. Diggs. Take care of it."

"Hell yes. Wait," Diggs said, putting his hands out and looking around with a devastated expression. "This is the first time without bandanas. Should we have a moment of silence? This is huge and kinda sad."

"Jesus, Diggs. Go," Dare barked.

I watched the twins leave, then asked, "What the hell do bandanas have to do with someone coming onto the property?"

Dare pulled the neck of his shirt up so it was resting just below his eyes and gave me a sidelong glance before letting it fall into place.

Knowing who he was, it was oddly unsettling.

"Wait, that's our property?" Ledger asked, just now catching on. "You're watching us?"

"How long have you been watching us?" Jared demanded, his tone hinting he was more impressed than annoyed.

Einstein grinned over her shoulder as everything on the screens started disappearing.

"I think I love her," Lincoln whispered next to me.

"Don't go there."

Einstein shut the laptops and hopped off the barstool, her head already down and fingers flying over her tablet. "Dare and Lily, be ready to go. You," she said, stopping next to me. "You're going with

Conor and me . . . I'll get you a weapon."

"He's not even here," I said through clenched teeth.

And he was the last person I wanted to see.

Just then the door flung open and a massive brick wall of a guy stepped in, face impassive as he gestured behind him. "Dead guy out front."

The guy from Libby's apartment . . .

"Is *this* Conor?" I asked on a stunned breath.

"Yep." Einstein turned toward him, calling out behind her, "Let's go."

"You. I'm gonna fucking kill you."

Conor held up his hands in surrender. "Man, it wasn't my idea. Swear there's nothing going on between us. You gotta take it up with Libby when we get her back."

I followed Einstein to the door. "Fuck you."

He nodded. "Deserved."

My bandmates were whispering curses of shock and confusion and trying to figure out what was happening and where I was going, when Ledger suddenly laughed. "Holy shit, no way. We're being Punk'd."

If only it were that simple.

Forty-three

Libby

I WASN'T SURE HOW LONG it had been since the phone call.

But I'd stopped screaming at Gabe that I was going to kill him.

I'd stopped yelling my hate for him.

He'd started pacing again. At some point, his gun had made it back into his hand.

And the frequency that he checked his watch was increasing, as was his agitation.

"Is he not checking in?" I asked, taunting him. "Did your guy not make it? Or maybe he failed . . ."

He shot me a warning look, but continued pacing.

After another few minutes and a dozen watch checks, he grabbed his phone and called.

I knew there was no answer the moment Gabe's feet stilled.

He rubbed his forehead with the back of the hand holding the gun before letting it drop heavily to his side. With a harsh breath, he turned and charged toward me.

I grounded myself and prepared for the hit, but it never came.

He stopped right before me and holstered the gun before roughly turning me to the side.

My heart took off when one of the ankle cuffs fell away, but I didn't react in any way to give my thoughts away.

But he knew them. Of course he did.

The instant both feet were freed, he shoved me face first against the wall and drove his shoulder into my back so I couldn't move.

I tried to clear my mind. Tried to only focus on what was crucial so I could make a move when the cuffs dropped from my wrists.

And *failed*.

Steel rattling.

Maxon, I'm sorry.

Slight shift in Gabe's stance.

Maxon, forgive me.

Another hitch in Gabe's breathing.

Maxon, I love you.

I was suddenly yanked away from the wall and dragged away, my stunned and horrified gaze dropping to my hands.

In front of me. Two sets of handcuffs now on each wrist. Gabe's white-knuckled grip on the long lengths of chain connecting my hands.

I looked to the door Christian had walked through earlier then to the gun in Gabe's other hand again, my mind racing as I thought of dozens of scenarios.

None of them ended in my favor.

Others ended in unknown.

Better the unknown than the alternative.

I fought against his hold, pulling back until I could feign stumbling and falling backward.

Gabe's grasp slipped. He lunged for me at the same time I pushed forward and rushed him. I twisted away from his reach and jumped onto his back, bent and ready for me.

Before he could react, I locked my ankles around his waist and looped the chains around his throat, pulling tight and crossing my hands over each other behind the back of his neck.

The gun clattered noisily to the concrete floor when he stood, his hands going to the steel digging into his throat.

I pulled tighter and leaned closer, my teeth clenched tight and voice trembling when I said, "My family's gonna come through a door any minute. They'll make your death slow and painful for what you've done to me over the years . . . for the last two weeks . . . for tonight. If I haven't killed you first."

He yanked on the sides of the chains, only succeeding in tightening the twisted metal.

"This is for every man you killed. This is for Maxon. And this is for me." Tightening my thighs on his hips, I sucked in deep breath and flung all my body weight back, throwing us off-balanced and sending us crashing down to the floor.

Just before we hit, I released the breath, shut my eyes, and made my body go limp.

It was such a bad fucking idea.

My head cracked on the concrete, sending blinding pain spider-webbing across my skull and black spots dancing across my vision when I could see at all.

What air remained in my lungs was forced from them when Gabe landed on me.

It felt like he'd shattered every bone in my body.

My head lolled to the side, and a weak cry left my lips when I saw the gun just feet from me.

I unwrapped the chains from Gabe's neck and struggled to stand when he rolled off me, sucking in deep breaths that sounded like inverted screams. When my legs continued giving out, I crawled to the gun and gripped it in my trembling hand.

Each breath was agony.

I felt seconds from passing out.

The image of the enraged Gabe wouldn't stand still.

But I knew he was standing. I knew he was unfurling to his full height. And I knew that murderous gaze was locked on me.

I lifted the gun and prayed to God I was aiming at the man in front of me.

I gritted my teeth. "Contract void."

He lunged.

I fired.

Forty-Four

Libby

SANK BACK ON THE floor, crying out when the movement shifted parts of my body that ached and screamed in protest.

Two Moretti were dead on the floor of the warehouse . . . and I didn't know if that made the contract void, or if it was the spark that ignited a war.

And I didn't care.

Years of wondering, waiting, and worrying were now dead at my feet.

I dragged myself to where Gabe lie and searched his pockets for the keys to these cuffs and his phone.

My eyes skipped over his bloodied chest to his glassy eyes, and for a second, sadness tugged at my chest.

Because the guy I thought I knew hadn't deserved this. Parts of the man who spoke to me tonight weren't bad. But other parts were impossible to ignore. Parts I knew all too well having lived day in and day out with Johnny.

That crazed darkness that was as uncontrollable as it was volatile.

Normal men—even by mafia standards—didn't kill the men you slept with out of jealousy and rage.

They didn't stalk you, while openly trying to befriend you as a different person.

They didn't order your fiancé's death to keep a claim on you.

Not if they expected to live.

I palmed the keys to the cuffs and his truck, and gripped his phone in my hand as I struggled to stand.

Each inch felt like it took a lifetime, and my legs were begging for the reprieve of the floor again.

I wheezed and reached for my ribs when I tried to straighten, my face pinching in pain.

Yeah. Definitely a bad fucking idea.

I slowly trudged toward the door, tossing Gabe's locked phone on the floor on my way there, praying to at least make it into his truck. Then I'd worry about getting home.

But as soon as I stumbled out of the warehouse, two cars tore onto the nearly indiscernible U-shaped drive. My eyes filled with tears when I recognized the cars, and quickly raced down my cheeks when the passenger door of one was thrown open and someone stormed out.

And there he was. Maxon James. Eyes locked on me. Wrath and dread streaked across his devastatingly handsome face, making my heart ache.

The rock star who wrote our future in lyrics.

The boy who vowed to be my forever.

The man who promised me the world.

I loved him.

An exhausted cry fell from my lips when he let the object in his hand fall to the ground and raced for me.

I only made it a step before he had me in his arms, his head buried in my neck.

I cried out and winced when he squeezed too tight, but held on when he tried to let me go.

"What did he do?" he demanded, his tone rough and dripping with hatred.

"No, they did . . . they didn't. I—"

"They?"

"What do you mean *they*?" Dare asked, suddenly beside us.

I lifted my head from Maxon's chest and wanted to cry at the thought of having to explain everything when all I wanted was to lie down. "Cousins," I finally said. "Both dead. One killed the other, I killed the second. I think I cracked a rib . . . probably have a concussion."

Maxon went still, but Dare was looking at me like he was trying to figure it out. "Cracked a rib, huh?"

My mouth twitched into a smile. "It was a bad risk. You would've been pissed."

He cupped his hand around my neck and placed a gentle kiss on my forehead. "I'm sure I still will be when you tell me."

The cuffs fell from my wrists, and I looked up to see Einstein wink at me.

The key had never left my hands.

Maxon pulled me gently into his arms, his mouth going to my ear. "Libby, I love you. I'm sorry, I'm so damn sorry."

"Don't," I pleaded. "I have to apologize for so many things, but just know that I love you. I've always loved you and everything I did was to keep you safe."

"I know." His fingers trailed to the pulse point at my neck. "Your heartbeat will always be my favorite song."

My eyes slowly shut when his mouth moved across my jaw but popped open before he could reach my mouth. "Did I see you drop a tire iron?"

He shrugged and grinned mischievously. "It was the only weapon they'd give me."

I shouldn't laugh.

Nothing should be amusing after what I'd just done.

But I was beyond exhausted from the last few hours, and the thought of Maxon armed with a tire iron was too ridiculous not to react to.

The laugh was short-lived and ended on a hiss. "You were gonna run in there with nothing but a tire iron?"

His face fell, those whiskey eyes boring into mine. "I would've gone in there with nothing to get you back."

I was swept up in our next kiss.

Nothing ever felt like this.

Nothing ever could.

Wild and calm.

I could see it all in that kiss, just like every other. The house, the kids, the life I wanted.

Words he'd laid out in every achingly beautiful song.

Everything we would finally have.

My future with the boy brave enough to love a rebel.

Epilogue

Maxon
THREE MONTHS LATER

ROLLED OVER AND PASSED a soft kiss to Libby's jaw, then pressed my mouth to hers, full and pouty in sleep.

I let my fingers find her pulse and lay there for a while.

Felt her. Memorized her.

Waking to a song none other could compare to.

"Your heartbeat will always be my favorite song," I whispered against her shoulder, then slipped out of bed.

A couple days after everything happened, Dare went with Kieran Hayes to Chicago to meet with the Moretti family.

After realizing Gabe had been here, watching and studying Libby ever since her twenty-first birthday—longer than the seven years Libby had known him—Dare demanded the old contract destroyed.

A new one was drafted and signed.

The alliance was restored.

And Libby's marriage never happened.

Apparently even the Moretti family feared Kieran Hayes.

I was halfway down the hall when Einstein came trudging into the entrance, looking mostly asleep.

"When did you get here?"

"Slept here."

I just watched her walk past me to mine and Libby's room, shaking my head when I heard her flop onto the bed.

"Good to know," I murmured, and continued walking toward the kitchen to make coffee.

When Libby and I moved into our house, I'd offered Einstein a room.

As a joke.

She said she'd already picked one out and made a copy of the house key, and she'd use it from time to time.

I didn't ask how. I wasn't sure I wanted to know.

But true to her word, a few mornings a week, I woke up only to have her pass by me in the hall so she could cuddle my wife. How she knew I was awake and not in bed with her . . .

Again . . . I didn't ask.

Besides, they'd spent most their lives together. I wasn't going to be the one to separate them.

That hadn't stopped Einstein from calling me a best-friend thief the entire week leading up to the wedding and after.

Our mob-style wedding.

It was casual. Fun. Perfect.

Libby's mom even showed.

We had cupcakes and skipped the flowers. Libby wore a skirt and shirt that were so Libby and opposite of what you'd expect on a bride . . .

And I'd counted down the minutes until I could tear them off and bury myself inside her.

When the guys had asked about the ceremony, I'd told them the truth. That Libby came from a mafia family and this was how they did weddings.

They'd laughed. Ledger thought they were being Punk'd again.

None of them knew exactly what had happened the night Libby was taken, only having caught pieces and thinking most of it was pranks—including the man the twins killed in their driveway.

I planned on keeping it that way.

"Freaking cold toes."

I looked over my shoulder, a smile pulling at my lips as I watched Libby walk into the kitchen in nothing but my shirt.

I wrapped an arm around her waist, pulling her close to kiss her. "Wife."

"Caveman."

I smiled against her mouth. "Something like that."

"Come back here," Einstein yelled from our bedroom.

Libby stared at me. Her face was blank, but her eyes were light and excited.

Before I could ask what was going on, she groaned and headed back to our room.

I grabbed a mug and poured coffee, and was headed to the fridge for creamer when I heard it.

I looked over my shoulder and around the room when it disappeared.

I had the fridge open when it started up again.

"The hell?"

I shut the door and followed the sound out of the kitchen, but it disappeared.

I'd started rocking back when it started up again, coming from . . .

From my bedroom.

I walked faster than before, my mouth open to call for Libby when the sound shifted.

The amplified dragging and scratching sound was gone, and in its place was something I'd never heard.

Not this way at least. But I knew it just the same.

A rapid *whom whom whom* filled the house and slowed my feet.

I walked into my room, my steps hesitant and eyes wide.

Libby was lying on the bed with her shirt bunched under her breasts.

Einstein was kneeling next to her, pressing something to her stomach.

Both were staring at me and smiling wide.

I lifted my hand and pointed.

Tried to point.

"What . . . what is that?"

Einstein sighed. "Oh, come on. You're not that dumb."

Libby hit her without ever looking away. Her smile never faltered. "That's our baby."

I was suddenly on the bed, kneeling on the other side of her, and Einstein was pressing that thing into my hand.

"Rebel . . ."

She placed her hands on her stomach tenderly and whispered, "I'm almost three months." When I looked at her again, her eyes were bright with tears.

I bent to kiss her, long and slow.

Pulling back slightly, I murmured, "Listen."

Libby released a shaky breath and smiled as that *whom whom whom* surrounded us.

"That heartbeat . . . that's my favorite song."

The End

Look for more *Rebel* novels
from Molly McAdams, coming soon!
Lock
Limit

Coming soon from
New York Times bestselling author, Molly McAdams . . .

The mafia's hacker and the man who's always been her comfort. Her everything.

She loves him, but she's paid the price of love in the mafia before.

Now she'll do anything to keep him from the pain haunting her. Even ruin him.

But when a threat comes to town, he won't let her continue pretending what they have isn't real.

Acknowledgments

Cory—Thank you for being my constant support. I would never be able to do what I do without you. I love you!

Molly—What would I do without you? Thank you for the never-ending plot sessions and just being completely amazing. You will always be the best half of Molly Squared.

Amy—Thank you, thank you, thank you for everything. Your support and encouragement means the world to me. Ramblers forever.

Regina, Letitia, Malia, Marion, Shannon, & Christine—Thank you for making this book what it is! From the photos, illustrations, and cover, to the edits, proofs, and formatting. You're all such rock stars!

Made in the USA
Lexington, KY
23 June 2018